THE SECRET

JENNIFER WELLS works in Market Research
when not writing. She lives in Devon with
her young family and cat.

THE SECRET

Jennifer Wells

First published in the United Kingdom in 2018 by Aria, an imprint of
Head of Zeus Ltd

9 7 5 3 1 2 4 6 8

A CIP catalogue record for this book is available from the British Library.

ISBN 9781786691095

Aria
an imprint of Head of Zeus
First Floor East
5–8 Hardwick Street
London EC1R 4RG

IVY

Prologue

1943

From the moment I saw Mrs Cuthbertson in the garden that day, I knew that I was not safe. She was a woman who appeared quite harmless to those who did not know her – her hair was starting to grey and her outfit had the refinement of any middle aged woman of her class – but for me the sight of her was enough to send a chill racing through my body.

It was a cold Sunday in early autumn and I had spent the morning in my lodgings at the nurses' house, warming my feet by the kitchen stove while I studied a medical textbook. When I looked up from the page, I glimpsed movement through the window and saw a woman emerging from the low clump of trees that separated the nurses' house from the cottage hospital. She was a tall, thin woman in a long elegant coat, her hair scraped into a tight bun. It had been a year since I had last seen her, but I knew instantly that it was Mrs Cuthbertson. She had returned, but she was not welcome.

She stopped at the bottom of the lawn and then stood with her hands on her hips as if she owned the place and gazed across the sloping lawn, her hand shielding her eyes from the low autumn sun. She looked first to the buildings of the cottage hospital and then across the lawn to the nurses' house, holding her gaze for so long that I feared that she could see me watching her through the little kitchen window. She made her way across the lawn and up the slope to the nurses' house and I felt the quickening of my heart in my chest, my book falling to the floor.

I stood up slowly, my legs quite numb, and took a deep breath. Then I walked shakily over to the kettle and put it on the burner, setting out two tin mugs with a milk bottle and sugar bowl. There was no use in hiding – Mrs Cuthbertson had always known that I had no nursing duties on Sunday mornings, the sitting room curtains were open and there would be smoke coming from the chimney. She must have known that I would be at home to receive her, and to not welcome her in would be to admit something was amiss.

I opened the cutlery drawer and rummaged round for a teaspoon, but then I stopped, my heart pounding. My eyes fell upon a small paring knife that had been pushed to the side of the drawer. I took it out and touched my trembling fingertip to the sharp blade. Then I loosened my grip and slid the handle into my sleeve so it was covered by the fabric of my housecoat, my fingers forming a loose fist around the blade. Then I twisted my arm behind my back and waited for the knock on the door.

I

One year earlier – September 1942

I had first met Mrs Cuthbertson one evening in the September of 1942, but it was not until a week later that I actually learned her name. The first time I came across her, she was pacing the kitchen of the nurses' house, and she looked quite annoyed when I entered, tired and dirty from my shift on the ward.

In those days it was not unusual to find a lady waiting in the kitchen in the evening. The war had depleted the nursing staff and extra beds had been squeezed into the wards as we took in the overspill from London hospitals which needed the space for the wounded. We worked long shifts and the little time that we had back at the nurses' house was usually spent sleeping, meaning the lady 'visitors' we received in the kitchen would often have to wait for a nurse to come off shift.

The woman who I found in the kitchen that night was a stranger to me, but it was her manner that struck me first – the agitation in her steps and the wringing of her hands – and when she saw me, she addressed me as if I was a shop girl who had been slow to answer the bell.

'Is the matron not here?' she said in a voice that seemed used to giving orders.

'She has been called away to a military hospital in London,' I said.

'Bridget, then,' she said shortly.

'Nurse Bradshaw has the evening off,' I said quietly, as if apologising for the fact that it was me she found in front of her and not the more senior nurse who had been left in charge. 'She will not be on duty again until half past seven tomorrow morning. The ward is being staffed by the trainee, who has instructions to fetch me if I am needed, but I am the only qualified nurse on the hospital grounds tonight.'

'The hospital is woefully understaffed,' she said, looking me up and down, 'and I see from the plainness of your cap that you must only be a junior nurse.'

'If you haven't noticed, there is a war on!' I said, finally finding my voice. 'We are only a small hospital, but you will always find someone on the grounds. Nurse Bradshaw and I live here in the nurses' house so can usually be found.'

Her pupils were wavering slightly, there was a tremble to her hands and I began to suspect that, despite all her complaints, it did not really matter who answered to her call of 'nurse'.

'I am afraid that you will have to make do with me,' I said firmly.

'Indeed,' she sniffed, 'and you are…?'

'Nurse Watts,' I said. 'Ivy Watts. We usually offer our lady visitors some tea. I will make a pot.' I lit the burner, putting the kettle over the flame and then I turned back to her: 'Then we can discuss what ails you, whether you need prevention or cure.'

The words were the standard introduction that we always used, for it would not do to give away the nature of the services that we offered from the nurses' house. Most of what we offered was no more than advice – from educating young women before their wedding night or giving help to mothers who already had too many mouths to feed – and what we provided was little more than what could be purchased at the chemist or from the advertisements in magazines. Yet such services could not help all the women who visited us and sometimes we would help those who had come to us too late for such things. My role was to introduce women who could not keep their babies to childless couples, but the services offered by Bridget were of a different nature and, if discovered by the wrong people, could lead to a call from the constable.

'Please, won't you take a seat?' I said, pulling out a chair for her at the large kitchen table, but she did not. I took the large leather notebook that we used for such visits down from the top of the cupboard and laid it open on the table, smoothing my sleeve down a blank page. I drew up a chair and took a fountain pen from the drawer, marking the date at the top of the page. When I looked up, she was still standing and I started to wonder who she was and why I had never seen her around Missensham town before.

She was a tall woman with long thin limbs and a very distinctive way of holding herself, straight backed and elegant, which I put down to a mix of deportment lessons and a noble bearing. Her hair had lost its colour but was not yet grey and was pulled into a tight bun, exposing a high forehead. I thought her to be approaching fifty, although that in itself was not unusual as we often helped older ladies. I would not feel so bad with the older ones. Theirs was an unfortunate position but they tended to know the ways of the world and knew that they could not face bearing another infant. Yet this woman did not look like the older ladies we saw – those whose bodies were already ravaged by pregnancy and those who were exhausted by childcare and could not face going through it all again. This woman was well turned out. She wore a wedding ring and not the cheap brass kind that Partridge's Department Store would sell to the unfortunates who needed to pass as respectable – it was a shiny gold ring with a large diamond engagement ring nestled into it.

'I hear that nurses are poorly paid,' she said, completely without invitation, 'and that you and your colleague have this little business set up to make ends meet.'

I snapped the book shut. 'We provide a service for lady patients,' I said. 'We charge the ladies only what they can afford to pay us. We are available as long as a nurse is here and...' but as I looked at her, I realised that although she must have known the nature of the services that we documented in the leather book, she was not in need of them herself. The services that we offered relied on secrecy. We urged our visitors to mention it only to others who could be trusted and those in need, and I wondered how a woman such as herself had heard about us. The ladies who visited us in the kitchen would usually come at night, looking about them anxiously as they walked up the path to the nurses' house. They would never give us their real names and we never asked them to, yet they would mostly keep their heads low when they spoke to us, mumble, blush and try to excuse their situation, although we would never ask for any explanation. The woman who stood in the kitchen before me was different and she looked me right in the eye.

'Bridget might have mentioned some medication that she has to deliver to me,' she said. 'She has been coming to me on Sundays, but this week I am in need of it early.'

'She did not mention anything and she has not marked anything in the book,' I said, patting the leather cover. 'We record everything outside the main hospital work in here, and it would be most unlike Bridget to—'

'Bridget would not record it in there,' she said, 'but I know that she would have put it aside for me in her nursing bag.'

'We don't usually put medicines aside—' I began, but her face told me that she would not be satisfied with any explanation that I could give her.

'One moment,' I said. 'I will need to check. Do help yourself to tea while I am gone.'

Bridget's nursing bag was in the hallway under the hat stand, the place we always kept them – clean, tidy and fully stocked, in case we were ever called away in an emergency. I picked it up and carried it back through to the kitchen and put it on the table on top of the leather book. I snapped open the catch and peered inside. I saw what she was referring to immediately – a small glass bottle, resting on top of the instrument towel as if it had been thrown there in haste. It was quite out of place among the bottles, rubber tubes and metal instruments which were all carefully stowed. The bottle was small but long, with a blue label, and the tablets that were visible through the glass appeared pretty standard – small, round and white, revealing nothing of their potency. 'Luminal' was printed at the top of the label in block lettering. It was a brand I was not familiar with, but there was so much fine print on the label that I could not have imagined the contents for sale over the pharmacy counter. There was no prescription with it and nothing to indicate for whom it was intended.

'Nurse!' said the woman sharply. 'Is there anything in there that Nurse Bradshaw has put aside for me?'

'No,' I said, a little panicked, 'there is not.' I snapped the bag shut. Bridget and I were strictly forbidden to supply medicines without a prescription and there was something about this woman, with her agitation and her directness, that made me uneasy.

She sniffed impatiently. 'Nothing?' There was something in the way she said the word that made it sound more like a threat than a question and suddenly I became aware of my slight build and scrawny limbs compared to this tall and forceful woman who could easily overpower me.

'There is nothing that is accompanied by a prescription,' I added shakily. 'Our pharmacist has been called away, along with the matron, so we have to be strict with the medicines.'

'I see,' she said. 'I think I will have that tea after all,' and she sat down in a way that suggested she had no intention of moving and forced a smile.

'I will see to that now,' I said.

The kettle had started to whistle, so I lifted up Bridget's nursing bag and put it under the table, but, not happy to leave the medicine while my back was turned, I took the bottle out and put it in my pocket. I went to the draining board, arranged the cups and put a small spoon of tealeaves in the pot, then I returned the bag to the hallway. When I returned to the kitchen the woman seemed a little brighter, as if she'd had time to reflect.

'I have a son,' she said with a smile as if the making of tea signalled a break for idle chat. 'He is twenty – that must be about your age.'

'It is,' I said, perching on the chair opposite her.

'The war…' Then she stopped as if choking on a word, but she continued: 'Well, after all that has happened to him I must care for him at home now, it is a tragedy as he is so young. On top of everything else, his nerves are frayed and we are so far from the town. With that bomb falling in the lido last year, well, now we fear the sirens at night. Dr Crawford has prescribed him pills to help him sleep. I think they were called…' then she stopped, a slight crease on her large brow.

'Luminal?' I said, recalling the blue label on the little bottle that I now fingered in my pocket.

'Yes,' she said. 'So they were in Bridget's bag after all!' She smiled, although it seemed to take her some effort to pull her mouth into position. I noticed a bead of sweat on her brow and remembered the tremble in her hands that I had seen earlier.

'I did not say they were not,' I said. 'Only that they were not accompanied by the prescription you mention.'

'Oh,' she said bitterly, twisting her fingers together. 'How frustrating.'

'I am sorry,' I said, 'but, as you said yourself, I am just a junior nurse, I could get into trouble.'

She said nothing but stared at me as if waiting for me to realise how silly I was being, but when I remained silent, she pressed her lips together until they became quite white and I noticed a little streak of blood where she had bitten down on to her bottom lip.

'Look,' I said. 'I can come out to your son tonight, but I cannot bring you Luminal without a doctor. We are just a cottage hospital, we are more used to dealing with gout and bronchitis. If your son's symptoms get worse, he can come here or we can take him to Oxworth General where he can be monitored.'

'It is only Luminal that works,' she said firmly, raising a pointed eyebrow like a dagger.

'All right,' I said. 'I might be able to give you a small amount for tonight and you will need to return and see Dr Crawford for a prescription.' I took the bottle out of my pocket and read the back. As she had said, they were a sleeping aid, but they were strong enough to be used for grand mal seizures and warned of the risk of habit forming. 'It says to not exceed the dosage,' I added, reading the label, 'and they are dangerous if taken with alcohol, and do not—'

'I cannot come back so easily,' she said firmly. 'I am in need of the whole bottle, and I will take that.'

'You may indeed be able to take it,' I said, unscrewing the bottle cap and tipping one tablet into my palm, 'but it will be tomorrow when Bridget is back and we are expecting Dr Crawford to come over for his rounds.'

'But—' she protested.

'One pill will be enough for tonight,' I said, handing the single tablet to her. 'There must be ten tablets in this bottle. One will help your son to sleep, yet ten would be enough to kill an ox!' I resealed the bottle and put it back in my pocket. 'You will not have need for all of them tonight.'

She stared at me, and then at the single white tablet in her palm. 'You are just like her,' she said, 'your silly friend, Bridget.' She took a large leather purse from her handbag and put the tablet inside. Then she took out a roll of pound notes wrapped as tightly as a cigar and fastened with a rubber band. She removed three notes from the roll and lay them on the table in front of me. It was about what I earned in a whole week, enough to tempt me, but also enough to tell me that something was wrong. I stared at the notes and when I looked up from the table I saw that her eyes were fixed on me, the pupils wavering wildly and the blood on her lip swelling into a crimson bead.

'I cannot accept money for such medicine,' I said, my voice becoming weaker, 'not without a prescription. I can come out to your son or there are things such as Chlorodyne from the chemist in the high street. They do not need a prescription for everything they sell, but they keep a proper poisons book. If you want anything stronger, you would have to go and see them, Mrs…'

'I should go,' she said, snatching the pound notes back from the table. She stood up and I noticed she had gone quite pale. Only then did I realise that her behaviour might be due to the pills that she so desperately wanted, or more likely, the lack of them.

'Look, I have a little Chlorodyne in the bathroom cabinet,' I said. 'Will you take it home with you? It will take the edge off tonight, until we are able to…'

She licked the blood from her lip and stared at me, and for a moment I feared what someone in such need might do, but then she nodded wearily and dropped her head into her hands. 'Go and get it, then,' she said, 'and be quick about it.'

I did not hesitate and ran up to the bathroom, glad to find the little blue bottle of Chlorodyne still half full.

When I returned, she was standing with her coat and hat on and her bag in her hand.

I held the Chlorodyne out to her. 'Remember what I said to do if he gets worse,' I said, but her expression was quite blank and her eyes were large. 'Your son?' I ventured.

'Yes, yes,' she said automatically, 'of course,' and I wondered if she even remembered what she had told me about her son. Then she pursed her lips and nodded to me briefly, letting the back door bang on its hinges as she left.

I ran to the door and locked it behind her, then I hurried to the window and watched her go – her silhouette fading into shadow and her footsteps lost in the quiet of the night.

2

I could not sleep after the woman's visit. I lay awake in the darkness listening to the scrape of the ivy on the window and watching the dapple of moonlight on the ceiling. Even the knowledge that I had checked the locks several times did little to help my sleep and my thoughts were filled with memories of the desperate woman with the wavering eyes who had let herself into the kitchen and demanded drugs in return for money.

The sound of footsteps outside made me jump, but then came the jangle of keys and a curse as Bridget dropped them on the doorstep. I squinted at the clock – the hands were clumped together over the twelve. Bridget was due on the early morning shift and would get very little rest, but I was glad she was home and that I was no longer alone in the house. I drifted off to sleep.

Bridget rose to the drill of the morning alarm bell with a groan and, when I did not hear the clank of the water pipes, I knew that she must have put on her uniform without washing. I went into the kitchen in my housecoat but found her staring at a triangle of toast. Her usually delicate features now seemed drawn and pale and she had pinned her long chestnut hair tightly under her cap without styling it. She shook her head when I offered to make her tea, but when I asked her if she'd had a nice evening, her face broke into a wide grin, although she said nothing further and walked shakily to the front door, letting it bang behind her.

There had been a time when I first moved in to the nurses' house that I had admired Bridget – she was only a few years older than me but was able to speak to both the patients and doctors with the authority typical of her class. Her face had a daintiness to it, and she had a warm smile for those she favoured. In those early days, Bridget had chatted to me about her life – of her smart family home in west London and the society parties she frequented with her sisters and cousins, but when I told her that I had only ever lived with my crippled mother in a tiny house in Missensham, her friendliness had faded to politeness and all that I learned about her life after that was what I overheard as she sat on the stairs and gossiped to her friends on the telephone.

Bridget's short exchanges with me made it quite clear that the friendship I had longed for would not grow and we moved separately, inhabiting the same space but nothing more. On that morning, with her messy hair and her hangover, it had not seemed right to mention the woman who had visited in the night.

I watched Bridget through the sitting room window as she walked to work, the blue of her uniform flashing through the trees at the back entrance of the hospital. Had we been closer, she might have asked for my help that morning, but she did not and I felt that it was not right to offer it, so I consoled myself with the thought of her facing the stench of the morning round of bedpans alone.

I returned upstairs slowly. A glance through the open door of Bridget's bedroom told me a little of her evening – there was an imprint of mascara on her pillow and an evening dress left on the foot of her bed where she had fallen in a drunken stupor. On her nightstand was an expensive bottle of perfume, still in a bag from Partridge's Department Store. I wondered how she might have afforded it, but then I remembered the unwelcome night visitor and how she had thrust money at me, saying that I was just like my silly friend. I imagined Bridget taking the little rolled pound notes and folding them carefully into her purse.

I washed, dressed and ate breakfast. Then I remembered the little bottle of Luminal that I had put in my pocket the previous evening. I fished it out and returned it to Bridget's bag. I felt that she was suffering enough that morning so did not need the extra worry of a little bottle of pills that was at worst stolen and at best mislaid. I walked down the path to the hospital in time to join the doctor on his morning rounds.

The church bell struck nine as I entered the back door of the hospital. I just had time to straighten my cap and run into the hallway and stand next to Bridget to welcome Dr Crawford as he entered through the main entrance.

The local doctor's rounds were always a formal occasion, yet there was rarely anything that could not be handled by a good nurse. Most patients just needed the reassurance that only a man in a white coat could give. We trailed after Dr Crawford smiling and saying very little as he squinted at charts, held wrists and listened to chests.

Missensham Cottage Hospital only had two wards – one for men and one for ladies, each with eight beds. There was one toilet and one bathroom and a sluice room which also housed the medicine cabinet. There was also a little room at the back with only one bed, secreted away from the rest and unknown to most. It was cleaned regularly and the bed made, but then the door would always be shut again – it was a room kept clear for an emergency, the serious case that we hoped we would never see.

As for staff, there were few for the doctor to inspect. The matron had left for Queen Alexandra's military hospital in London, leaving only Bridget, and I had joined fresh from a hurried period of training. There was a local girl, Violet, who covered the gaps in our shifts, but she had received no training other than the instruction to run to the nurses' house should a problem arise.

Meals were brought in by a local woman, who also cleaned once a day, and the doctor from the surgery on the village green visited twice a week. There was also the odd visit from a district nurse or midwife. For the most part it was only Bridget and myself who staffed the wards. We would even take most of our breaks in the nurses' house in case there was an emergency which required us to return to the main hospital building.

The doctor's rounds were usually brief, but in recent weeks the war had provided a little more interest and Dr Crawford took an unusually long time tending to the patients. There were a couple of soldiers – local men who had been brought back from their postings, the nature of their wounds meaning that they would survive but would not be returning to combat – and some bronchial patients, transferred from London to make way for the wounded. Otherwise, the patients were what could be expected in a small town that straddled the London suburbs and countryside – a farm hand whose leg had been crushed by machinery, old women with swollen ankles and a pregnant farmer's wife who always ignored the doctor and said she would rather wait for the midwife.

I noticed that Bridget was lagging behind the doctor, her face was still pale and strands of hair crept from her cap on to her moist brow. Dr Crawford glanced at her disdainfully over his spectacles and, after the rounds were over, he permitted me to end my shift but asked Bridget to stay behind and help him with the medicines. She complained that she was due off shift, but he was insistent and I realised that he had a lecture on appearances planned for her as they dispensed the medicines.

I returned to the nurses' house and made a cup of tea to take up to my bedroom, but as I passed Bridget's room, my eye fell on the bottle of perfume again. Bridget was from a good family but the war meant that everything was becoming scarce and few people could afford such things. There were really only a couple of places that her good fortune could have come from, but only one place where I might find out.

I went back downstairs to the kitchen and opened the cupboard under the stairs. It was the place that we kept the medicine chest for our lady visitors, but it also contained equipment that Bridget would sometimes use when the ladies had come to us too late. As a nurse who had trained in war time, most of my experience had been with the wounded and I lacked Bridget's knowledge of such things. My role had always been limited to private adoptions – finding suitable homes for infants whose mothers had no alternative but to give them up – and the contents of the kitchen cupboard seemed strange to me. I did not know what the rubber tubes and syringes were for and it was something that Bridget would not tell me. When she had a patient in need of them, she would send me upstairs and I would hear nothing more than the grate of the kitchen table as it was pulled away from the wall and I would return to find nothing amiss except a strong smell of Dettol.

Bridget had told me that the war had brought more work than in previous years, but when I pulled out the tubes and syringes, they had become quite dusty and the smell of Dettol had faded. I realised it had been many weeks since I had last heard the scrape of the kitchen table as it was dragged in to position.

I pulled the large leather book from the top of the cupboard. It fell open where I had noted the date and time the previous evening. I leafed through the entries. There had been a couple of sheaths purchased, a Dutch cap fitted and a woman who had thought better of it and left, but nothing more than that in nearly a week. The visitors were described as 'farmer's wife, twenty-six', 'typist, twenty-one' and 'mother of four' and by each entry was the amount that the lady had been able to pay us. Bridget had made less than a pound in the last month, but then my eye fell on an entry from the previous Sunday. It was no more than a line long: 'Mrs Cuthbertson – the usual – 10 a.m.' and then the flourished symbol for a pound, with no amount written next to it, but the symbol was repeated several times, saying more about the amount than any number could.

I leafed back through the book, looking carefully for another of these one line entries which were written in a slightly smaller hand. I found two others, each with the same wording: 'Sunday, 10 a.m., Mrs Cuthbertson'. It was a name that implied familiarity in that it was a name at all and not just a string or words which said little more than the patient's age and status, but it was not a name that that I knew, and I thought of the woman who had come searching for Bridget and the little bottle of pills in her nursing bag the previous night.

Sunday was an unusual day in our schedule. It was the only day of the week that neither Bridget nor I worked a shift in the late morning or early afternoon. On Sunday mornings, Bridget would go in to the hospital at dawn and I would arrive later to join the doctor's rounds. After that we were both permitted the morning off, providing that at least one of us stayed in the hospital grounds in case we were needed. For the last few Sundays I had returned to the house a little later than Bridget, only to find that she had already left without explanation. Today was a Sunday and Bridget had been held up by Dr Crawford. The page in the book was empty.

Then I heard the scrape of the latch and the turn of a key in the front door. I shut the book quickly and returned it to the top of the cupboard. The tubes and syringes were still out and I leant into the cupboard, trying frantically to stuff them back inside, the click of Bridget's heels echoing on the hallway tiles. Then suddenly all was quiet and I fancied that she had stopped by the mirror in the hallway to check her hair, but there would not be enough time for me to put everything away and I feared having to explain myself to her.

The ring of the telephone drilled in my ears, but it stopped abruptly and Bridget answered with the usual salutation of 'Missensham Cottage Hospital – Nurses' House.'

I coiled the last tube and shoved it back in the cupboard, shutting the door quickly. I drew a long breath as I sat down in the armchair by the stove with my cooled mug of tea.

It was a few minutes before I heard Bridget's voice again: 'Yes, Mrs Cuthbertson. I can be with you in a quarter of an hour.' And then: 'Yes, I manged to get another bottle for you. No, it won't be missed.' Then nothing more but the clunk of the receiver as if both speakers understood a farewell was not required.

I opened the door to the hallway.

'Oh, Ivy, you startled me!' She had been gazing into the mirror and I saw that her cheeks were quite flushed and her hangover seemed to have eased. 'Were you eavesdropping?' she said, but there was no bluntness in her tone and I fancied that something about the phone call had taken away her annoyance at being overheard.

'I heard the ring,' I said. 'I just wondered if you had to go out and whether you needed me to stay in the hospital grounds?' I did not sound convincing, but she did not notice.

'What?' she said. 'Yes, you had better stay here until the afternoon. Violet is on the ward and will be for the rest of the morning. I shall be back here before lunchtime, so you can have the afternoon off to visit your mother as usual.' She said it as if she was giving an order. It was a tone that she often used with me, but I did not mind as she was slightly older than me and had more experience, but then she added: 'I am going out. Can I borrow your lipstick?'

I thought of her expensive perfume but nodded. After all, I had inherited my mother's reddish hair and freckled complexion and had never really found a shade of lipstick that suited me. 'Are you going anywhere nice?' I asked.

'Oh,' she said, as if not expecting the question. 'It is nursing duty of course, but as I am not due on shift, I am doing this one privately. It is nowhere nice,' but then her face softened a little. 'Just someone nice.'

'Oh, do tell!'

'A soldier recovering from leg wounds,' she said, 'rich and quite dashing. I'm sure that I can rehabilitate him. He won't talk about what happened, but I am sure with a bit of therapy I will be able to get his legs working again.' She laughed. 'And his other parts!'

'Bridget!' I could not help laughing. 'Where did you find him?'

'That's my business,' she said, ending our brief moment of intimacy.

I thought of the twenty year old son that my night visitor had mentioned – the man who had been through a lot and could not sleep – and how he could be the same person as Bridget's beau, but to mention the woman and how I knew that she had been paying Bridget for Luminal would only sour things further and no amount of swapped shifts and shared lipstick would ever make up for it. I said nothing more.

'Well, I must go up and get ready,' said Bridget. 'I mustn't be late.'

'I was going up to my room to read anyway,' I said. 'My lipstick is in the bathroom cabinet, you can help yourself.'

I followed her slowly up the stairs and went to my bedroom. I sat on my little bed and looked at the clock on my nightstand – it was a little after ten o'clock, a time that Bridget was yet to record in the pages of the leather book, together with the date, a repeated pound symbol and a single name: 'Mrs Cuthbertson'.

I heard the clank of the water pipes as Bridget turned on the taps, followed by the hum of her hairdryer, then her footsteps on the stairs.

I went back out on to the landing and looked down the stairs. Bridget stood in the hallway and I watched her as she peered into the mirror by the hat stand, drawing my lipstick carefully around her mouth. It was only then that I realised she had removed her cap and apron but still wore her plain blue dress. She swung a coat over her shoulders and leant towards the mirror as she pinned her hair into a neat wave. Then she pulled her nursing bag from under the hat stand and opened it up, glancing quickly at the contents. I held my breath, fearing that she would notice that the little bottle of Luminal had been moved, but she snapped the bag shut and tucked it under her arm. She opened the door and checked the mirror one final time, before blowing a kiss to the glass and closing the door behind her.

I returned to my bedroom and peered out from behind the curtain, watching the triangle of her long coat disappearing into the trees. Somewhere in her bag she had the Luminal, taken without prescription and probably without the knowledge of Dr Crawford. She was taking it to the woman who had scared me the night before, the Mrs Cuthbertson whose name appeared in the leather book and who she visited on Sundays – the Mrs Cuthbertson to whom she would go when she was called.

3

I thought nothing more of Mrs Cuthbertson for almost a week. It turned out that she was Bridget's problem and I was glad of it. Even when I walked in on Bridget fumbling through the medicine cabinet, her hands full and her face guilty, I said nothing and turned on my heel. Over the week, however, I did notice some changes in Bridget; she had a new coat from Partridge's, had lightened her hair from its original chestnut to a shade that was almost blonde, and when I borrowed one of her textbooks, I found six new pound notes which sprang into tight curls when I opened the pages.

But Bridget's luck did not last and she was called back to her family home in Fulham on Friday morning as an unexploded bomb had been found at the back of her parents' garden, leaving them shocked and in need of their daughter. It was customary for a nurse to have twenty-four hours off for a family emergency and I wondered how I would cope without Bridget, but between us, Violet and I managed to tend to all the patients, changing dressings and administering medicines as if we had been doing it for years.

It was not until I came off shift on Sunday morning that I felt I could really relax. I left the hospital and went straight to the nurses' house, putting the kettle on before slumping down in the armchair by the stove without even changing out of my uniform. An hour had passed since Bridget had called the main hospital from a telephone box outside Parsons Green tube station with the news that she was on her way back to Missensham and, although she missed the doctor's rounds, I was relieved to know that she was returning.

When the phone in the hallway rang, I answered, expecting Violet's voice on the hospital line with a request for help on the ward or a notification about more patients transferring in from London. But when I took the call, I knew instantly that it was not Violet.

'Nurse, are you there?' Despite the crackle on the line, the woman's voice was unmistakable and as I heard the words, I could imagine them on the lips of the night visitor, the woman who had sat opposite me at the kitchen table and demanded medicine that had not been prescribed.

I glanced at the clock, the hand clicking on to the hour as I did so. It was ten o'clock. This was the call that Bridget usually took from the woman known in the book as Mrs Cuthbertson and as she spoke her name, I remembered how I had heard it on Bridget's lips exactly one week ago when she had stood in the hallway and answered the telephone just as I was now. As I had suspected, the woman who had visited me in the kitchen and the woman Bridget listed in the book were the same.

'With whom am I speaking?' she said, but the words had a tone to them which made me unsure whether she wanted an answer or just to know that someone was listening and ready to take orders.

'This is Nurse Watts at the Missensham Cottage Hospital Nurses' House,' I said, but my greeting seemed to be a detail that did not matter to her.

'I need someone up at Elmridge House today,' she said. 'As soon as you can, for I must attend a church service and my son cannot be left alone for long.'

Her voice was sharp and somehow I felt as if I was being scolded for breaking an engagement I did not know I had agreed to. I took a deep breath. 'I am afraid that there are no nurses working at this time,' I said. 'If you have a medical emergency, I can telephone a doctor or ambulance for you, but if you require a routine visit from a nurse, you may telephone Dr Crawford at the surgery on the green and he can get you added to the rounds of the district nurse...' but my last words were lost under her own as if they did not matter.

'I cannot wait for the district nurse,' she said. 'This is a private appointment and I will pay you directly. I understood that a nurse would be free from duties at this time. I assume you are not on duty as you have answered this number.'

'Well, I...' I glanced at the clock again, but it told me only that it was a few minutes past the hour and not what time Bridget would arrive back. 'All right,' I said, reluctant to let down Bridget's patient. 'A nurse can come out to you this morning, but it will not be Nurse Bradshaw, for she has been called away unexpectedly. It will be me, Nurse Watts, and I—'

'I shall need to leave Elmridge House on the half hour,' she said, 'so be prompt. It is on the Oxworth Road. I need you at half past ten, it will only take you half an hour, so you have sufficient notice, and don't come smelling like a brothel this time.'

'Please,' I said. 'I am not the nurse who—'

'Oh, and be sure to bring the medicine.'

'Which medicine?' I said. 'For I cannot bring anything that has not been prescribed by—'

But the line was already dead.

I put the receiver down and stared at my reflection in the mirror above the telephone table. I took off my cap and smoothed my hair back into a bun, then I removed my apron and belt, leaving just my blue dress. We were forbidden from wearing our uniform off duty, but the plain blue dress was the only thing I could imagine a private nurse wearing and I remembered how I had seen Bridget leave the nurses' house without her cap and apron the previous Sunday. I sat on the floor next to my nursing bag. I checked the contents – everything was clean and replenished, but it was just the usual array of metal instruments, tubing and jars, and I did not know what else to take. Then I remembered the little bottle of Luminal and the caller's insistence that I bring 'the medicine'. Maybe now she had a prescription to show me – I would take some just to be sure.

I ran across the lawn and through the trees to the back of the hospital, passing a startled Violet as I barged through the back door. In the sluice room I found the key to the medicine cabinet under the kidney bowl and rummaged for the little glass bottle with the blue label among the packets and jars. I found the Luminal near the back. There were a few bottles and I fancied that one would not be missed and thought that I could always sign it out later if Mrs Cuthbertson did have a prescription to show me after all. Then I ran back to the nurses' house to collect my bag and burst in through the kitchen door.

'Nurse?'

A girl perched on the chair by the fire. She was barely bigger than a child and wore a floral print pinafore and a cardigan which seemed two sizes too big for her. By her feet was an old-fashioned wicker basket lined with straw and as many real eggs as I would usually see in a whole month.

Her face was not one that I had seen before and something about her made me think of an evacuee, although since the bombs had started to fall on the outskirts of London, Missensham was no longer considered a safe area and most evacuees had returned, which made me wonder if she had anywhere left to call home.

'Can I help you?' I asked impatiently. 'For I must go out to a patient.'

'I heard that you can do things for ladies in trouble,' she said in a voice with more depth than I expected and I realised her a woman, but only just.

'Oh!' I said. 'Yes, of course,' but could manage nothing more. To see such a girl sat where I had seen so many others was a shock to me. I was more used to dealing with middle aged women who could not afford another mouth to feed, farmers' wives fearing they had no strength left to carry another and women who were having flings with soldiers. That someone like her would come to me asking for help was something that I could not quite understand. Somehow she was in the same situation as these women, yet she was so unlike them.

'Is this not the right place?' she said. 'For I heard that—'

'Yes, yes,' I said quickly. 'Yes, this is the place, but surely it can't be for yourself...'

She nodded. 'There was this gentleman,' she said, 'and now I am late.'

I could not imagine such a girl with any gentleman, let alone a farm hand, and I knew there would be no ring on her finger. I realised that my face must have fallen, for she forced a weak smile, revealing a slight overbite. I noticed that the flowers on her dress were daisies. It was a childish pattern and I fancied that Daisy would be a name which suited her – the name of a farm girl or the shy flower that went unnoticed.

'How late are you?' I said.

'I don't know,' she said, blinking quickly as if she did not understand the question. 'I just don't know.' I wondered if coming to the nurses' house had been her own idea or if she had been left here by her so-called gentleman and told what to say.

'Where is the man that did this?' I said. 'Could he marry you?'

'No, I don't want any of that,' she crossed her arms across her lap, her voice cracking, 'not again.'

I felt a weight in my stomach. I could not ask her any more about what had happened to her because I couldn't bear to think about it. 'Don't worry,' I said, hearing a catch in my own voice.

She cast her eyes down and shook her head slowly from side to side repeatedly.

'Maybe you should go to the police station,' I said, 'or maybe—'

But she cut in, her voice now hard as if she had already suffered enough and wanted an end to it: 'I heard there is something you can take. Some kind of mint called royal penny or something.'

'Pennyroyal,' I said. It was an old remedy used to slip babies and quite out of touch with modern medicine, but I knew that we kept some as the older farmers' wives knew about it from their mothers and would sometimes request it from Bridget. She would only ever give them a little and request that they stayed with us after they took it. I knew of nothing else I could give her as Bridget usually dealt with that side of things. 'I will see if we have any in the medicine chest,' I said, 'but you may need to wait until the other nurse gets back before you can take it because I'm not really trained for this.' I went to the under stairs cupboard, but as I did so she stood up and her cardigan fell open and I saw the daisy fabric clinging to a small round bump where the cardigan had been. 'No!' I cried. 'I am sorry, but you are too far gone!'

'Please,' she said, clutching my hand.

'I cannot help you,' I said, 'but others can. If you explain what happened to you, and what this man did, you may be able to find someone sympathetic, but you would need to go to a clinic in London.'

She looked doubtfully at me and we both knew that she could not.

'I only have until noon,' she said. 'I am only in town today and I am already supposed to be at the market. I cannot come back. They said you could sort me out in a couple of hours.'

It was then I looked at the clock and heard Mrs Cuthbertson's words again in my head: '*On the half hour… be prompt.*'

'I'm sorry,' I said, 'but I have not been trained for this.' I took her hand in mine. 'Listen, I have to go out, but there is another nurse. She was called away, but she is on her way back from London as we speak. She will be able to help.'

'I thought you were a nurse,' she said, her voice trembling. 'Why can't you help?'

'I don't know how,' I said simply. 'You will have to wait or come back another day.'

She sat back down and stared into the fire. She nodded when I offered her tea but would say nothing more to me as I busied myself with the kettle and pot. When I brought her tea to her, I handed her one of Bridget's books called *Wise Parenthood*, although I did not even know if she could read. The time kept clicking by so fast that the hands seem to have moved further to the half hour every time I checked.

'I have to go,' I said at last. 'Stay here as long as you can, ask for Bridget if someone comes, she is another nurse and she should be here very soon.'

She nodded, but as I shut the door behind me, I wondered what would become of her.

I did not realise it as I rushed down the garden path with my bag in my hand, but that was the first day that Mrs Cuthbertson had forced me to do her bidding. I had jumped when she had called, and it would not be the last time.

4

I did not leave the nurses' house until a quarter past ten. I ran through the garden and then down on to the hospital driveway, only slowing to a pace that was respectable for a nurse once I was in view of the hospital windows. I took one of the staff bicycles from the shed on the driveway and put my nursing bag in the basket, together with my gas mask, a loaf of bread, a tin of corned beef and some rather wizened apples that I had taken from the larder. Then I pedalled furiously across the village green and cut across the grass by the church and pub. I continued past the tea room and doctor's surgery and took the Oxworth Road past the entrance to the high street and the new housing estates which clustered round the Metropolitan line station.

Once I was out of town, the road became narrower and lined with high hedges, with nothing but an old church tucked away in a dark copse and the rumble of a train in the cutting somewhere below a canal bridge. It was a road that I rarely ventured down as there was nothing along it for several miles and I only knew of it as the road which would swallow up the number 34 bus after it had left the station.

The tarmac was ridged with regular furrows of mud, a pattern left by the caterpillar tracks of tanks on their way to the training ground in Evesbridge, and my boots became speckled with muddy spray from the bicycle tyres.

I came upon a sign for Elmridge House after twenty minutes on the road, it was a small entrance, just a gap in the high hedge wide enough for a cart or motor vehicle, and one that might be mistaken for a farm track. Behind the entrance was a driveway which led up a hill through a long field. At the top of the hill a small clump of trees obscured the skyline, but there was no sign of a house of any sort. I got off the bicycle and pushed it up the steep hill, walking for several minutes before I came to the trees which I had seen from the bottom of the driveway.

Here, I stopped for breath, and when I turned to look behind me, I saw that the view stretched across the whole valley, with the town of Missensham nestled in the bottom. I could make out the green snake of the railway cutting, the neat patterns of housing on the estates and the dense row of buildings in the high street. Rising above it all on the opposite slope were the old workers' terraces of Drover's Hill, the house in which I had been raised somewhere among them. The fields and foliage were still green, with only the odd rusting canopy to show the arrival of autumn.

I turned away from the view and forced my way up to the top of the hill. As I neared the trees, I found that they were not the clump that I had first thought but old cedars and hollies spaced over a wide lawn. The driveway widened into a large sweep of gravel, as if an announcement for the grand house which rose above it.

Elmridge House reminded me of a large Victorian hunting lodge, with a jumble of pitched roofs and long windows set high into the gables. The walls were set with jagged grey flint, covered in wilting boughs of wisteria which lent an air of romance to the place. In the middle of the gravel sweep was a circular flower bed sprouting with deep green pointed leaves – a few curled trumpets of white petals still blooming despite the season. An old-fashioned car sat on the driveway – rusty brown with a long bonnet and round headlights perched on the end like pince-nez. The engine was idling and a large man in a chauffeur's uniform sat hunched over the wheel as if both he and the car were ready and waiting for their orders.

The woman who had visited me at the nurses' house stood in front of a large arched doorway. Her hair was set tightly in the same neat bun and she wore a long black coat which accentuated her thin body. I had thought her a strange creature when I had seen her before, for I had seldom seen anyone with her demeanour, the length of her limbs accentuating her every movement. Yet now, as I watched her in front of her grand house, everything about her physicality seemed to make sense, and I felt as if I was watching an animal in its natural habitat.

'Mrs Cuthbertson?' I said. For she had not left her name when she visited the kitchen and I only had the name she had given me on the phone.

'You are not Bridget?' she replied and I realised that she did not recognise me from our strange meeting in the nurses' house. I recalled how she had acted that night – her trembling hands, the wavering of her pupils and the bead of sweat on her top lip – yet now her manner was quite different. I wondered if she even remembered sitting in the kitchen with me that night, or if she only remembered a girl in a uniform – my reddish hair and freckles identifying me only as someone who was not Bridget.

'I am afraid Bridget is detained in London,' I said. 'Her parents found an unexploded bomb in their garden…'

She glared at me with one eyebrow raised as if I was a child making up an excuse for lost homework and that another's family misfortune counted for little.

'But that is all right,' I continued, trying to appease her. 'There are always two nurses at the cottage hospital. It is not a busy time; I took the call, so here I am. My name is Nurse Watts.'

She looked at me doubtfully, and suddenly I regretted leaving the shy daisy girl alone in the kitchen in favour of a woman such as her and prayed Bridget's train home had not been delayed.

'I suppose that Bridget did not brief you,' she said.

'No,' I replied, 'but I brought my nursing bag. I didn't know what to expect, but there is usually enough in there to cover any eventuality.'

She did not answer, but I was glad that she had not asked for any more Luminal and I was relieved that I would be able to replace the bottle in the medicine cabinet without detection.

'My son suffers from a nervous complaint,' she said. 'It is due to this awful war. We are quite isolated up here on the ridgeway so he is in need of a new face to take his mind off things. I want no more from you than to take him round the grounds in his wheelchair. He needs to be kept calm, so don't babble away to him like Bridget does.' She fixed her eyes on me, her words becoming slow as if she was talking to a child about a very serious matter. 'My husband is suffering from the advanced stages of tuberculosis and must not be disturbed, he keeps a room at the back of the house, so under no circumstances go further than the cottage with the dovecote where you might stray into his view.' She raised a bony finger to emphasise the last words. 'Girl, what did I just say?'

'To not speak to your son unduly and go no further than the cottage with the dovecote,' I repeated, although my eyes had not left hers and I had given her no cause to think that I was not listening.

She nodded and seemed satisfied.

'Bridget really does send her apologies,' I said, feeling that if I could not defend myself I could at least defend my housemate.

'Oh?' She seemed to hesitate, her large brow furrowed, and I realised that she was one of those people with whom it is best to say very little – she would only hear what she wanted to and the parts that she did hear would never match together well. Before she could question me, the sound of a clock chiming the half hour rang out from somewhere inside the house. 'I have to go!' She ran to the car and I followed her slowly. 'I will miss most of the service now,' she shouted at the driver, 'but you can at least put your foot down and get me there for the

Eucharist.' She opened the car door, but then turned to me. 'You will find him in the corner room to the right of the landing. Hannah will show you up.' She jabbed a bony finger in the direction of a grand stone porch. 'Remember, don't go beyond the dovecote, because my husband must not know of your visit.' Then she thrust a roll of banknotes tied with a rubber band into my hands. Her eyes locked on mine for a brief but intense moment and then, without a farewell, she got into the back seat of the motor car and slammed the door. As I watched the car crawl away down the long sloping driveway, I imagined her leaning forward and berating the driver for the lateness she blamed him for.

I leant the bicycle against the trunk of a cedar and took my bag into the stone porch. Inside the house was a dark wood panelled hallway and a large staircase which rose in a wide arc of bannisters to the floor above.

A dumpy, middle aged maid stood by the hat stand and, when I greeted her, she gave a start as if waking from a daydream, and took my bag from me without a word. We climbed the stairs together, but when we reached the top, she just pointed to a doorway and handed my bag back to me. I smiled, but she did not return it, repeating only the instructions her mistress had given me. It was then that I got a strange feeling about Elmridge House – something about it was not right, although I could not think what.

The room was the first one along a wide corridor, the only one with an open door and, by the wear in the carpet, I thought it must be the only one ever used. When I put my head round the door, I found a large white bedroom with a window overlooking the garden at the side of the house, and another to the front. There was a bed in the corner of the room, with an antique chaise longue, wardrobe and chairs, and a grand fireplace with silver candlesticks on the mantelpiece. There was a bookshelf stacked with military manuals, the polished case of an artillery shell used as a bookend, a Persian rug on the floor and a miniature Eiffel Tower on top of a writing desk – souvenirs collected from service abroad.

It was in this room that I found him, seated in a wheelchair which faced the front window. From the back, I saw that he was broad shouldered, his dark hair cut short at the sides in the standard military way and, when he turned the chair, he met me with a wide grin.

'Hello, nurse calling,' I said a little awkwardly because the introduction had come too late and he could see exactly who I was.

'I see you met my mother,' he said, pointing to the rolled banknotes in my hand, which I only then realised that I was still holding.

'I'm afraid so,' I said.

He smiled again, this time with a slight chuckle in his throat and revealing a chipped tooth at the front, which I thought made him look quite rakish.

'I'm Nurse Watts,' I said and then, for some reason, added: 'Ivy.'

'You did not know about the chair?' he said, his large hands gesturing to the wheels that rose either side of him and the red tartan blanket that covered his knees despite the heat of the day.

'No,' I said. 'Well, actually yes. In fact, I forgot about it as I would not have expected it on the first floor.'

'I like a view,' he said, pointing to the windows, 'and despite what my mother says I am not completely helpless.' Suddenly I thought that this must be the man that Bridget had spoken so dirtily of, her 'someone nice', the man who was dashing and rich, and I could see none of the pitiful creature with frayed nerves that his own mother had described.

'Well, she might have called you helpless,' I said, 'but then everything that came out of her mouth was objectionable.'

I realised too late that I had allowed the words I thought in anger to leave my mouth and I was relieved when he laughed.

'That is just her way, I'm afraid. Well, she can't have given you much of an introduction then.'

'Not even your name.'

'Hugo.'

And I could not help laughing when he said it.

'Well,' he said wearily, 'that is probably why she did not tell you.'

'I think she was just in a hurry,' I said, relieved that he had laughed with me.

'Yes, I'm afraid I am an inconvenience to her. She only ever leaves the house to go to church these days, yet she still feels that she needs someone to babysit me. Hannah would be perfectly capable, but she calls her an imbecile. It's as if she fears being apart from me,' and at this his voice faltered just a little.

'She did not say what I am doing here,' I said awkwardly. 'Only that I am to wheel you around the garden.'

He nodded. 'That's about it.'

'But surely there must be something else,' I said. 'I am a nurse after all. I think that Bridget said you were injured – we have a couple of soldiers who were at Dieppe recovering in the cottage hospital, I am getting quite used to bullet wounds.'

'I just get a few aches and pains sometimes,' he said. 'The main thing is that I keep up my exercise, but just getting down the stairs will be enough for today. Once I have done that, a push around the garden will be fine.' He pointed the wheelchair in the direction of the door. 'There is another chair in the cupboard in the hallway and I can make my own way down the stairs.'

'But...' I removed the rubber band from the banknotes and counted them. 'She gave me three pounds!' I said, somewhat embarrassed that my brief encounter with Mrs Cuthbertson had given me no time to discuss the payment. 'Are you sure that is right? I cannot take three pounds just to push you round the garden!'

'I think the money is in exchange for your discretion,' he said. 'She does not want someone who will make a lot of noise and—'

'Disturb your father,' I added, remembering Mrs Cuthbertson's words.

'She is very particular about having the right person,' he said. 'To be honest, she did not really take to Bridget.'

'Well, you could not call Bridget discreet,' I said, thinking of the telephone calls that I had overheard when

Bridget chatted with her society friends and the way she would try and gossip with Dr Crawford, who she saw as her own class. After all, I already knew of her intention with Hugo.

He laughed. 'Come on, we had better get going, for my mother would want you gone before she returns from church.'

I went back on to the landing and down the stairs. The second wheelchair was where he said it would be; in a cupboard in the hallway and by the time I had got it out and sitting on the flagstones, Hugo was already resting on the bottom step, grasping the bannisters and breathing heavily, his pale skin quite flushed.

'I will have to help you from here,' I said.

'Just bring the chair closer,' he said, 'I—'

I took the wheelchair right to the foot of the stairs where he stood shakily, but then fearing he would fall, I grabbed his arm and drew it round my shoulders, taking his weight just long enough for him to pivot on his feet and slump into the chair, allowing his shoulder to rest on mine for just a second as he did so, and I was suddenly aware of his warmth and the hardness of his muscle.

'You have done that before,' he said, pulling the blanket back over his knees, 'but you seem too young to have much experience with cripples.'

'No,' I said. 'Just my mother. She had polio as a child. She walks with a stick around the house but would need a chair outside it, although she does not like to go out much. She...' but here I stopped myself. Hugo had been so open about his own mother's nature that I felt him someone that I could confide in, but I realised that it was too soon to tell him of my childhood spent caring for my mother and avoiding her sharp tongue. She was a woman who I loved and resented in equal measure, the weakness of her body the only thing that compelled me to keep close to her.

'I thought you must have been training in the military hospitals or something,' he said.

'I am sorry I have not,' I said, 'but I hear there are a lot of men recovering from leg injuries in those places. Were you at Queen Alexandra's before you moved back home?'

But at the mention of the hospital, his manner seemed to change. 'It is your first visit,' he said, 'we have just met and there is so much to talk about, so just for today can we not discuss such miserable things?'

'Of course,' I said, it was a common feeling among the soldiers who had returned home and I quite understood. I remembered what his mother had said about his nerves and I took his request for one of general silence. After all, that was easier than trying to dismiss the horrors of war with some awkward comments on the weather or the fading of the summer flowers in the garden.

I pushed the chair out of the hallway and into the bright sunshine on the drive. A gravel path led round the side of the house and I followed it on to another stretch of lawn which sloped away into an area of low shrubs. There was a little iron bench by the path set back into a long flower bed full of the same dagger like leaves that I had seen in the flower bed on the driveway, the white curls of the blooms starting to brown and wilt.

I paid little attention to the garden as, ahead of me, I could see the lawn fall away and the sky open up into a wide hemisphere of blue. The view of the countryside from the back of the house was even more beautiful than the view of Missensham that I had seen when I paused for breath on the driveway. As I walked further, I could make out the rolling hills on the other side of the valley and the patchwork of fields that were the farms of Evesbridge. I longed to see right down in to the bottom of the valley, but I noticed that I was nearing a small brick building with a tower that was pitted with neat rows of holes – the dovecote cottage that Mrs Cuthbertson had spoken of. I pushed the wheelchair level with the building and stopped the chair on the gravel. We had not reached the end of the path, nor come to any obstacle, there was nothing to stop me going further but Mrs Cuthbertson's words echoing through my head, and I knew that the walk ended here.

Neither Hugo nor I said anything I and wondered how often he was really taken to see this view.

In the middle of the far hill was a field, larger than the others, with a gentler slope. It was lined with grey rectangles spaced evenly and following the contours of the land. Parts of the field were green, but there were areas that looked like tracks, smudged with brown.

'What are those? I asked. 'Are they tents?'

'They are huts,' he replied. 'It is the army training ground at Evesbridge.' He turned his head slightly to look away and I could see the grind of his jaw.

'Do not think about it,' I said quickly. 'You have done your bit, and paid the price,' although the last part of this

I said only to myself. 'It is a shame we cannot go further,' I added, remembering Mrs Cuthbertson's words and hoping that he would contradict her.

But he said nothing to encourage me.

'Well, this is a lovely garden anyway,' I continued.

'I never thought about it,' he said, 'but I suppose it is.'

'There are so many of these white flowers.'

'Calla lilies,' he replied. 'My father used to say that they were planted years ago, but they keep coming up everywhere, even this late in the year. He can't get rid of them.'

'I always thought flowers were a woman's obsession,' I said.

'Well, my father liked to keep things ordered,' he said. 'You may have heard of him – his name was Dr Clive Cuthbertson.'

I shook my head. 'I haven't.'

'Well, I suppose that it has been many years since he practised in Missensham. Most of his work was in Oxworth. He has a reputation as a very dutiful man, but he is very strait-laced.' Then he added bitterly: 'He only likes things that he can control.'

'You mean the lilies?' I said.

'The lilies and everything else.' He laughed. 'Look behind you.'

'What?'

'Look behind you and tell me what you can see.'

I did as he said, but there was nothing notable about the path we had walked down. In fact, the only thing that was different was that a dumpy woman in a dark uniform now sat on the bench by the shrubbery, her head bent low.

'There is nothing but the maid,' I said. 'The one who showed me upstairs.'

'Her name is Hannah,' he said, without turning his head. 'She will be sitting on the bench by the shrubbery, watching us.'

'She is on the bench,' I said, 'but...' As I spoke I saw Hannah's head turn a little in our direction, but she drew it back quickly when she saw me. 'Yes,' I said. 'I suppose she is watching us.'

'My father has always favoured Hannah as she is a little slow and easy for him to control. Even now that my father is starting to lose his mind, she will still report back to him. Hannah sees it as loyalty because she is family, in a way.'

'How is that?' I asked, as I could not see any part of Hugo or his mother in Hannah.

'She has no Cuthbertson blood,' he said laughing. 'The driver that you saw is Edgar, my father's brother. Edgar was badly wounded in the Great War, but his body recovered better than his mind; he daydreams and rarely talks. My father thought he was doing him a favour by employing him here – he gave him lodgings in the old dovecote cottage and helped him to court Hannah.'

'Well, it sounds like a kindness to me,' I said.

'He did it because he knew that Hannah is barren,' said Hugo, lowering his voice. 'He encouraged them to wed because he thought that Edgar could never be a responsible father.'

'Oh!' I said, but nothing more. I thought that it was strange for him to be so open about his family on our first meeting, but his voice was calm and he did not turn to see my reaction and I fancied that he rarely got to talk about his frustrations with another person. It was something that I understood only too well.

'For a long time, Edgar had to put up with driving my parents everywhere and my mother's insults,' he continued, 'but he has always enjoyed the garden and didn't like removing the lilies. Now my father's TB has left him barely strong enough to give an order, and Edgar has had enough of removing the lilies, so now my father has control of neither the lilies nor who tends them.'

'Well, I cannot imagine anyone controlling your mother!' I said, trying to lighten his mood.

He laughed. 'My mother spent the first few years of their marriage on his arm at committee functions, but then became quite important in herself. It is only since my father became infirm that she has spent so much time with me. Church on Sunday morning is the only thing that she now attends on my father's behalf, although she was brought up godless and I don't think that she understands a word of the services. She even gets Edgar to drive her there to make her look important.'

I did not ask more about his family. It clearly wasn't a happy arrangement, but this was something that I could understand. My own small family was very different to Hugo's, but just like him, I found my mother's neediness quite suffocating and in this, I felt we shared a bond.

'This is such beautiful countryside,' I said, 'and quite far from the battlefield. You must be glad to be home.'

But he did not answer me and I thought it a reminder that he did not want to speak of his injury and its cause.

'I tire of this view,' he said at last. 'I would rather look the other way.'

'Of course,' I said and turned the wheelchair round on the path and started pushing it back the way we came. Hugo did not even acknowledge Hannah as we passed the bench, so I nodded to her awkwardly and continued towards the front of the house.

Hugo was silent for a while and did not turn to me, and I supposed him to be deep in thought and quite a different man to the one who had joked with me when I arrived. I stopped the wheelchair on the lawn by the driveway, in the shade of a large cedar tree, and sat down on the grass beside him.

'Will you come again?' he said suddenly.

'I don't know,' I said, surprised by his request. I had seen my visit to Elmridge House as honouring an appointment that Bridget could not keep, and it had never occurred to me that I might return. 'We are not really supposed to take on private nursing jobs,' I explained. 'Besides, it is up to your mother – I will have to wait to see if I am called.'

'I cannot suffer Bridget again,' he said, 'with all her endless chat of parties and the love lives of people that I do not know. She is like a wireless that I cannot turn off.'

I laughed, because it was the kind of chatter that I did not hear from Bridget any more. It was gossip and anecdotes reserved only for those she saw as her social equals and I wondered if money was the only reason she came to Elmridge House, or whether it was for the grand house with its fine rooms and this well spoken young man.

'She never mentioned coming here to me before,' I admitted. 'I thought she had found herself a rich fellow and was spending her Sunday mornings on glamorous dates.'

He laughed. 'You are not like her,' he said. 'I find her quite conceited and you are not. You do not even speak in the same way.'

'Oh!' I said, suddenly embarrassed, for I had always thought that my accent had softened over the years to one that was more like Bridget's – an accent that was more in keeping with the town, more becoming of a nurse, and more acceptable.

'Don't worry,' he said. 'I can see that you need to fit in with the likes of Dr Crawford and Bridget and you pass well enough, it was just you said that you thought Bridget was having glamorous dates with someone – a "fellow", but the word came out flat and I can't imagine Bridget ever saying it that way.'

'You mean that you can't imagine someone who has been brought up properly ever saying it that way!'

'No,' he said. 'I would not have put it like that.' But he did not explain further and I worried that my words had sounded harsh.

'Well, you are right,' I said. 'You need money to train to be a nurse and then, after you qualify, you earn little. It is beyond most of us. That is why nurses are usually from good families, not like me.' But I felt a little unkind as I said it because I knew that he did not think badly of me.

'Are you not from a good family, Nurse Ivy Watts?' he said, the wide grin returning to his face.

'I am not,' I said slowly. 'At least, not in that respect, but I suppose that I am lucky.'

He raised his eyebrows. 'How so?'

'I only have my mother,' I said, 'but I have a guardian angel. She trained as a nurse and a midwife – that is why I wanted to be a nurse too, and so that I could care for my mother when she needs it. This nurse is an old friend of my mother's. When her son left home, she rented her house to us and she brings work for my mother to do – sewing and mending that she can do at home – and that covers the rent. She lent me the money to help me train and helped me with the exams.'

In fact, she had done so much more than that, but to give Sadie her full credit would be to reveal more of the background I was ashamed of and was trying to overcome. I could not tell Hugo that my father had died in the war, leaving my crippled mother destitute, and that all she had left of him was a little wedding photograph that gathered dust on the mantelpiece. I could not tell him that Sadie had met my mother in an infirmary and taken pity on her, and that the money my mother paid Sadie was well below the rent she could get from another tenant. I could not tell him any of that, and yet I had admitted more to him than I had to anyone in a long while.

'Well, I like your accent better, Ivy Watts,' he said. 'If I wanted to hear another stiff voice like Bridget's I could just turn on the wireless.'

'Thank you,' I said, although I was not sure how much of what he said was due to the politeness that came with his class.

I wheeled him back to the house, past the flower bed and up to the front porch. I did not feel ready to go, yet the clank of the church bell told me that our time together had come to an end.

'Will you come again?' Hugo repeated.

But we both knew it was not up to us.

5

I left Elmridge House at half past eleven. As I pedalled along the Oxworth road, a car passed me by the underground station, a bulky man in a peaked cap at the wheel. It seemed to be going much faster than the speed limit and I could not make out the passenger, yet the petrol rationing had made private cars a rare sight and I assumed that it must have been Mrs Cuthbertson returning to Elmridge House.

I turned into the empty high street and then into the maze of little workers' terraces that hid behind the neat shop fronts. When I reached the bottom of Drover's Hill, I got off the bicycle and pushed it up the steep slope, the houses becoming smaller and denser the further I went, until it seemed as if they were teetering on the top of the hill, holding on to each other for safety.

I stopped for breath at the top of the hill and looked across the whole of Missensham – to the other side of the valley. It was a view of roads and rooftops, but in the distance I could make out the ridge and the clump of trees that obscured Elmridge House from view and just spot the long driveway that I had cycled down barely half an hour beforehand.

I carried on to the end cottage with the blue door. I leant the bicycle on a lamp post, flipped over the 'nurse on call' sign and wrapped my knuckles hard on the door. There was smoke coming from the chimney and inside I could hear the whirr of a sewing machine.

'It's only me,' I called, 'Ivy,' but I knew that I would have to wait.

At last, I heard the rattle of bolts and the loosening of locks on the other side of the wood as the door was opened without greeting, and I took my bags from the step and drew a deep breath before stepping inside.

The little sitting room seemed smaller than I remembered and cramped and airless compared to the large open rooms of Elmridge House. In the middle of the room, a woman sat behind a workbench, her face hidden by a large black Singer sewing machine. The picture rails were hung with evening gowns of every colour, length and style, making the room seem even smaller and I felt as if I was in the middle of a busy ballroom, crowded with dancers and socialites.

The woman at the machine did not look up, 'Can't you see that I'm busy?' she spat. 'I'm still panting from having to get up to open the door.'

'Hello, Mum,' I said, trying to keep my voice light. 'It is good to see you. How are you keeping?'

She shrugged my hand from her shoulder, grumbling to herself, but I had dealt with her moods for many years and knew better than to enquire about her woes.

'I've brought us some lunch from the larder at home,' I said. 'I'm afraid it is corned beef again, but the greengrocer still had plenty of apples in.'

'I told you I am busy,' she muttered. 'Take them into the kitchen. Sadie is fussing with the tea in there and she says she won't go home until I have finished these for her. I'm making little over the extortionate rent she charges as it is. I have to keep her sweet.'

'I don't think she will mind too much,' I said, embarrassed that Sadie could obviously hear every word, then I added: 'Don't forget that she is your good friend not just your landlady.'

But my mother did not respond, so I just spoke to the machine and her hunched shoulders.

'This is nice,' I said, taking a green satin gown from the jaws of the machine.

'Some harlot put her high heel through the hem,' she said, wrinkling her freckled nose in disgust. 'There is red wine down the front. How do these people live like this when there is a war on?'

'I hardly think they are being frivolous, Mum,' I said. 'These ladies may be enjoying the odd evening out but it's not as if they are blowing all their clothing coupons on new gowns instead of winter coats. They want their dresses patched because they are not getting new ones and without ladies like them you would have no way to earn a crust.'

But she did not seem to hear me and just grumbled to herself. 'All these young things out dancing with the boys from the barracks, strutting about in their finery – they don't know how lucky they are, having all that fun.' But she said 'fun' as if it was a dirty word and that those who had it did so at the expense of others.

'They don't know if there will be a tomorrow,' I said. 'They are making the most of life, Mum,' I said, but my words were lost in the clatter of the sewing machine. 'Which is something that you never did.' I stared at her hunched body, her wide brow creased with concentration and her arm working the handle furiously, but she still did not look up. 'I will go and help Sadie,' I said to myself.

The kitchen door was propped open and Sadie stood outside in the alley, her squat frame propped up against the coal bunker. I dumped my bag of groceries on the draining board and stepped outside to join her.

From inside, the clatter of the machine stopped abruptly and a violent curse rose over the whisper of the boiling kettle. I raised my eyebrows and Sadie nodded.

'I just had to get out for a bit,' she said. 'She is particularly bad today. You will need to tread carefully.'

'Oh, I am used to it,' I said. 'Nobody escapes my mother's tongue, she does me no special favours, her own daughter.'

'Nor her best friend.' She shook her head sadly.

'How are you?' I said. I took her hand and squeezed it. I had known her my whole life, but she was not an affectionate woman, it was only recently she had stopped pulling away and allowed these smallest tokens of affection.

She looked down at her hand in mine. 'I mustn't grumble, but my ankles are swollen again,' she said.

'You are back in uniform!' I tugged at her old-fashioned midwife's cape. 'Will they ever let you retire?'

'The local midwives have gone to London on nursing duties for the wounded. They got me back doing some shifts. I've got a couple of jittery mothers on the estates and one out in Evesbridge, plus there is Mrs Cane lying in at the cottage hospital.'

'Mrs Cane from Longdown Farm?' I asked, thinking of the bloated red faced woman on the ward.

Sadie nodded.

'Well, I may see you back at the hospital again then,' I said. 'It must be over a year since you were at the nurses' house with Bridget and me. A year since we all sat round the kitchen table and you passed the book over to us.'

'So how is that all going?' she asked, lowering her voice despite the clatter of the sewing machine. 'Many lady visitors to the kitchen recently?'

'It is not going badly at all,' I replied. 'I have managed to find homes for a couple of unwanted babies in the last few months and the prevention side has picked up a little. When the bomb fell in the lido all those months ago, it brought things a bit too close to home, so there has been an increase on Bridget's side of things.'

'Ah,' she said. 'With all the bombs that fell on London last year, the young don't know if they will live another day, so they pay no heed to the consequences of their actions.'

'Or maybe they can't face bringing a new life into such a world,' I offered.

We said nothing for a while. I had come to learn that was often the way with nurses. We had to be chipper for the patients, but nobody could keep that up forever, not without a few moments to think on the things we had seen.

'I wish you could have taught me,' I said after a few minutes. 'The way you taught Bridget. Especially now there is more call for it, because I fear that we may not be able to help everyone.' I thought of the girl with the daisy print dress and the basket of eggs, but somehow to speak of her seemed too painful.

'I'm sorry,' she said. 'Bridget was with me first and she is older, she can pass her knowledge on to you when the time comes.'

I nodded, yet I could not imagine Bridget talking to me for more than two minutes or the time that it took to give an order.

'Come,' said Sadie. 'I do not hear the machine any more. It might be safe.'

We made tea and corned beef sandwiches and when we returned to the sitting room, we found Mum sat in the rocking chair by the fire. She had folded away her work table and the green satin gown hung from the picture rail with the others.

The evening gowns were indeed 'finery', just as my mother had described them – sequins and feathers and silks – but every one of them was a faded glory. There were the long hems from when the century was new, the fringing and beading of the twenties, and the clinging silk of the past decade, but each of them was now patched or had the waist taken in, a collar added or removed, a hemline taken down, or lace sewn over a stain. They were fond reminders of evenings that were not blighted by rationing or blackouts but whose owners still tried to make the best of what little life was giving them.

We sat down with the sandwiches. Sadie took the stool opposite my mother, leaving me the window seat.

'Your hem is muddy, Ivy,' my mother spat. 'You haven't walked mud into the house, have you?'

'Oh, I am sorry,' I said, remembering my journey that morning and the muddy caterpillar tracks on the Oxworth Road. 'I was…' But there was no reasonable explanation for pushing a man round in a wheelchair for three pounds, so I said nothing further.

My mother stared at me, so I unlaced my boots and put them by the door.

'Sorry,' I said again. 'I actually stepped in mud by the Oxworth Road, the verge has been chewed up by some sort of army manoeuvre. It looks like some tanks went through to the training ground. These things will do some damage in battle, if only to the fields of France.'

They tutted as only women of their age and class did; in a kind of unspoken agreement that neat verges were more important than all that silly fighting.

'There is an old house there,' I said. 'Some kind of grand Victorian lodge. I had just thought it a farm track that led up there before, but the storm last year must have taken down a few trees, for I had never noticed the house before. In fact…' I was about to tell them of my visit to Elmridge House, but I noticed something pass between them; a look of understanding and my mother seemed to tense.

'There is a woman who lives there, Mrs Cuthbertson, who has no favour in this town,' said my mother, her face quite grim. 'People keep away from there, and you would do well to do the same.'

'Oh,' I said. 'Why is that?'

'She is on a charitable committee which serves a few Hertfordshire hospitals,' said Sadie quickly. 'Many years ago she tried to stop all of the funding that went to Missensham Cottage Hospital and, if she had got her way, the hospital would have had to close. For a long time it looked certain that she would win. It was a tough time for us all.'

'Why would she do that?' I said. 'Elmridge House is not far out of Missensham. The cottage hospital and the people that it helps are on her doorstep!'

'Well, the *Missensham Herald* got hold of the story and a journalist started investigating her,' Sadie continued. 'The newspaper ran some stories about her big house and motor car and then the *Herald* discovered that she was recommending that the money be spent elsewhere – on the development of a new wing at St Catherine's in Oxworth – a ward that would be run by her husband. She wanted to use the money to benefit her husband's career. She is not a pleasant character.'

'But it must have been so long ago,' I said, 'for I never heard anything about it from the matron when I arrived at the hospital, nor Dr Crawford or Bridget. It surely can no longer matter if it—'

'Ivy, enough!' My mother's face was suddenly furious, her hands braced against the arms of the chair as if to lift herself up to scold me.

'I am sorry,' I said, 'but I just don't...' But then I realised it was not worth protesting because any more words on the matter would cause her to get up too quickly and curse with the pain in her hip. I would then have to watch in silence as she hobbled to the kitchen and slammed the door behind her, leaving only a chink of light from under the kitchen door. I had seen my mother's temper many times before and I did not want to suffer it that afternoon. 'It does not matter,' I said quickly, wondering what I had said to offend the women. 'I just happened to go past the house on the way to see a patient in Evesbridge. I don't expect I will need to go that way again for some time.'

My mother slumped back into her chair, then lifted her mug and took a slurp of tea as if to signal that the conversation was over and I did the same, glad that we could move on to our lunch at last. After my busy morning I had been ravenous, but the atmosphere in the room turned the sandwich to cardboard in my mouth and we all ate slowly. I tried to make conversation about the weather and the bomb that had nearly destroyed Bridget's family home, but my efforts were met only with nods and grunts. Sadie said only that the meat was delicious but voiced it in such a way that I thought it more a wish than a fact.

My mother ate in silence. This was not completely out of character for her, but I missed her usual interruptions and scolds. She did not seem angry any more and spent most of the meal staring at the dying embers in the grate as if imagining a roaring fire. After a while, her silence made me feel as if I was intruding.

When the clock on the mantelpiece struck the hour, I got up from the window seat, glad of an excuse to leave.

'I will see you out,' said Sadie quickly and I nodded, although it was a strange thing to say as the front door was only a few paces from where we sat.

Sadie opened the door for me and waited until I was over the step before handing me my bag. Then she leant close to my ear.

'I would not mention that old house again,' she said, 'not in front of her.'

'Why?' I mouthed.

The sewing machine had already started to clatter again, but Sadie still lowered her voice. 'Your mother was just concerned for me at the time. She thought I would lose my job if the cottage hospital was shut down, but she did not know any more than what the newspaper said about the new wing at St Catherine's.' She paused, her voice becoming a whisper. 'The woman at Elmridge House found out about what we were doing at the nurses' house. Her husband is very religious and did not approve of…' But they were words that she could not finish in a street where the houses were so tightly packed and we stood only feet away from the neighbours' windows. 'That woman never told anyone but the nurses what she knew,' Sadie continued. 'She told us not to oppose her shutting the hospital down or she would report us to the police. If it was not for the newspaper finding out about her husband's work at St Catherine's, she would have succeeded.' She drew back from my ear and faced me, looking me in the eye. 'You should never go to Elmridge House. People keep away from there and you would do well to do the same.' It was a strange turn of phrase and

I realised that I had heard exactly the same words on my mother's lips when I had first mentioned the house.

I nodded but could not look her in the eye. I had been captivated by the old house and the family that lived there and already knew that I wanted to return.

6

In the fortnight since I had first met Mrs Cuthbertson, I had learned so much about her, and none of it was good: she was rude; she was a bad mother; she had tried to close down the cottage hospital and had threatened the nurses; and she was most likely a drug addict. All of that mattered very little to me as there was something about Elmridge House that intrigued me and I realised that I would be willing to put up with Mrs Cuthbertson's unpleasantness if she asked me to visit the house again.

The nurses' house had not received a single visitor all week. Daisy did not return and when I mentioned her to Bridget, she just shrugged her shoulders and said that she had seen no such person, unmoved by my story of the girl who had been too scared to wait for her.

I put off telling Bridget about my visit to Elmridge House. I suppose that I feared her jealousy, but when I heard the long grate of the telephone in the hallway at exactly ten o'clock on Sunday I knew that she would find out. I jumped up from my chair in the sitting room, my novel falling from my knee, and ran across the room, only to hear the tumble of Bridget's footsteps on the stairs and the rattle of the receiver that silenced the ring.

'Ah, hello, Mrs Cuthbertson' she said, with an excitement in her voice.

I leant against the door and waited, but when I heard nothing more, I ventured into the hallway to see Bridget stony faced, her arm stretched out to me, the receiver dangling from her fingers.

'She wants *you*,' she spat.

I ducked past her and took the receiver.

Ten minutes later I was pedalling hard along the Oxworth Road on my way to Elmridge House, Bridget's protests still ringing in my ears. Mrs Cuthbertson had said no more than usual, but I had put a bottle of Luminal in my bag just in case she managed to produce a prescription for it. It was not until I felt the breeze on my shoulders that I realised I had forgotten my coat, but somehow I did not feel that I was breaking any of the hospital rules. My visits to Elmridge House were as a nurse, but it was private work – Mrs Cuthbertson was paying me directly and there was no way that I could record them as official business when all I was required to do was push a wheelchair.

When I reached the entrance to the long driveway, I got off the bicycle and pushed it up the steep slope. I thought that I had made good time, but, as the house came into view, I realised that my efforts were not good enough for Mrs Cuthbertson.

'Where were you, girl?' she snapped as she stood by the motor car, the door held open for her by the burly chauffeur. 'You are late – I shall miss the first part of the service again!'

'Well, I couldn't possibly have got here any quicker,' I said under my breath as I tried to pin my hair back. 'You didn't give me much notice.'

But she did not seem to hear me and pointed towards the porch, the slenderness of her arm accentuated by the point of her bony finger. 'Go and help Hugo down the stairs,' she said. She rummaged in her bag and thrust a roll of banknotes into my hand. 'Go on!'

I propped my bicycle up against the nearest tree, dumped my nursing bag on the driveway and ran into the hallway, but Hugo was already sitting on the bottom step, the red tartan blanket wrapped round his legs. I turned back to get my bag, but he grabbed my arm and shook his head. 'Best to wait until she has gone,' he said.

We listened in silence to the curses she directed at the chauffeur, then the slam of the car door and the crunch of the gravel, not daring to speak until the clatter of the engine faded away to nothing. Our eyes locked together as we listened, smiles and raised eyebrows at every rushed footstep and curse. Only once we could hear birdsong again did he loosen his grip and I went back to the driveway.

In the distance, I thought that I could see the roof of the motor car skimming the hedge which lined the Oxworth Road and I watched it until it was out of sight. My nursing bag was next to a sweeping tyre track where the car had narrowly missed it, flecks of flint and mud speckling the leather. I remembered my mother's warning

again and thought that maybe she and Sadie were right –
Mrs Cuthbertson should be avoided, but at least that
morning I would not have to suffer her.

I rescued my bag and held it aloft as I carried it inside
so that Hugo could see what had happened. I put it on the
flagstones and wrestled the wheelchair from the cupboard.
Then, without a word, I helped him into it and began the
journey through the grand doorway and out on to the
driveway.

'I wish you wouldn't sulk,' he said. 'I was looking
forward to your cheerfulness.'

'Well,' I sighed. 'I suppose I should be grateful that she
has a driver. I am sure that if she had been driving herself
she would have run my bag over, not just ruined it. In fact,
she would have probably run me over too.'

He laughed, and I was glad for it because I could not
see his face.

'There!' I said, pointing to a small black cloud on the
horizon. 'She means it to rain on me too, she saw that I
had forgotten my coat.'

'You're wrong,' he said. 'If she could control the
weather, it would rain all the time.'

I laughed, the knot in my stomach that I had felt when I
saw my bag covered in gravel slowly easing. 'Well, we had
better get going on our walk,' I said, 'before she notices
that the weather is still fair.'

I pushed the chair on to the path which led round the
side of the house and past the bench and the beds of dagger
shaped leaves, the flowers now browned and fallen. In
the distance, the hills on the other side of the valley were

blunted by mist. Hannah had not followed us outside this time, but I fancied that I saw her face watching from one of the downstairs windows.

'Actually I think that my mother quite likes you,' said Hugo suddenly, but then he added: 'Well, actually she likes no one, but she at least favours you over Bridget, so I would almost say that she has a soft spot for you.'

'I'm not sure that I want her soft spot,' I said, but this time he did not laugh and I thought that maybe my rudeness had gone too far. After all, no matter how objectionable the woman was, she was still Hugo's mother, she had raised him and spent every minute that she could with him, so they must have some kind of connection.

We continued in an awkward silence, somehow made worse by the fact that I could not see his face, only the swirl of dark hair on the top of his head and his broad shoulders, which told me nothing of what he was feeling.

After a few minutes I stopped the chair on the path, the swish of gravel replaced by only the silence of the valley. We had drawn level with the old dovecote cottage, yet the path carried on ahead of us as if tracing the journey I was forbidden to take.

We looked at the view in silence. The sky was a dull white and the once vibrant green of the fields was muted by mist. A long grey cloud had blurred the line of the horizon, drawing a smudge of rain down across the distant fields. We watched the rows of little grey tents in the training ground as they slowly dissolved into the clouds. Then a dull rumble rolled over the hills.

'Is that the army guns?' I asked.

But my question was answered as the sky above us darkened and heavy raindrops streaked through the thin fabric of my dress.

I heaved the wheelchair in a circle and I pushed it as hard as I could away from the dovecote and the dagger leaved beds and back in the direction of the front porch, the rain already soaking my dress and slicking my hair against my scalp. Back at the house, I pulled the chair inside the hallway and helped Hugo out of it and on to the bottom stair.

He settled himself and shook the raindrops from his sleeves. 'I do hope that Hannah does not tell my mother of this,' he said. 'She would worry that I might get a chill.'

'Oh, you must pass on my apologies...' I began but then I saw that he was smiling and cared nothing for his mother's concerns. 'Well, you had better go up and get warm before you get that chill,' I said.

Hugo began to heave himself up on the bannisters, pulling his legs after him while I wheeled the chair across the flagstones and wrestled it back into the cupboard.

When I got upstairs, I found that he was already in his room, sat in an armchair by an empty grate.

'I had better light a fire or we will never dry out,' I said.

I knelt by the hearth, but the coal scuttle was empty and there were only a couple of small logs and some bits of kindling in the wood basket. I arranged the kindling in the grate and watched the flames leap from the match, the fire taking hold with a contented crackle.

We watched the flames in silence for a few minutes, but when lightning flashed through the window, he jumped and I did too, and we both laughed.

'Those are still the blankets that you wore outside,' I said, pulling at the tartan on his lap, 'let me air them for you.' But as I reached for his lap, he grabbed at the material.

'No,' he said quickly. 'They are not wet.'

'As you wish,' I said, but I had already felt that they were slicked with rain. 'I'm sorry,' I added, although I was not sure what I was apologising for. 'Well, I will just sit here for the rest of my visit, if that is all right,' I said awkwardly. 'I am going to my mother's house for lunch and it may take me a while to dry off before the walk.'

'The rain doesn't look like it will stop,' he said, but neither of us bothered to look out of the window as the whole room had dimmed.

'Well, I will look like a drowned rat for the rest of the day then,' I said, 'because there is no airing space at my mother's, she has patched up ballgowns hanging from every hook.'

'Can you not stay longer?' he said. 'Until the rain stops.'

Then there was another rumble of thunder, the sound seemed to intensify and I realised that several seconds had passed since the lightning; the main storm was still to come.

'I will have to risk it,' I said. 'I am worried about how long the journey will take me in this rain. The roads by my mother's house can turn quickly to mud and it might be hours before it stops. Can you lend me an umbrella?'

'I wish I could,' he said, 'but I can't use them in a wheelchair and my mother has never needed one as she is driven everywhere, although you could borrow a coat of hers.'

'No,' I cried. 'I would not dare wear anything of hers! What if she passed me on the road and saw me from the window of her car?'

He shrugged. 'Honestly, she has so many things she would not notice one missing.'

'No,' I said, 'I—'

'Look.' He pointed to the corner of the room. 'She keeps a box of old clothes on the top shelf of the wardrobe in here. There must be a raincoat in it. It has been up there for years, so I am sure she won't even remember that she has it and would not recognise it if she saw it again.'

'All right,' I said reluctantly. I went to the wardrobe and opened it. There was a large cardboard box on the shelf above the rail, just as he had said. I got it down and put it in front of the fireplace, a musty smell rising from it as I took off the lid.

'There,' he said, peering into the box. 'I knew there would be something.'

'What do you mean?' I asked, pulling out the only garment I could see. 'I can't go out in this!'

It was a pale yellow coat made of a very fine leather with a trim of black fur and a few large black buttons. It seemed to be a very loose fitting style, and when I held it up to my face, the hemline fell to my ankles.

'Well,' he laughed. 'It will certainly keep you covered.'

'I have seen this kind of coat before,' I said. 'On grand old women. Aren't they what women used to wear for journeys in those old open motor cars twenty years back, so that all their puffy blouses and long skirts wouldn't get covered in dust from the road?'

'I believe so,' he said. 'The car that Edgar drives must be equally old; she probably got the coat at about the same time.'

'I can quite imagine your mother with the roof down in that rickety old car,' I said, 'but shouldn't this coat also have a ridiculously large hat with a dead bird on top to match it?'

'Well, I'm sure there will be a dead bird in there if you want one,' he said.

I laughed. 'Well, something smells like a dead bird.' I knelt down and folded the coat into my lap. 'Seriously,' I said, 'I can't wear this. There must be something else...'

But there was not. There was some kind of headdress – a little tiara but made of no more than wire and rhinestones – and some large corsets, the boned panels still laced tightly together. At the bottom was a large bouquet of artificial flowers – swirls of white silk each wound loosely round a roll of yellow felt at the centre.

'Well, there are no dead birds,' I said. 'Not even a feather.' I took the yellow coat from my lap and unfolded it once more. 'I'm not even sure that it is wearable,' I began. 'The leather at the waist seems to have stiffened with age or...' but my voice became quieter for it was not an aged leather panel that I was feeling but a large pocket that contained something hard and flat and I pulled it out to see a postcard.

No message was written on the back, except for one faded word – *memories*. On the front was an old photograph – a group of people posed round a tall woman, her neckline bare down to her breast and a tight bodice hugging her tiny waist. Her skirt billowed out at the hips and fell in waves of taffeta to her knees. To her right was a man in a dark tunic with puffed sleeves, and to her left was a man in an evening jacket holding a top hat. There were about ten other women in the picture, all wearing similar white dresses and each of them extending a leg or holding an arm in a graceful arc. Every eye socket had been shaded to a dark pit, every limb was naked and every shoe tapered to a fine point. 'This is some kind of performance,' I said. 'This is...'

But there were words too, printed in a flowery typeface along the bottom of the postcard:

Leonid Postov's Ballets Spectaculaire, The Crown Theatre, Covent Garden.

I felt the silk of the flowers between my fingers and realised that the bouquet in my lap was the same as the one held by the woman in the centre of the photograph. She was a thin woman and as tall as the men on either side of her. There was something about the way that she held herself, the straight back and the raised chin, that I recognised, and there was something familiar about the poses of the dancers around her, the way their fingers and toes were pointed to lengthen the slender limbs.

I thought about my meeting with Mrs Cuthbertson earlier that day, how she had told me to help Hugo on the stairs and directed me towards the porch – the line of her slender arm, accentuated by the point of her finger. I had thought her skinny when I first met her, but she carried herself without awkwardness and I realised that the elegance I had mistaken for good breeding was in fact down to years of training.

'Your mother was a dancer!' I said. 'A ballerina.'

'You are surprised?'

'Well, yes, I suppose I am. But now I think of it, she does have some elegance about her.'

There were other things about Mrs Cuthbertson that were starting to make sense – her receding hairline I now realised had been caused by years of drawing her hair into the tight bun that dancers favoured and she was still in the habit of wearing heavy make-up as if she was on stage. But there was a lot that I did not recognise.

'She is smiling.' I said. 'I never would have thought!' and she was, the young dancer had a brightness to her eyes and her rounded face did not seem so severe. 'She looks so different,' I added. 'I never would have guessed it if the postcard had not been here.'

Hugo laughed. 'My mother used to be softer, believe it or not. She was even well liked, or so I have heard, but she said that she always felt trapped at Elmridge House. I think she missed the dancing. It was having a baby – me – that trapped her here away from everything that she loved.'

'That's not your fault,' I said quickly, but his expression told me that my words would make little difference to what he thought.

'My father has always been a dull and pious man,' he continued. 'I think she was worn down over the years and she changed into what she is now.'

'Your father?' I asked, pointing to the man who held the top hat.

'Yes,' he said, 'but he is somewhat older than her, so how did you know?'

'Your mother is holding this bouquet,' I said. 'I just thought that this gentleman had given it to her. These flowers are only silk and wire, but they look so like the ones that grow all over the garden here.'

I looked at the picture again. There was something about the young Mrs Cuthbertson that was enchanting. The glamour of the ballet was a world very different to my own and she was at its centre. She was young, admired and she was beautiful, and when Hugo turned his head to me, I realised that I had said the word out loud.

'You think my mother was beautiful?' he repeated.

'Oh,' I said, embarrassed. 'Actually, I meant the whole thing – the poses and the costumes and everything.' I put my fingertip on the centre of the postcard. 'I suppose she is, although so much time has passed and the stage make-up is so heavy, it makes all the dancers look the same... and her hair is pulled so tightly...' But my thoughts were wandering. 'I can imagine she would finish this performance,' I said, 'and then have some champagne at the Savoy, then she would step outside, taking this fine gentleman's hand, and they would get in to a beautiful motor car...'

'And she would be wearing the ugly coat,' he finished.

I laughed and he did too and I suddenly realised that I had been lost in the glamour of the photograph. I returned the postcard to the pocket, then I put on the coat. It seemed to swamp me at first, but when I did up the buttons, it cinched a little at the waist and fell just short of my ankles and I caught the reflection of myself in his dressing mirror and suddenly felt glamorous. I spun round slowly, the coat billowing at my waist.

I saw Hugo's grin reflected in the glass. 'It fits,' he said. 'So you have no excuse.'

'You mean I have no *choice*,' I muttered, 'and I shall have to use all my bicycle clips to keep it from catching in the chain.' I put the old corsets, the silk bouquet and the tiara back in the box and returned it to the top of the wardrobe. Now only the old coat was left.

Hugo must have seen the disappointment on my face. 'Why are you sad?' he said.

'I'm not sure,' I said. 'I suppose that all this just reminded me that some people lead very different lives to others. I have never even seen a ballet, and my own mother's life has been the opposite of the one that your mother has lived. My mother could never have danced, she has been crippled since childhood and was born into poverty. My father died in the war and all she has to remember him by is a cheap brass ring and a tiny wedding photograph that gathers dust on the mantelpiece. She spends her days mending other people's party dresses and complaining about the women who wear them – women she has never met.'

'I'm sorry,' he said. 'It is so isolated up here that I forget what the world is like for others. Why not give the coat to your mother? You are too young to wear it. Then she would at least have a tiny part of this life you imagine of champagne and motor cars. She could even pretend that her kitchen was the Savoy.'

'You don't know my mother,' I said. 'She would not see the funny side and she has never been a dreamer.'

'Well, I am glad that you are not like her,' he said.

'Oh, I am,' I said. 'Just half an hour from now, my mother and I will be sat together, with just one lump of coal burning in the grate, chewing Spam sandwiches and moaning about the weather.'

'I don't believe it!' he said.

'In fact, I should already be heading back to the nurses' house in case Bridget needs to call me to the ward to lance a boil or cut an old man's toenails.'

He laughed. 'All right, I have heard enough!'

'I am so late that I will have to run across the driveway in this coat. That won't be glamorous,' I said, heading for the bedroom door.

He smiled. 'Goodbye, Ivy.'

'Goodbye, Hugo.'

But then he turned his chair to face me. 'I will maybe see you next week,' he said.

I nodded. 'I hope so,' but we could say no more than that because we both knew that it all depended on a phone call that his mother would make the following Sunday morning at ten o'clock.

7

I arrived at the bottom of Drover's Hill wet and exhausted from my long journey from Elmridge House. I had kept my head bowed most of the way, forcing the bicycle through the rain and trying to keep the wheels steady on the muddy roads. The only people I had seen on my journey were huddled under shop awnings in the high street or peering from the windows of the bus as it sprayed my skirt with muddy water. The yellow leather coat had dampened to a dull beige, rainwater seeping in at the seams and fur collar, but it had kept parts of me dry and for that I was grateful. The potholes on Drover's Hill were pooled with a brown soup of water, muddied rivulets chasing along the gutters. The narrow streets gave a little more shelter from the rain, but my arms ached as I pushed the bicycle up the final slope to the little house at the top of the road.

I leant the bicycle against the wall of the house, undid the clips, picked up my nursing bag and flipped over the nurse on call sign. Then I took a loaf of bread I had brought with me from the basket, the sodden paper bag dissolving in my fingers.

I hammered on the door. 'It's me – Ivy!' I yelled over the clatter of the sewing machine. 'I'm sorry I'm so late, but the roads were terrible. Open up!'

Inside, the noise stopped and I counted the seconds as I imagined my mother hobbling over to the door with her stick. Then came the sounds of the key in the lock and the bolts being drawn one after another and at last the door swung open and I followed my mother as she hurried back inside.

'Shut it quickly. I don't want rain on the mat,' was her only greeting.

She sat back at the sewing machine and put her head down. 'I will be done by the time the tea's brewed,' she said, waving a bony finger at the kitchen door.

I obeyed the order and hurried into the kitchen, putting the kettle on the burner and the loaf of bread on the board, glad of a chance to peel the wet coat from my skin at last.

'Am I just setting out two cups?' I called once the din of the machine had lulled.

'Yes,' she called. 'You just missed Sadie. You are over an hour late and she had a shift to work up at the cottage hospital.'

I joined her in the sitting room again. 'That's a shame, but maybe I will catch her there later,' I said, trying to make my voice sound light but really fearing a lecture about my lateness. 'I'm afraid that I won't be able to stay for long as I am already supposed to be on my way back to the nurses' house. I'm not due on the ward, but I have to be somewhere in the grounds in case they need me.'

She snapped off the thread and pushed her work table against the hearth, only then did she look up, her mouth dropping open and her eyes staring right through me.

'What?' I said. 'What's wrong? I'm sorry about not being able to stay but...' My voice trailed off when I realised it was not an apology that she wanted. 'Mother?' I said. 'Mum, are you quite all right?'

'You have been to the Cuthbertson house,' she said slowly, a slight catch to her voice.

'Well, yes,' I said. 'I—'

'The house you spoke of on the Oxworth Road, the one I told you to stay away from.'

'I don't understand,' I said. 'How did you...?' But then I saw that her eyes were resting on my arm and I realised that I had folded the coat over my wrist like a waiter's cloth, the fur trimmed neckline on the top fold. 'You've seen this before,' I said slowly. 'You have seen this coat before!'

She had a slight wobble to her lip, but she bit down on it quickly, forcing her mouth into her familiar look of disapproval.

'Look,' I said. 'I don't like that woman much either – she accused me of being late to a time I had not agreed to, and her car nearly ran over my bag and all my equipment – but really I have seen very little of her. All I have been doing is pushing her son around the garden in his wheelchair and getting well paid for doing so. I am taking her money for very little. There is no harm in that.'

'Harm!' she spat. 'What do you know of harm?'

It was then that I realised how little attention I had paid to my mother's warning. I had sat for so long in this room listening to her moaning about grass verges chewed up by caterpillar tracks and women who could afford evening gowns and dared to wear them that her warning about Elmridge House had seemed no more than another gripe at the end of a long list of things that she was bitter over.

'If she tried to shut down the cottage hospital it is all in the past and she failed anyway, didn't she? Whatever you feel towards her is no more than a grudge,' I said. Then remembering what Hugo had told me, I added: 'I hear that there was a time when Mrs Cuthbertson was actually well liked, sweet natured even, when she was newly wed, at least.' But now, as I repeated Hugo's words, they seemed to fall flat and I began to realise that my mother's reaction must be nothing to do with some petty act of committee bureaucracy that Mrs Cuthbertson had committed.

My mother stood up shakily and took a couple of stumbling steps towards me, tearing the coat from my arm. She grabbed my wrists to steady herself, straightened her back until she was almost my height and raised her chin so that she could look me in the eye. 'You are never to have anything more to do with that place,' she hissed, 'nor that woman.' Then she turned and walked quietly back to her seat, sat down heavily and turned her hunched body away from me.

On the floor was the long leather coat, soaked with rain and trodden under my mother's feet.

LILY

8

'Lily?' there was a knock on the dressing room door. 'Lil, are you there?'

In the mirror, a woman stared back at me with heavily made-up eyes, a trail of sweat creeping from the clump of white flowers on her hairline. I pulled the tiny lace sleeves of my costume back over my shoulders and tried to smile, the pale foundation on the face of my reflection spidering into cracks.

'Come in,' I called wearily.

Grace burst into the dressing room, the sound of distant applause rising and falling with the swing of the door. She clutched a large bouquet to her white bodice. 'They are from Dr Cuthbertson,' she said, setting the flowers down on the dressing table. 'Lilies for our Lil. Although I'm buggered if I know how he got hold of them in February!'

I took the bouquet from her and rubbed the petals between my fingers. 'They are fake,' I said, 'but they are proper silk, not like the little rolls of white paper we have been using on stage.'

'Well, it looks like he has gone to some effort, Lil,' she said, grinning. 'Silk lilies for the great Liliana Postova. These are not just cheap carnations like the other punters throw. You are more to him than just any old bird dancing in frilly knickers.'

'He probably just knows that lilies are often used in performances of *Giselle*,' I said. 'That is all that he is thinking. Liliana Postova is hardly a famous name, but who knows? Maybe next season Len will be able to get us into a theatre bigger than the Crown and things will really start to take off for Ballets Spectaculaire. Then every gentleman in the audience will throw lilies for me.'

'Pigs might fly,' she said flatly. 'It might help your career having your brother as the company director, but Len is no miracle worker, so you can forget your dreams of the Opera House! No, I think Dr Cuthbertson's attentions are your best way out of the Crown, there may not be another. After all, the war took away the best of our dancing years.'

It was the kind of comment I had come to expect from Grace. We had been friends since our first childhood ballet lesson in an old pumping station in Hackney, and even in those days she would always smile sweetly at the decrepit pianist in the hope that he would buy her new practice shoes. Grace had never had any commitment to dance and was always happy to remain in the corps de ballet, dreaming that one day a rich gentleman would be lured by the naked limbs that her costumes revealed. For just a moment I hated her for it, but there was truth in what she said and that's what hurt the most.

'Maybe you are right,' I replied quietly, but could not manage any more.

'I would jump at a chance with a bloke like Dr Cuthbertson,' she continued.

'It is just silk flowers,' I said. 'Not a diamond ring.'

'Oh, come on,' she sat down next to me, nudging me along the bench with her hips. 'I have seen the way he looks at you. He can't keep his eyes off you. On stage or off.'

'Do you think so?' I said, my face warming a little under my mask of greasepaint. I had always known that I was no great beauty, but the stage make-up hid my pale complexion and darkened my eyes, and while my long, thin limbs and small breasts would not catch the eye of any gentleman, they were ideal for success as a dancer.

'Well, a lot of gentlemen come to the ballet to see women dancing in their smalls,' said Grace, elbowing me in the ribs. 'It is no surprise!'

'Oh, Grace!' I laughed, embarrassed that I had let her flatter me.

'Come on, Lil,' she said. 'You know I don't mean it. You were great tonight. It is the end of the season and we have flowers, admirers and booze!' She took a half empty bottle of crème de menthe from the dressing table and threw her head back as she put the bottle to her lips. Then she slammed the bottle back down, the liquid tinkling in the glass.

I couldn't help laughing. She was still in full costume, green drops of liquid sinking into her lace bodice, her lips now a dark circle in her chalky greasepaint and her hair coming loose from her floral headdress. It had only been minutes since her exit from the stage, but all the elegance of the ethereal sprite had left her when the curtain closed.

She passed me the bottle and I took a sip but without her enthusiasm.

She fingered the silk petals of the lilies. 'Well, no matter what happens, you have him captivated.'

'I don't know,' I said. 'I fear there is something not right about the whole thing. I just cannot think what. He does seem to stare at me now and then, but the expression on his face is a little odd. It is not one that I can read.'

'Well, he comes with the approval your own brother, they fought together after all. Len will have seen him at his worst, that is for sure, yet they are still chums.'

'He is a major benefactor of Ballets Spectaculaire,' I said. 'I think that is enough to make a friend of Len, if nothing else. Len just has ambition for the company, and money will do that.'

'Well, who else has money to give away these days?' she said. 'He can bloody well send some my way if he wants rid.'

I laughed.

'Oh, Lil!' she cried. 'Has it not escaped your attention that he is a doctor?'

'No, it hasn't,' I said. 'He promised that he will take a look at my aching bunion and I can't wait!'

She laughed. 'Are you sure that it is just your bunion that he wants to look at?'

'I think my bunion would be enough to put him off,' I replied.

She rolled her eyes. 'I think any man would overlook a bunion when they see how wide a dancer can throw her legs. I have seen Dr Cuthbertson in this dressing room many a time. Don't think I haven't noticed him sneaking in. Don't tell me you haven't shown him already!'

'He is a gentleman, Gracie, we just talk a lot,' I said. 'I feel that I can talk to him and tell him anything, and he likes to listen.'

'Well, if nothing more, he is a man, for God's sake! There are so few of them left. On top of that, he is eligible – a doctor, a theatre benefactor. He must be rich because he has a car – I would even settle for that burly chauffeur who follows him everywhere; I like the strong silent type.'

'That chauffeur is Clive's brother!' I said.

'Ooh, *Clive*!' she shrieked. 'So you are on first name terms with this doctor you pretend to show no interest in!' She winked and patted my knee. 'And he is even introducing you to his family!'

'No,' I said quickly. 'He has not introduced me to his brother or anyone in fact. Clive...'

Grace raised her eyebrows dramatically.

'I mean *Dr Cuthbertson* just told me about him. His brother doesn't say much because his mind is still on the battlefield. Since the Great War he has only been capable of doing the work that Clive can give him.'

'Pity!' She tilted her head on one side and pouted at her reflection. 'One brother has the looks and the other has the brains. It just goes to show that you can't have everything. Well, I will just have to seduce the handsome one then, distract him from those dark thoughts, while you are dancing on your back with the other—'

'Grace!' I tried to nudge her off the bench, but she pushed back, laughing.

'Oh, come on, Lil! Dr Cuthbertson is a trusted friend of Len, a man who listens to you, a war hero and barely in his thirties. Is none of that good enough for you?'

'Grace, I have only really got to know him in the last few weeks!'

'You are right,' she said. 'With his kind you can cross your legs and hold out for a proposal. Has he given you a ring yet?'

'No,' I said, but I was not sure if I was ready to tell her any more.

'What?' she said. 'Come on, I can tell you are keeping something back! Am I not your best friend?'

'Well, it is not a ring,' I said, 'but he did give me this.' I handed her a small card with a picture of a grand house on the front. It was a romantic looking house with a jumble of pitched roofs and arched windows, perched at the top of a lawn dotted with cedars and neatly clipped hollies. A motor car was parked on the driveway next to a circular flower bed. Dr Cuthbertson's brother – the man we had spoken of – stood by the car, complete with goggles, long coat and peaked cap.

She squinted at the card, her stiff lashes curling into spiders. 'Elm-ridge House,' she said, pronouncing every syllable. 'Blimey, is this his place? It looks like a manor house or something.'

'He just called it his house,' I said, 'but yes, I suppose it is rather big. He has invited me there. In fact, I am being driven there tonight.'

'Oh, Lil!' She grabbed my arm excitedly.

'Well, I think it was at Len's suggestion,' I said quickly. 'He wants me to rest my joints for a few weeks and, to be honest, I think he just wants me far away from here so I can't sneak back into the practice room. I think it will do my dancing some good though. Clive is a doctor after all – he can advise on some of those new treatments, like physiotherapy, and I could do with some country air – these London smogs are no good for a dancer's lungs. When I return, I will be invigorated and ready for the next season.'

'Oh, to be a ballerina!' She laughed. 'I wish I had such bonuses. What will I do here all on my own with you out in the countryside? Who will help me finish this off?' She held up the bottle of crème de menthe which I saw was now almost empty.

'I don't think you'll need any help!' I laughed. 'Anyway, I will not really be out in the countryside. It is actually in Missensham, not thirty miles north of here.'

'My aunt is in Oxworth,' she said. 'I don't think it can be far from her place, then. I will pop over for afternoon tea while I am visiting her.'

'I would love that,' I said. 'I hear that Dr Cuthbertson is a religious man, I will probably be as bored as hell. Len is going up there with me, but he won't be able to stay, and I fear the lack of booze and ragtime.'

Grace nodded enthusiastically. 'Well, whether you bed him or not, it seems a good idea. At least a break will help you to get over...' But then she stopped for just a second, her mouth open as if struggling to find the right words to say. 'Well, it will help you get over what happened here.'

'I don't know what you mean,' I said, but I was fooling neither of us.

'I think you should take his picture down,' she said, waving her hand towards my dressing mirror.

I followed her finger to the photograph of the dancer tacked to the mirror. The man wore the costume of Albrecht; the duke – a short velvet tunic with puffed sleeves and pale tights, his eyes heavy with kohl. It was the type of outfit that no respectable gentleman would wear, yet the camera had captured the vigour of the dancer's pose – the knot of muscle as he held himself on the point of his toes and the thrust of his raised arm.

'Yes,' I said. 'I should do that.' But although Grace kept her eyes on me, I made no attempt to remove the photograph. 'He was a bastard for leaving,' I added, though the words were no more than what she wanted to hear from me.

She nodded and we fell into silence, each one of us expecting more from the other, but neither of us willing to oblige. She took a cigarette from my case on the dressing table and touched the tip to the mantle of the oil lamp, waiting for the end to spark before she put it to her lips and blew a jet of smoke into the air.

'It's been a long season, Grace,' I said at last, 'and I am sorry for—'

'Don't be,' she said. 'Think of it as in the past. Just make sure that you get better – bunions, exhaustion, broken heart, whatever, and come back soon and get back to your dancing, whether it be at the Crown or the Royal Opera House.'

'Thank you,' I said.

'Or you will find yourself in the corps de ballet again and I won't be clearing up the flowers; I will be the one getting them.'

'Yes,' I said, 'and the bunions that come with earning them.'

She clamped the cigarette in her lips and gathered up the bouquet of silk lilies. 'Here, you will need to pose with these,' she said, thrusting the lilies towards me.

'Why?' I said, taking the flowers from her.

'We must go and get our photograph taken,' she said.

'What?'

'Oh, Len wants us to do it while we are still all in costume. The audience have left the theatre and the dancers are waiting for us on the stage. Dr Cuthbertson and some of the other benefactors will be there too. It is what I came to tell you.'

'Shit, Gracie!' I said. 'Why didn't you say something earlier, my make-up will have run.'

'Well, you won't be the only one who is a bit worse for wear,' she said. 'They wanted a few of the corps de ballet in the photograph as well, but most of the French dancers are already on their way back to Paris, so I said that I would do it.'

'No, you cannot!' I said, pointing to her reflection in the mirror. I handed her a rag and she started to rub the smudges from under her eyes.

'Shit! I never thought about all that,' she said, trying to fan the cigarette smoke away from her chest, 'and now Len will know I have been smoking around the costumes!'

I took the cigarette from her and stubbed it out on the mirror. 'Have another swig of crème de menthe,' I said. 'You are always saying that it covers the taste of anything, so it will probably take the cigarette off your breath. You will seem fresh as a daisy.'

She took another glug from the bottle. 'You are a good friend, Lil,' she said, 'but you will be sick of me when we have been bunking together in Paris for a whole summer.'

'Yes,' I said weakly, but the tour of Paris that I had longed for would now not happen the way that I had hoped – someone would be missing. I could not help but look at the photograph on the mirror once more. I had not spoken of what happened with Grace, but she must have had her suspicions about what had caused Alexander, our best dancer, to step from the stage the previous evening, demand his payment and leave without waiting for the curtain call.

I had been forced to dance the final performance of the season partnered by Len, the understudy, the ballet director and my own brother. Alexander must have known the pain of every step that I took with Len at my side, for, as we danced together, we must have both been imagining Alexander among us, and our pas de deux felt passionless.

'You know, I think I will have more of that booze,' I said.

I clutched the silk bouquet to my chest as we staggered through the maze of narrow backstage corridors, arm in arm, Grace giggling as we stumbled against walls and into the dark stage wings. We tripped over coiled ropes and bits of scenery and emerged on to the stage that was still bright with the arc lights.

The set from the final act had been replaced with a plain backdrop curtain. The dancers mingled on stage, the bright white of their billowing skirts blurring together as they moved, but among them I caught a glimpse of the man that Grace and I had discussed – Dr Cuthbertson in his evening jacket and top hat, flanked by his bulky chauffeur.

'Dr Cuthbertson!' I called, letting go of Grace's arm. 'Clive!' But then the dancers were all around me and I lost sight of him as I was jostled against elbows and skirts stiff with starch.

'Liliana!' Len grabbed my arm and then repeated the name, louder this time with the flourish of a fake Russian accent. He still wore the duke's velvet tunic, but there was nothing regal nor Russian about him when he linked his arm into mine and hissed: 'Where the bloody hell have you been, sister dearest?'

Len pulled his mouth into a smile and we pushed through the throng of dancers, nodding and smiling until we were at the curtain. He beckoned the dancers towards us, fanning his hands effeminately as they grouped around us. In front of me was a strange wooden box with bellows at the sides, like a stretched concertina, the bulge of the photographer's head moving under the black hood, his raised hand holding the trough of flash powder aloft.

Then an arm took mine; a man's arm in a sleeve of fine fabric, and I turned to see a tall man with a long, distinguished face. He was a man with smooth skin, his hair untouched by grey – his youth disguised only by the stiffness of his suit and the little half-moon spectacles perched elegantly on his nose.

'Dr Cuthbertson!' I said.

'The great Liliana Postova!' he said, his smile softening his features. 'You were enchanting tonight, Lily.' He held his top hat in his hands, yet he still wore his dress coat despite the heat of the lights and I thought that, from even once glance, one would know that he moved in educated circles. As I stood beside him, I realised that he was taller than I had remembered and his arm felt firm and muscular.

'I am so glad the season is over, Al—' I said, my voice trailing off when I realised that I had almost called him by the name that had been on my mind so much. But Clive was not Alexander, he never would be. I remembered Grace's words – Clive was a doctor, he was rich, a family friend, a war hero – and suddenly I wondered what it would be like to have him in my affections in place of Alexander. 'So much has happened since we last spoke,' I said. 'Clive, I have so much to—'

As if reading my thoughts, he said: 'Don't worry, Lily, we will have plenty of time to talk about it.'

'For God's sake everyone, try and look like dancers,' barked Len. 'It's the last night of the season – you will have plenty of chances to get wasted after this. Everyone face Lil and I want you to hold your positions for the camera – whatever you can hold for a few seconds without moving, we don't want any blurs. Come on.' He clapped his hands loudly. 'Épaulé, écarté, Arab-bloody-esques, whatever your pissed up limbs can manage!'

I held the bouquet of lilies to my chest and faced the camera. Grace appeared in front of me and lowered herself into a curtsy, her skirt billowing around her. Around us, taffeta swirled and rustled and arms were raised and toes pointed.

Len stood to the right of me and took my arm. 'Chin up and just get through it,' he hissed through a toothy smile. 'You will be on your hols in the country soon; there's no escape for the rest of us.'

From somewhere behind me, a hand smoothed my hair and another picked at my bodice and angled my head towards the camera.

'Smile,' hissed Len. 'Try and look like a ballerina.'

'Do not worry,' said Clive calmly. 'You will be away from all of this soon enough.'

'Yes,' I said. 'I am looking forward to it.' And then I realised that I actually was.

The photographer barked some orders from underneath the black hood. I felt the heat from Clive's body as he was jostled next to me and inhaled the scent of his cologne. Alexander had left me heartbroken, but could the man who stood next to me really desire me? Could I love again?

As I looked into the lens, I knew that this moment would be captured forever in light and shadow. It was a moment that would change everything.

The flash powder in the trough ignited in a blaze of light, sealing the moment in memory forever, I took Clive's hand in mine, then I looked into the future and smiled.

9

April 1920

I first saw the woman on the bench when I woke from my nap and glanced out of the window to check the weather for a walk in the shrubbery. She was a woman of middle age but her hair was already quite white and she was dressed in the uniform of a postwoman – a long heavy coat, skirt and stockings – despite the warmth of the spring sunshine. I would not have thought it so strange, but the usual man had already brought the mail and it was almost noon. She held a large leather postbag on her lap, which was fit to burst, but I could see a knot of wool poking from the top. A pair of knitting needles worked furiously in her hands and she sang to herself with neither tune nor words. I raised my hand and rapped my knuckles on the glass, but she did not look up from her knitting and I wondered if she could hear at all.

My first thought was to call for Clive, but it was Saturday and he was in his study as usual and had asked not to be disturbed. I went to the bell pull to call for Hannah, but the sash fell slack in my hand and I could not hear even the faintest of jangles from the bell ringing downstairs. I called out for Hannah, but as soon as I heard my voice echoing in the corridor I realised that she would be in the kitchen preparing lunch.

I returned to the window and tried to heave it open, but the lock had rusted shut and the heavy frames just banged together. Hearing the noise, the woman looked up and I raised my hand to wave, but she jumped to her feet, clutching her bag to her chest, and ran off into the shrubbery. I watched her disappear into the trees, my hand falling back to my side, and suddenly I realised that despite my attempts to scare her from the garden, I was now sad that she had gone.

Since arriving at Elmridge House two months previously I had been able to rest my body and even forget about my turbulent season at the Crown Theatre. I had spent most of my days walking in the shrubbery or sitting at the back of the house admiring the view over the valley of Evesbridge, but I had been neither relaxed nor happy. Missensham village was pleasant enough, but there was little to do there and I missed the bustle of London. During my stay, Clive had only had one visitor, his boss from the hospital – he was a charming man, but one whose manner was so similar to Clive's that they might have been twins and they did little to entertain me. Clive played gentle piano music over and over on the gramophone, he said that he found it relaxing, but I longed for a little ragtime or to go out dancing at the clubs I used to frequent.

Elmridge House also seemed to have very few staff for such a large estate. There was Dr Cuthbertson's driver, Edgar, who also tended the garden and seemed to be treated as staff rather than family. He was a man who I would sometimes see from my window as he readied the motor car or tended the flower bed, but I knew that he would spend many an hour in his quarters at the dovecote cottage, reliving the horrors of a war that had left him working in the service of his brother. There was also Hannah, the maid who was Edgar's fiancé, and sometimes other women who Clive said were hired from a domestic agency. They were women who seemed to come and go quietly and I would never catch more than a glimpse of their uniforms as they hurried from room to room.

I had seen a lot of Clive in the first couple of weeks, but since then he had started working long hours at the hospital and retreating to his study in the evenings. Clive's study was down at the other end of the corridor. I could call to him, but only if I shouted and I seldom heard anything from his room. Despite this, I was always aware of his presence due to the creaking floorboards, which would relay a single footstep from one end of the house to another, and the clank of lead, which rattled through the pipes with every turn of a tap. Clive was everywhere and nowhere and I felt his presence as if it was a haunting.

While I longed to see more of Clive, it was female company that I missed the most and I would often end up trying to make conversation with Hannah, who seemed quite nice but her speech was slow and she tended to hang her head when I spoke to her.

Downstairs, the heavy front door grated across the flagstones of the hallway, then came the creak of the stairs, followed by footsteps along the corridor.

Hannah stood in the doorway, staring at her feet. 'Madam, there is a lady—'

'I know,' I said. 'I have seen her sitting on the bench by the shrubbery.'

'No,' she muttered. 'She came to the front door, she—'

A woman barged past her, one full of life and energy, wearing a fashionable coat that looked as if it had been dragged through a haystack.

'Grace!' I cried, flinging my arms around her.

'Well, there's a welcome!' she said.

'But I was not expecting you. Is everything all right?'

'Yes, yes!' she said. 'I bumped into my auntie on her fruit and veg stand at Covent Garden, she was bringing the cart out this way to collect rhubarb from the market garden at Missensham Grange, so I hopped in the back. I've only got an hour before she picks me up and then I've got to squash back in with the rhubarb.' She pulled back and held me at arm's length. 'I smell of manure, don't I?'

'Yes,' I said, picking a piece of straw from her coat. 'Yet somehow I am still so glad to see you.'

'Madam?' Hannah looked uneasy as Grace took off her coat and dumped it on the velvet chaise longue, straw wafting across the fabric. 'Does Dr Cuthbertson know that you have a visitor? I should—'

'Don't worry yourself about it, Hannah,' I said, 'but please will you bring us up some tea?'

She nodded, scooping up Grace's coat as she went.

We stood rigid and silent as she left the room, then burst out laughing.

'Well, this is a change from swigging crème de menthe from a bottle!' she screeched.

'Oh, come and sit down,' I said, 'on this straw covered chaise longue!'

We sat together and she looked round the room, her eyes wide. 'This room is huge,' she said. 'You have windows to the front and the side.' She jumped up and ran to them in turn. 'This way a view of whatever it is – is this what they call an arboretum?'

'It is only a shrubbery,' I said.

'And from the other window you must be able to see all across the valley. Can I see my auntie's place from here?'

'No,' I said. 'It is just Missensham down in the valley and on the far hill.'

'But this is your bed,' she said. 'You have a whole private sitting room in your bedroom.'

'Well, it is just a chaise longue and a couple of chairs and a little table,' I said, embarrassed.

'You are quite right,' she said. 'It is actually no bigger than my family's bedroom in Stepney, although that is their only room, mind, and my dad has squeezed in six beds, a dining table, basin, all my brothers and sisters and a chamber pot or two!'

I laughed.

She walked to the side window again and looked out over the shrubbery and only then did she fall silent. She stared into the trees as if she had forgotten all about me and the room in which we stood. 'I ain't never seen anything like it,' she said quietly.

'You would tire of it soon enough,' I said. 'There are no music halls here, no Lamb and Flag, no Trocadero.'

'Of course,' she said quickly and she joined me back on the chaise longue. 'Well, Lady Lil, life in the countryside must be treating you well, because you ain't written, only one of your postcards to tell me that you have some big news, a real mystery that cannot be told in a letter.'

'Well, actually I started to write, many a time, but there was nothing to say,' I said. 'It is dull here and I miss all my old chums. Whatever happened to—'

'No, no, no,' she said, waggling a finger at me. 'What about your big secret?'

And with that question I suddenly forgot the world that she had brought with her into my room – the world of dancing and pubs and nightclubs and youth in London – and something unwelcome resurfaced, something that I had not yet had the courage to write on paper or even bring to my lips.

'I am with child,' I said quietly.

'With child,' she repeated the words as if they were foreign to her. 'But…' Then she recovered herself. 'I just did not expect it, not like this!'

'I know it has not been long,' I said, 'but it has been just me and Clive in this big house for two months now and we became close many weeks ago, just as you thought we would.'

Her mouth fell open a little. 'Clive?' she echoed.

'Yes,' I reminded her. 'Dr Cuthbertson.'

She nodded slowly.

'I am sure that Clive will marry me,' I said. Grace must have known that I had no support other than Clive. She knew that my parents were religious zealots and had disowned me when I became a dancer, but I was not sure if it was her that I was trying to reassure with my words, or myself. 'It need not be a big wedding,' I added.

'It has just happened so quickly,' she said, her voice was flat, without the excitement that I had come to expect from her.

'Well, I guess for some people it happens that quickly,' I said, 'but you look at me as if it was an immaculate conception.'

'Well, I...' But then she fell silent, her eyes drifting for a while as if she was deep in thought; an expression on her face that I could not read. At last she said, 'I don't know what to think actually, Lil. It must be a bit of a shock to both of us. I suppose that there is nothing wrong with it, not really.' Then she took my hand and squeezed it. 'I only think that I am not feeling happy because you do not look it.'

Grace was my best friend and I knew that I could not hide anything from her, and then we hugged, for what reason I don't know – a combination of celebration, commiseration, shared experience and an uncertain future, any and all of those things. I would not dance again, and it was something that we both understood.

'Well, at least you will be well off,' she said, 'you have this lovely room and—'

'The love of a man,' I said. 'I know that he loves me because,' I grabbed her hand and pulled her over to the side window, 'look!'

'The shrubbery?' she said.

'No, the lilies,' I said, 'in the flower bed around the bench. He has planted them so that they are the first thing that I see when I look out in the morning.'

'The plants with the leaves that are like daggers?' she asked.

'Yes,' I replied, but then I saw a crease in her forehead and the tense of her jaw and I realised that we were only looking at one flower bed of pointed leaves. The lilies had been bought in from a nursery only a fortnight ago and had not had the chance to flower.

She could not see what they meant and suddenly neither could I.

'He gave me the silk lilies too,' I persisted weakly.

'Lil, I—' She took my hand and held it tightly.

'What is it?'

'Well, I shall have to talk to Dr Cuthbertson about this,' she said. Then she smiled a warm, happy smile at last, 'And make sure that he takes good care of you.'

'You make it sound as if I will never see you again!' I said. 'My life is not over!'

'Of course,' she said, but this time her smile seemed forced as if I was a child that she was trying to reassure.

'I think things have been changing too quickly,' I said, but I could not hold the last word and felt a sting in my eyes.

'It will all be well,' Grace said softly. 'I did worry about you moving out to a place like this, but now I have seen it, it is not so bad, it may not have the society that we are used to in London, but you have the garden, and the...' But then she stopped, as if wracking her brain for something more.

She was right, of course. It had not been my intention to marry Clive and to live at Elmridge House. I had merely been a visitor, come to rest from a stressful season, and yet that had all changed in one evening.

It had happened on the evening of my final performance of *Giselle*, after the photograph had been taken, yet it was not the scene from the photograph that stuck in my memory but what had taken place after in my dressing room.

I tried to block the memories from returning to my head, but there were some snatched sensations that I couldn't help reliving: the emerald glow on the dressing room wall as the bottle of crème de menthe caught the light from the oil lamp; the muffled laughter from the corridor and the distant tinkle of a piano in the orchestra pit; the smell of the rug I lay on – old sweat and the rosin from hundreds of ballet shoes; my bodice crumpled underneath me, the lacing frayed where it had been torn from my body; the blanket under the small of my back, the fabric warm and damp; slow breaths and aching muscles; and the dull throb between my legs – the place where he had been.

I remembered the smell of his cologne, the smoke of his cigarette still hanging in the air and the warmth of where he had lain. I closed my eyes and felt the bulge of his muscles once more, my hands gripping the curve of his back as my body rose up against his. Then I saw his face again, his eyes large in the darkness and I felt the warmth of his breath as he whispered in my ear: 'I love you, Lily.'

Yet it was only one evening. It was only one memory.

Then Grace said: 'Chin up, you've got a face like a smacked arse!' and I couldn't help laughing, embarrassed that I had become lost in my memories once more.

We did not mention my pregnancy again after that. Grace's visit was a welcome break from my time at Elmridge House and I knew that I would not have another for a long time.

Hannah brought up a tray of tea and biscuits and we sat together on the chaise longue. I was happy to listen to Grace's gossip about the Ballets Spectaculaire and her excited chatter about the company's trip to Paris in the summer. It was an adventure that I had longed to be part of, but, as we spoke, we both knew that Paris would be no place for a dancer who was pregnant and already exhausted and Grace chose her words carefully, never using 'we' or 'us'. I could not help but feel a little excited for her and I even lent her one of my outfits for the Paris trip – a coat of pale leather with a black fox fur trim around the neckline and a matching hat. The coat was really far too long for the season, but Grace insisted – it was the type of outfit one would wear to travel in a motor car and she said that if she was disguised as an upper-class lady, she would be sure to attract a wealthy Frenchman.

We talked until we heard the chime of the grandfather clock from deep down in the hallway and then I called to Hannah, who came panting up the stairs, only for us to send her away again for Grace's coat and a bag and we stood in silence as if the presence of the maid had reminded us of the formality befitting the grand house.

As Hannah's footsteps faded, Grace glanced quickly down the stairs and whispered: 'There are always two nurses at Missensham Cottage Hospital.'

'What?' I said. 'What do you mean—'

'I just thought you should know,' she said.

'I still don't understand,' I said.

'My aunt knows this area and I remember her talking about such things a few years back. Apparently it has been the way for many a year.' She stopped then and I felt uneasy about a topic that would cause someone as blunt as Grace to hesitate. 'One nurse will work a shift on the ward, leaving the other free to receive visitors in the nurses' house out the back. The nurses at the cottage hospital receive private lady visitors.' She paused and looked me in the eye. 'Ladies in your situation.'

'Oh!' I said, feeling my face warm. 'Oh, Grace, I don't know. Clive would not allow it of course, he is so devout and it is against everything he—'

'Clive need not know,' she said. 'It is not up to him, or me – in fact, I am just telling you what you might need to know, because as long as you know all the options, then you have a choice. I just think every woman in Missensham should know these things, and now you do.'

I could not feel her goodbye kiss as I had gone quite numb.

'Just in case you feel you need me,' she whispered quickly over the plod of Hannah's approaching footsteps. 'You know where I am.'

Then Hannah appeared and Grace took her coat with a little nod, folding the leather driving coat over her arm and fixing the hat at a fashionable angle on her head. I walked with them to the top of the staircase and waited on the landing.

It wasn't until Grace was in the doorway putting on her coat that I found my voice again. 'Thank you,' I called shakily.

She turned back, looking up to me as if waiting for more, and there was so much more that I wanted to say, but in the end I could only manage a mumbled, 'Goodbye.'

She nodded. 'Goodbye, Lil.'

I waited until the door was shut behind her and her footsteps had faded before I went back along the corridor to my room and sat on the chaise longue and gazed out over the trees, hoping to see a lady in a postwoman's uniform looking back at me.

10

'*The nurses at the cottage hospital receive private lady visitors, ladies in your situation.*'

They had been Grace's words. The ones that she had whispered as we stood together in my bedroom at Elmridge House just minutes after I had told her of my pregnancy. She had told me of the nurses' house and how there would be a nurse there to receive me, but she had said no more than that. I had not pressed her for more – the shock of her suggestion had weighed heavily in my stomach, but, over the following days, I came to realise that the idea of carrying a child and giving birth was causing me equal worry and the weight in my stomach had lifted.

Almost a week after Grace's visit, I left Elmridge House with the excuse of posting a letter and walked along the Oxworth Road in the direction of the village. When I reached the cottage hospital, I went round the back and through a clump of trees which led to the garden of the nurses' house. I was greeted at the back door by a stocky woman in a large white cap and a tight uniform who, without a word, ushered me into the kitchen and sat me at a large table. She put the kettle on to boil, without even querying my need, and pulled a chair up for herself, sitting opposite me. It was not until then that I realised coming to the nurses' house was just the beginning and I had not thought what might happen beyond this point.

The nurse looked me up and down and lowered her brow into a frown, her thin lips pulled into a little kiss of disapproval and I suspected that she would have no sympathy for a dancer who would risk ending a pregnancy just because she wanted to keep her figure or spare a year from a career that would be over in five.

For a long time she did not say much. I fancied it was because she risked a visit from the constable if she did, but I suspected just as much that it was her way. Then she told me that her name was Sadie.

Sadie put a large leather book in front of me and laid it open on the table, smoothing the crease with her sleeve, and then she printed the date in slow, curling figures, with her arm shielding what she wrote. Only then did she look up at me.

'Is it prevention you are after,' she said, 'or cure?'

'Cure,' I said, although the word sounded strange.

She wrote in the book some more and then her pen stopped, but she did not look up. 'What should I call you?'

'Giselle,' I said.

She raised an eyebrow but still did not look at me. 'Age?'

'Twenty-five.'

'Missed bleeds?'

'Two,' I said, 'maybe three, I am not sure.'

Her eyes darted to my hands. I realised that they were clenched in front of me on the table and I put them in my lap quickly, suddenly feeling the absence of a ring.

'Oh,' I said. 'I have no ring yet, but I am to be married soon.'

'Of course,' she said but nothing more and I was glad that she did not question me, because the truth was I had not told Clive of my pregnancy as I was hoping that one day soon my bleed would come and I would never have the need to do so. I did not think that I was lying to her though, Clive would marry me when I told him, I was sure of that.

'My fiancé is a doctor' I said, hoping that it would give me an air of respectability and convince her that I was not just some silly girl who had been tricked by a farm hand. Then I thought it best to say no more in case she knew Clive, but she said nothing, her lips pressed firmly together as she wrote.

For a long time the only sound in the room was the breathy whistle of the kettle, but then Sadie got up from her chair and went to an under stairs cupboard. She took out an old Victorian medicine chest, like something one might find on board a ship, and sat it on the table between us. She opened the lid and looked at the contents, then she looked back at me and gave me a long stare.

'You are to be married,' she said after a while. 'You have a man when there are so few left to go round. You wear expensive clothes. You are not wasted by hunger nor weakened by the flu, your body is fit and strong, you are of a suitable age. You have so much more than many of us women have right now. Why do you want rid of it?'

I found that I could not answer because, after all she had said, my reasons suddenly seemed selfish considering the plight of so many.

'I dance,' I said eventually. I wanted to say more by way of explanation, but there was nothing that I could say to a woman such as her with her stout frame and coarse manner. I had offered no explanation to Grace for I knew that I did not need to – she was a dancer and would understand, but this woman was approaching middle age, her hands were red and cracked from her work, her face was without make-up and her hair was greying under her cap.

I could not explain to her about how I had been replacing my meals with cigarettes or the times I had wondered whether my dressing mirror was warped or if my waist was already thickening, or the way I had envied the fashionable coat that Grace had worn or the way I felt her ribs when we embraced. I could not tell her of how I still practised dancing when I was alone, using the mantelpiece for a barre, keeping my muscles strong and my stomach tight. They were old habits but my life had changed too fast for me to leave them behind. Now I had new obsessions – I had ordered new corsets from the small department store in the village and bright white knickers which I could check for blood.

'You dance?' she said flatly, her pen stopping dead on the page.

'Yes,' I said, 'but there is something else, you see, everything has happened so quickly for us, I suppose it is all a bit of a shock, but my fiancé has said that we will make plans.'

She looked up at me. 'He has said a lot of things then. Has he said that he actually wants a child?'

'He holds religious beliefs,' I said. 'He would not approve of me even being here.'

'That is all very well,' she said, 'but what I asked was whether he wants it.'

'Yes,' I said and then, 'no, I don't know,' and then I realised that I could not answer for Clive because I did not know him. He was a man who had seen me dance and been enthralled by it and there had been that evening in my dressing room with the warmth of the blanket, the distant tinkle of the piano and the green light dancing on the wall. Then there were the long days he spent working in his study, and I realised that he was actually a distant man and one lacking in affection and within weeks the lithe dancer that had entranced him would be gone forever. We had lived under the same roof for more than a couple of months now, but when all was said and done, I did not know him. 'I don't know whether he wants this baby,' I said, my voice wobbling, 'but if I were to have it, I fear that he would not want me.'

The woman took her handkerchief from her pocket and passed it to me.

'Oh, no thank you,' I said. 'I don't need...' but as I spoke, I felt a warm tear on my cheek.

She got up and emptied the whistling kettle into a teapot and set out two tin mugs on the draining board. Then she locked the medicine chest and put it back under the stairs.

'You have more thinking to do,' she said.

11

The nurse swiped her pen across the notes she had made in the leather book. They had been words which recorded my life as a dancer, a life which, with one streak of ink, she ended. But there had been other words on that page, ones which spoke of a comfortable home, of a healthy body and a wealthy fiancé – a kind and honourable man who would provide for me and the child. They were words which said that there was a chance I could still want the baby. Then the nurse had closed the book.

She did not say a word in judgement, nor a single word to influence my decision. Instead she stood up slowly and stoked the stove, then she found some biscuits, thin slices of garibaldi – she had little to spare, but they were offered anyway. She did all this while I talked, my words telling of a broken heart I had sought to escape and a career to which I might not return, of a body I feared would weaken – muscles which would waste and joints which would seize – of a comfortable home but a fiancé who could be distant, and about one evening in February which had changed everything. As I talked, I realised that my problems were no fault of the baby and that I still had a chance to change things.

When the nurse did finally speak, she said that she could not help me on that day, but if I did choose to come back to her in the little kitchen, it would have to be soon – I only had a week to spare as the baby would grow all the time. She said that I should make my decision after I had slept and had time to think and talk things over with my fiancé.

I said that I would.

As the days passed, my mind had become calmer, and I realised that I had not thought of returning to the stocky little nurse in the kitchen and that I could cope with my situation.

When I told Clive, I knew instantly from the look in his eyes and his trembling hands that he would do the right thing. He took my hand in his. 'I have a duty to care for this child,' he said, 'for it is my blood. I can care for it here and provide it with everything it needs and even when I am gone it will be remembered.'

But things did not change as quickly as I had hoped and in the following week I still saw little of Clive. He went to church on Sunday, as he always did. When he stayed later than usual I hoped that he had been talking with the vicar, but, when he returned, he said nothing of plans for a ceremony. He spent most of the week in his study, poring over textbooks for the new qualification he was working for, the specialism which he said would further his career, so I did not feel that I could disturb him for the sake of company or a conversation.

When Grace turned up again the following Saturday, covered in straw and clutching an expensive leather bag bursting with stems of rhubarb, I was glad for someone to talk to and welcomed her into my room.

'I shall wear this in Paris!' she exclaimed, twirling round the room in the outfit that I had lent her, the little hat positioned jauntily over one eye and bits of straw falling from the leather of the coat.

'Très belle!' Suddenly I could picture her in the Champs-Élysées or posing by the Eiffel Tower, all these places I knew from photographs but would never visit. Grace moved as she did on stage, with energy but no precision, a certain gaiety and wantonness to her steps. The billow of the soft leather as she twirled accentuated her tiny waist and I feared that my own was already fattening. I was still in my housecoat and I had not put on make-up and I worried that I was slipping into the lifestyle of a woman twice my age, a lady, a wife and a mother.

'Voilà!' she exclaimed, taking a bottle from her bag. 'A gift for you; something a little French to celebrate my departure.'

'Crème de menthe!' I said. 'It must be three months since we drank this from the bottle in my dressing room. I have crystal glasses now. But this is not the same bottle as it is almost full!'

'I got it from Len,' she said. 'He has still not forgiven you for what happened with Alexander so I took this from his dressing room to get back at him for taking you away from me. After all, if it wasn't for his friendship with

Dr Cuthbertson, you wouldn't be stuck all the way out here, so I think that he owes you something!'

'Of course,' I said, laughing.

'It might be three months since *you* last drank, but I have never stopped.' She laughed.

'I can believe it!' I said. 'Unfortunately Clive rarely drinks and even when he does it is only a sip of communion wine. He won't even allow cigarettes in the house, so I have few pleasures.' I had meant the words in jest but, as I said them, I heard a flatness to my voice.

Grace looked at me anxiously and I remembered that she was my best friend and someone who was able to read my every thought.

'I'm sorry,' she said. 'I thought you would be pleased for me. You know I have always wanted to see Paris.'

'I am, of course,' I said, embarrassed that she had seen through my forced smile. 'I suppose it just brings back memories of when I was Giselle at the Crown Theatre.'

'Well, at least you were Giselle,' she said. 'I doubt that I ever will be. I do not have your precision and I cannot bring myself to practise so hard.' She winked. 'Nor take it so seriously.' Suddenly I realised that maybe everything was not always a joke to her. She was fully aware of her flaws, she had just come to accept them as if they did not matter, and I admired her for it.

'Well, at least you have to time to practise,' I said. 'I do not have that.'

'Oh, please don't be sad again...' but then she stopped. 'You said you do not have time – you have made your decision then?'

'I suppose I have,' I said. 'I just had to accept that it would not be right either way, I just had to choose.'

She looked a little crestfallen. 'I really thought you would see one of the ladies I told you about – the nurses.'

'I did,' I replied, 'but she said that she would not help me right there and then and it turns out that I did not want her to.' She nodded, but I noticed that she had pulled her lips together tightly instead of a smile, so I added: 'But I can still go back, I am still not sure, and now seeing you looking so glamorous in my coat and soon off to Paris, I kind of wish that I had…'

'Oh, don't pay any attention to me,' she said quickly. 'I did not mean to be selfish. You see, I just want my friend back. I have to accept that you are moving on. You have a new life now. I suppose that I should say congratulations then.'

'Thank you,' I said glumly.

'It is a shame about Paris,' she said. 'I would have loved you to be with me. It would have been like the old days when we were young dancers not yet twenty, but the Great War put a stop to everything – we missed out – I just always thought that life owes us.' She drew the bottle of crème de menthe close to her chest. 'I suppose you won't need this then.'

'Leave me some pleasures!' I cried. 'I may not be going out to the clubs any more but a little drop won't hurt and will remind me of the old days. I can drink and think about you when you are in Paris. These things are not so available here as in London.'

'No!' she said quickly. 'I cannot leave it here now.'

'But you said it was a gift for me!' I cried. 'Clive would not let me buy any, but I'm sure he would put up with a gift in the house. I could pretend that I am going to give it to the church fete.'

'No!' she said, and the word was stern, almost a shout.

There were a couple of footsteps in the corridor and then silence and I fancied that Hannah had rushed to the noise but then stopped, listening for more. Then the floorboards creaked again and we listened in silence to the sound of her tread on the stairs.

'What?' I said quietly. 'What is it? You haven't become a drunkard, have you? You know that Len always has a way of getting his hands on more.'

'The thing is…' But then she stopped and heaved the heavy bedroom door shut. She sat down next to me and leant her head towards me. 'I already opened the bottle. You see, I did not know if you would have the courage to go to the cottage hospital, so I went to see someone myself. There is an old woman who lives on the canal in Camden that I heard about from the costume girl, she gave me something that I could mix into the alcohol. I thought that you might need it, but it turns out I was wrong.'

'I don't understand,' I said.

'I meant it as a gift,' she said, 'although it was never one that I would have been happy giving. You see, the woman in Camden said that the alcohol will dull the pain when the cramps come and the mint will mask the taste of the pennyroyal.' She paused. 'You know that I always say that crème de menthe can hide any taste.'

She put the bottle back down on the nightstand and I gazed into the swirling green liquid, suddenly realising what it contained.

'Oh, I see,' I said.

'Maybe you should keep it after all,' she said. 'Just in case you change your mind again, for I have no use for it and it seems that I have ruined a whole bottle of perfectly good liquor.'

'Oh,' I said. 'Thank you,' although I was not sure what I was thanking her for.

'Don't thank me,' she said. 'I feel bad about the whole thing; it is just that when I saw you last time you seemed so unsure about it, but now—'

'I was,' I said. 'I am,' and then, 'Oh, I don't know.'

Things were not the same between us after that moment. I tried to make conversation about how the lilies were starting to bloom in the bed by the shrubbery and asked politely after Len and a couple of dancers who I missed and Grace reacted enthusiastically to each topic, but her responses were short lived and we sat in awkward silences. I found that I was actually relieved when I heard the grandfather clock chime in the hallway and Hannah showed Grace out, leaving me with a hug that was no more than the lightest of touches.

I watched her from the window as she stepped out on to the driveway, drawing the fur trimmed coat around her shoulders despite the spring sunshine. She stopped and twirled round dramatically, the coat billowing around her. Then she waved, put her hand to her mouth and blew a kiss.

I raised my hand to wave back, but then I saw that the brim of her little hat was pulled low and she had not even seen me watching her.

'Au revoir!' she called to someone in the doorway. 'Mon Chérie!' Yet I didn't know what she meant by such playful words or who they were intended for.

I stepped back from the window and sat down on the chaise longue. Grace had left me again and she had taken so much with her – her London fashion, the news of my friends, her gossip about the ballet company, her excitement for Paris and my window to my old life. There was a space on the chaise longue where she was not, but on the nightstand was a tall green bottle.

12

'I used to dance,' I said.

'I don't understand' said Clive, adjusting his little spectacles, the light from the window reflecting on his lenses. 'Please, Lilian, you have to tell me more.'

I opened my mouth again, but the words stuck in my throat.

'Here,' he said. He took a glass of water from the nightstand and handed it to me. I propped myself up on my pillow and took a sip, but it revived a strong flavour of mint in the back of my throat and burnt a column of fire inside me, shivers of sweat running down my back. I leant my head back on the bedstead, the room spinning a slow circle around me. I did not remember retiring the previous evening. The sunlight bled through the top of the curtain and I thought that it must be nearly midday. I wore some kind of grey cotton nightdress which smelt fresh, but it was not my usual silk pyjamas and I did not remember putting it on.

Clive looked at me over the top of his spectacles, his long face angled in a way which I thought made him look even more distinguished, his eyebrows raised expectantly.

I cleared my throat but found that I could tell him nothing because I had no words that would mean anything to him. He leant forward in his chair and I noticed that he still wore his jacket despite the spring sunshine and that his arms and legs were firmly crossed, his hair already starting to grey. He was not like any other man that I had ever known, although I knew his type: he was the type of man that I used to see marching along the London streets with bowler hats and umbrellas; the suited men who stared at me from the auditorium and those who sat behind desks at the bank. He was one of these stuffy, grey men that I saw all around me yet never spoke to, and I was not part of his world.

Clive was thirty and still a bachelor, he was a scholar who worked late into every evening and he was a doctor – a man accustomed only to rational thought. The women in Missensham were sophisticated and demure. They had fine manners and social graces, and their bodies were corseted, swaddled and shrouded from neck to ankle, their feet laced into shoes as hard as stone. These were the women that Clive understood and I was not one of them and suddenly I fancied that he was looking at me as if I were an animal in a zoo with strange behaviours which he could not explain. There were no words that I could use to make him understand something that was a connection between body and spirit – the power in my muscles, the elation of a leap and the passion of the music. These were things that would mean nothing to him.

I pulled the blanket up round my neck. 'I used to dance,' I said again, 'and now I do not.'

Clive leant back in his chair. Gentle piano music tinkled in the corridor, the notes tumbling over each other until I caught the tune – the last bars of 'Clair de Lune'. It was a piece that I would often hear on his gramophone and I was reminded of how long I had been at Elmridge House.

'It has been three months since you danced, Lily,' said Clive as if reading my thoughts. 'I never knew that you desired to return, it is not something that we have spoken of.' Then his voice seemed to lose all of its refinement and education and he said simply: 'I just want to understand what happened last night.'

'Last night?' I said. 'I don't remember...' but then I realised that I did.

I remembered sitting on the window seat alone as the sun went down, hoping for Hannah or Edgar to pass and wave, or for the postwoman who trespassed to take her knitting to the spot of evening sunshine on the bench outside.

'You were busy with your work again,' I said. 'I think that I must have been lonely. I was thinking of how things used to be, so I think I had a little too much to drink and...' But then I saw a bottle on the nightstand, a tall glass bottle with no more than an inch of green liquid in the bottom which cast an emerald glow onto the wallpaper...

Suddenly I could taste it all over again; the mint no longer fresh but heavy and bitter on my tongue and a scour in the back of my throat. Then I remembered the globe of white light from the mantle above me, the hard floor tiles pressed against my cheek and the cold rounded curves of white enamel.

'The bathroom!' I said. 'I think I was in the bathroom.'

He nodded and suddenly his expression became pained and I realised whatever had happened to me in the night must have been serious.

I tried hard to remember. 'I think...' But there were no words to explain the memories that I had because they were just jumbled images and sensations which made no sense: a pain in my stomach so intense that all I could do was to gaze at the black and white pattern of the tiles beneath me; the tremble of my knees as I clutched them to my chest; a tall bottle tipped on its side, a green drip slowly swelling from its neck; a shattered crystal tumbler; a pool of emerald liquid creeping across the floor; a shard of glass and a streak of blood; the pounding of my heart in my ears; the chill of the porcelain; the creak of the pipes; the bitter tang in my mouth; the bright light high above me; and the echo of the dripping tap inside my head.

'No!' I said, but my voice was just a whisper.

Clive drew his chair forward and leant towards me. 'You had no need to do this,' he said shakily. 'I have given you everything you could want here. Why would you harm yourself? This is no good for you or the baby.'

'No,' I said. 'I didn't, I—' But then I saw the near empty bottle again and felt a coarse bandage wound tight on my wrist.

'Lilian,' he said firmly, 'is there something that you want to tell me?'

'That person who was in the bathroom,' I said. 'It does not feel as if that was me.'

'I just want to know why you did this, Lilian,' he said.

'Why?' I echoed. 'Why what?' But the memories were coming more quickly now and I felt that I could speak at last. 'I just wondered if a sip would work,' I said and, as I spoke, I could feel the bottle again, the glass neck trembling on my lips, followed by the burn in my throat. 'I did not know how much I would need.'

'How much you would need for what?' he said, unfolding his arms. 'You drank alcohol regularly when you worked in the theatres. Did you not know how much would make you intoxicated?'

'No,' I said. 'I was not trying to get drunk, I only meant to...' But I could not find the words. I pointed to the bottle on the nightstand. 'It was not just crème de menthe in that bottle,' I said. 'There was something else – something that would sort out my problem, sort everything out.'

For a moment my memories were of so much more than that night in the bathroom – they were of that week, that month and that year. I remembered what had led me to that place and why I had done it: there was the evening back in February and Clive's remoteness that had followed it; there was the end to my career as a dancer, and my farewell to the excitement of London and my brother and friends; there were the changes that were happening to my body – the tiredness and the thickening of my waist; and there was Grace – her fashionable outfits, her agility and her energy, and the way she had blown a kiss to someone who stood in the doorway as she had left the house. *Mon Chérie* – they were words meant in jest, but had the kiss been to Edgar, the burly driver that she had set her sights on, or was the kiss meant for Clive? There was also the woman that I had seen in the shrubbery with her postbag of knitting. Who was she and why did Clive care so little about a stranger on his land?

Then there was the life that lay ahead of me – a life which would be isolated from the city or even the village. It would be a life dictated by a distant and studious man, a life spent as a wife and mother, and a dutiful, regretful frump. Yet there had been another option for me, and it had been contained in a tall green bottle. It was the promise of an escape, and I had taken it.

Clive took the bottle from the nightstand. 'Where did you get it?' he said bitterly, 'this bottle and whatever poison it contained?'

I did not answer him because I did not need to – the bottle was never something that would have a place in his house; it was a relic from my old life back in London and he must have known that was where it had come from. He replaced the bottle on the nightstand and did not question me further.

As I lay in the bed, memories of what I had done slowly crowding my thoughts, I realised that there was something that did not add up – Clive had not once mentioned the loss of the baby. I could feel the sheets around me, fresh and warm. The pillow was soft, but there was the vague smell of vomit in my hair and somewhere the monotonous clank of a church bell – it was noon. The grey cotton nightdress that I wore was fresh and dry. While my throat had burned and my stomach had cramped, the body that I had strengthened over the years had remained strong and firm and fought back. I had tried to rid myself of the baby, but there had been no blood.

'Is the baby…' I began, but it was a question I was ashamed to ask.

'Everything seems to be in order in that respect,' he said coldly.

I took a deep breath and nodded. I thought of the nurse at the cottage hospital again and the kitchen where I had warmed myself by the stove. 'She did not want me to do it,' I said. 'I told her everything and she listened, but in the end she sent me away. She was trying to save me from this.'

'Who?' he said.

'That nurse,' but I did not say any more. I had probably already said too much.

Suddenly I felt that I longed to be in that warm little kitchen again, sitting at the table with the nurse I knew as Sadie, as we talked and drank tea. I had spent so little time with her, but she knew how my body worked better than any other. She had said that she would be there for me – whether it was to end the pregnancy or to bring the baby into the world – and now I knew that it would be for the latter. My last chance had been inside the bottle on the nightstand, I had taken it and I had failed. Three weeks had passed since I had seen the nurse and now I was too far gone, and the only time I would see her again would be for the birth of the baby.

'Oh, Clive,' I said. 'I know that we have not been together long. It is all just so unfortunate, for I know that it was only that one evening…'

He drew back a little, as if something I had said offended him.

'Clive?' I cried. 'I cannot do this alone, for it must look respectable.'

'You must not concern yourself,' he said quickly. 'You came here to rest, but things have just complicated themselves and I blame myself for that.' Then he paused. 'No matter what happens. I promise you that I will always provide for you. Elmridge House will always be your home. You must know that I have a duty to care for this child. It has Cuthbertson blood, after all. I can provide for it here and give it everything it needs and even when I am gone it will be remembered.' It was the words that he had used before when I had first told him of my pregnancy, words which were almost exactly the same and I wondered if he too remembered that moment as I did – a moment so powerful that we had both committed it to memory.

'Thank you,' I said and I reached out and squeezed his hand. It was all that I needed to hear for I knew that a proposal would follow. Clive was a traditional man and would want to buy a ring. It was an unspoken commitment, but it was a commitment all the same.

'You must rest,' he said stiffly, returning my hand to the blanket. 'You are still recovering.'

After Clive had gone, I drew the counterpane around me and stood up shakily so that I could look out of the window. The lilies had thrived in the milder weather, the dagger like leaves now spilling over the border, flowers unfurling among them – delicate orange spikes wrapped in curls of pure white petals. Clive was an old-fashioned type of gentleman, the type that was not comfortable expressing himself in words and showing affection, but I knew that the silk lilies he had brought to my final performance were his way of showing his desire for me. He had planted lilies in the bed outside my window, as he knew that they would be the first thing that I saw when I looked out every morning, and now he had planted more lilies in the flower bed on the driveway, so that I would catch sight of the flowers from each of my windows, and I thought that he planned to fill the garden with them. I knew that we would have lilies at our wedding.

I walked to the window. There were more flowers this morning and I could not wait until they were all in bloom. Clive's words had reassured me and the despair that I had felt the previous night was no more than a memory. I had a feeling of hope inside me, yet things were still not perfect, as, deep in the shrubbery, I could see the eyes of the postwoman looking up at my window, watching me.

IVY

13

The upturned wicker basket lay on the hospital driveway, wisps of straw snared in the bushes and broken eggshells scattered on the gravel. It was a basket that I had seen before, although it took me a while before I could picture it in the twig like fingers of the girl in the daisy print dress as she sat by the kitchen stove and begged for the help I could not give her.

It had only been a week since I had seen the girl, but the brief time we spent together now seemed long ago. In the seven days that had passed, I had discovered a new world at Elmridge House. It was a world that I longed to be part of and, when Hugo told me that he wanted me to return, for a brief moment I had actually believed that it could be. I had tried on his mother's leather coat and twirled in front of the mirror, the photograph of the dancers in my hand, and I had felt as if I was one of them.

Yet it was a dream that would not last and barely an hour after I put on the coat, it had been torn from my arms by my furious mother and trampled on her doormat. She had pushed me back into the street and slammed the door shut on my questions and pleas. As I rushed home down the muddy street with only my thin cardigan to shield me from the rain, I knew then that I could never return to Elmridge House and the world that I had dreamt of.

It was only when I arrived back at the hospital, my limbs aching from my rainy walk from Drover's Hill, my shoes muddied and my clothes damp, that I saw the upturned basket and remembered the life that I was returning to and the visitor who I had come to call Daisy.

I peered into the basket, hoping that there would be something that I could salvage from it and return to her, some unbroken eggs that could still be sold, but it was then that I saw a dark red pool sunk into the gravel and a trail of crimson droplets that led to the door of the hospital. I followed the trail, my heart quickening; sometimes it was a wavering line, sometimes a spatter of drops, and suddenly I felt that I could see the ghost of the girl as she staggered towards the door as the blood fell from her. There was a smear of bloodied fingers on the door frame where the wood had been grasped for support – the moment before a collapse or a cry for help.

I ran inside, hoping that I still might catch up with her, but the hallway floor was covered with a sheen of fresh bleach, the only trace of blood on the crimson head of the mop that was propped against the wall, and I wondered what had become of her. Then I saw a bucket of bloodied linen left in the hallway, outside a door that was shut. It was the door to the smallest room, the one kept free for emergencies. I stopped outside the door and took a deep breath before I opened it with a shaking hand.

She looked so tiny hunched in the bed, as if she were no more than a crease in the sheets. I sat down shakily on the end of the bed, watching for the rise and fall of her ribs, praying to see some movement. Her face was grey and her features seemed as delicate as the broken eggshells, wisps of her hair fanning out on the pillow like a muddy halo. I had met her only a week ago but remembered so little of her. To me she had been a girl with bright eyes, trembling hands and an overbite which showed when she smiled, but now even these things were gone from her and all that remained was a stone grey face and the tiny hump in the sheets. I took her wrist in mine, not so much to check for a pulse, but to feel for warmth and humanity. Then I placed my hand on the hump in the sheets, hoping to feel some movement.

I leant forward. 'Daisy?' I whispered, but the word felt ridiculous, it was not her name and she would not hear me. 'Please, you cannot be—'

'Dead?' it was my thought but not my voice. Bridget stood in the doorway, stuffing more bloodied sheets into the bucket. 'No, she is not dead, but that is no thanks to you. You are late. Where in hell have you been? If you had been back at the house when you were supposed to be, we could have sent for you,' but her voice lacked the venom of the words. Bottle blonde strands were coming out of her cap and her movements were slow and weary and I fancied that she had wanted to scold me some time ago, when I should have been there but was not. Several hours must have passed since Daisy came to this room and Bridget's fury had gone, with only the words remaining.

'What happened?' I asked quietly.

'She was with child,' she said. 'She tried to sort herself out.' She paused and her next words were shaky as if she had to force them from her lips: '... With a knitting needle, as far as we can make out.'

'A knitting needle,' I echoed. 'No, I don't understand, I...' But I was a nurse and I did understand. I knew the workings of the female body; I had washed and dried it, bandaged it and rubbed it with ointments. I had seen it laid open in the diagrams of textbooks and on the surgeon's table. I knew what she was saying to me, it was just something that I could not bear to think about.

Bridget cleared her throat, stood up from the bucket and straightened her shoulders. 'It has been a difficult day,' she said, her voice strong again as if suddenly remembering her class and status, 'but we must press on and all that, Dr Crawford is making the arrangements. The ambulance will be coming to transfer her to Oxworth General this evening, for there is a risk that she may haemorrhage again. We must continue with other duties, the wards have been quite neglected this afternoon,' she said, looking at me pointedly, 'and we should make a better show of things.'

'Maybe we should find out if she has family,' I said, 'and...' But I could not complete the thought.

Bridget smoothed her hair back behind her cap. 'Well, whatever family she has she will need to keep tight to them. The doctor does not give her much hope of ever having a family of her own now,' she said quite matter-of-factly.

'Oh,' I gasped, a trickle of ice in my stomach.

Bridget sighed. 'It is strange though, I have never seen her before, but I suppose now I will not see her again. In a way, she has sorted out her little problem and will never need our services. If only she had come to us in the first place.'

'Yes,' I said quietly.

'Well, are you going to get that mop and—'

But her words were more than I could bear. Suddenly I felt the room spin around me.

'I'm sorry,' I muttered and pushed past her, stumbling over the bucket of bloodied sheets in the doorway. I skidded across the wet hallway and ran for the back door, tumbling through it and out into the cold air. Daylight flashed through the trees as I ran into the garden of the nurses' house and, when I reached the back door, I shoved it open and hurried into the kitchen, acid rising from my stomach as I leant over the basin, letting a stream of vomit spatter onto the enamel. I hung my head in readiness for more, my lungs heaving and my back wet with sweat.

Then, somewhere behind me, there was a faint noise – the tinkle of metal on china as tea was stirred in a cup. I took a long breath, wiped my mouth on my sleeve and smoothed back my hair, then I stood up straight and turned round.

Sadie sat quietly on the armchair, her eyes fixed on me.

14

'Why didn't you teach me?' I yelled. 'She came to me. She needed my help, but I could do nothing for her but leave her in the kitchen with a cup of tea and a textbook and hope that Bridget would turn up. That is all that I could do for her and now she comes back to us –' I flung my finger in the direction of the cottage hospital and the room where Daisy slept – 'broken!'

Sadie shook her head slowly. She was slumped in the chair by the stove, and, from her weariness, I knew that she must have been at the cottage hospital when Daisy was admitted. She would have seen her when she collapsed in the driveway and was hauled over the steps as the blood drained from her and spattered onto the floor.

'Did you hear me?' I yelled. 'Why didn't you teach me? You could have taught me what you taught Bridget – those things that you had learned from the clinics in London – but you did not. Instead you put me in charge of the adoptions book – you had me matching up those little mistakes in their rags and cardboard boxes to bored broody housewives, but here was a girl in real need and there was nothing I could have done to help her!'

Sadie did not open her mouth nor raise her hand to silence me. Her face was stone as she listened to my words, just one eyebrow raised in disapproval to show that she had heard me.

'Why didn't you teach me?' I said again, but now my fury was leaving me and I pulled a dining chair over to the stove and sat opposite her. I still wanted an answer and I would not leave until I got one.

'It felt wrong,' she said at last and just that, wafting away my stare with the back of her hand.

'Wrong! How could it be wrong?' I said. 'You are always talking of the good it does – the lives that these women get back and the poverty that is prevented. Did you not believe in anything you were saying?'

'I didn't mean what I teach is wrong,' she said. 'It just felt wrong to teach you.' She folded her arms and looked away. 'I just could not, not you of all people,' and I started to realise that no matter how long I worked at the hospital and how much time she had to spare, she would never teach me a thing.

'Why not me?' I questioned. 'I don't understand.'

She rubbed her eyes but still would not look at me. 'Well, there is your mother—'

'My mother!' I cried. 'What has she to do with this?'

'She would not want me to teach you,' she said plainly.

'Why ever not?' I said. 'She was married, she gave birth to me. She has lived in poverty all her life, she knows the ways of the world. She must surely know of the kind of things we do in the kitchen for our visitors. You are her best friend and you have been helping the ladies for longer than anyone. She must know what you did here.'

'She knows what we do here very well. She...' And then she seemed to hesitate a little.

'What?' I said.

'Well,' she began quietly, 'there was a time when she too was in need of such services and she knew where to go to find them.'

'What?' I said. 'I don't understand.'

'I first met your mother when she was looking for help,' she said. 'I saw her in this very room. She was sat on the same chair you are sitting on now.'

'No!' I said. I thought of my mother with her long skirts that would cover her ankles, and how she would criticise the immodest fashions of the women whose dresses she mended. I thought of how she would only ever take a nip of alcohol at Christmas and how she would sneer at the young men she thought too friendly towards me. 'She would never get herself in that situation,' I said. 'She is just not that type of person.'

'What type of person is that?' asked Sadie.

I thought of the overworked farmers' wives who could not physically bear another child, the fourth time mothers who were too poor to feed another mouth, women who had the act forced upon them, or those whose pitiful circumstances had left them craving just one night of intimacy. There were those who were too old or weak for their bodies to carry a child, and those who had feared the loneliness and separation brought by war. Every woman and every circumstance was different and I could not think of a story recorded in the leather book which I could not relate to. My mother could have been in a similar situation to any one of these women, and I realised that her decision to seek help would have been a difficult one for her to make. It was something that she had never told me about and I began to wonder about the situation that she had found herself in – one that had led her to such secrecy.

'Well,' I said, 'I expect my mother had her reasons for coming to you, but if you had helped her all those years ago, she would surely understand what the women we see are going through, she would want you to teach me.'

'Maybe you are right,' she said, 'but it would also be difficult for me. I could not have you sit at this table and talk to women about…' and suddenly I realised that she could not bring the words to her lips, the words I had heard her use day in, day out with neither blushes nor hesitation, the words she recited from the books and handed out on leaflets. 'Oh, Ivy,' she cried. 'Of all people, I could not teach you!'

'I still don't understand why I am any different from any other nurse,' I said. 'Just because my mother came to you once, a long time ago. I don't see how that is enough to make any difference. My mother came to you for help and would have been grateful for it. You have to remember that you helped her.'

She looked at me squarely. 'No,' she said. 'I did not.'

'You turned her away?' I cried.

'Yes,' she said wearily. 'Please don't judge me for that. I offered her some alternatives, some ways out, and I said that she could come back to me when she was ready, but in the end she chose not to return here and I was glad of it, for I still do not think that I would have let her go through with it.'

'Go through with it,' I echoed. It was not a phrase that Sadie used for the women whose babies were only just off the breast and wanted a break before conceiving another, nor the newly betrothed who were nervous of their wedding night, and I realised that my mother's situation had been more complicated. When Sadie had opened the leather book on the table and enquired about the patient's needs, I realised that my mother had asked for the 'cure'.

I tried to understand what had brought my mother to this place all those years ago. It was a part of her life that I had known nothing about until now, and I realised that there was so much about her past that she still kept secret. It was Sadie who had told me that my father died in the Great War, but my mother had never spoken of her marriage. When I was a child I would sometimes ask about my father, but at the mere mention of her husband, my mother's face would fall and her whole body tense, her silence more terrifying than any of her usual shouts or curses. Then she would stand up shakily and hurry to the kitchen, slamming the door behind her, and I would sit alone listening to the shudder of the water pipe and the angry clatter of dishes on the draining board.

Like me, my father had the surname of 'Watts', but my mother had told me no more than that. He was a man that I knew only from the wedding photograph on my mother's mantelpiece. It was a small photograph in a blackened frame, coated with dust as it was never cleaned nor handled with any affection, yet in my childhood it was an image that I had come to know well. The couple in the photograph stood close together in front of a plain studio backdrop. My mother's veil was pinned against her hair with pale flowers and she held a bouquet to her chest, but years of exposure to the morning sun had bleached the bottom of the image and I could only guess at what her gown had been like – whether there had been lace, a train even, or if my mother had dared to show a little of her ankles. But it was the man at her side that would hold my attention. He was clean shaven, wore a dark jacket and a high white collar, just like any bridegroom, and his face seemed like that of any man that I might pass in the street. One day I had returned the photograph to the mantelpiece for the last time, realising that I could learn nothing about a man who was no more than light and shadow.

I wondered if the man in the photograph could have guessed what was to become of him. Whether he even knew that my mother was carrying his child when the photograph was taken. It can only have been weeks after their wedding day that my father left to fight and my mother found herself alone and with child. She had cared for me, but she had not been a natural mother, I saw that now, and suddenly what Sadie had said made sense.

'I was the baby she didn't want,' I said. 'She was pregnant and she wanted to get rid of it. She didn't want me!'

'Oh, dear girl!' Sadie rose from her chair.

I stood up quickly, grabbing her arm so that she could not leave, but she turned towards me, flinging her arms around me, and I stumbled in the surprise of the embrace. The woman who could not bear a squeeze of the hand nor a pat on the shoulder held me as if I was a child and I felt the shudder in her chest as if she was fighting tears.

'It was only you,' I whispered into her ear. 'She wanted rid of me, it was only you that stopped her!'

She broke away from me quickly and sat back down as if suddenly remembering her place. 'You must remember that your mother thinks differently now,' she said flatly, smoothing down her apron. 'She loves you. She has a funny way of showing it, but she does. It is why I did not teach you what I had learned. Your mother sat in that chair twenty years ago, but you were here too, inside her. She came close to losing you in this place. She cannot forget that and we cannot remind her, if she knew you were carrying on the work that I did here, it would be too much for her.' They were strange words to hear said of my mother for she had never shown me any tenderness herself, and they were words which had come at the wrong time – just moments after I had learnt that my mother had sought to have me, her unborn child, destroyed. Sadie was still talking but I barely heard her words. My mother had not wanted me, so whatever feelings she had about how I could help other women, surely did not matter.

'We do not have to tell her,' I said, trying to keep my voice steady. 'It is not as if what we do is common knowledge. I am sure that Bridget's parents in their respectable part of Fulham have no idea about what she does in this room. You can teach me what you know, we can just keep it secret from my mother.'

'No,' Sadie said flatly.

'No!' I echoed. 'If my mother does not know about it, what possible reason can you have for saying "no" now?'

'I gave the other women that came here options,' she said. 'They would take them or they would walk away and I would not see them again. You are the only baby that I watched grow. You have been like my own daughter. To think that if I had not stopped her, you might not be here now. I could not bear that!'

'You did stop her,' I said, 'yet you cannot have known how things would turn out. You always said that the women are the best judges of their own circumstances. My mother was poor, widowed and crippled, she had as good a reason as any to end her pregnancy, yet you stopped her, why did you do that? You have helped countless other women, what was so different that time?'

'I just knew that something wasn't right,' she said.

'The polio?' I said. 'Did you perhaps think that she was frail and might never conceive again?'

'No,' she said. 'It was not that.'

'What then?'

Sadie opened her mouth a little, but then hesitated as if she was searching for the right words. 'There was nothing wrong with your mother's body,' she said at last. 'There was something not right with her mind.'

15

'There was something not right with her mind.'

They were the last words that Sadie had said about my mother before she stood up from her chair, brushed down her apron and straightened her cap as if our conversation had been about household chores or the weather. Despite my pleas, she would tell me no more. She had told me too much already, she said, and if there was anything more to be said on the subject, it should come only from my mother's lips. From the look on her face, I knew that she meant it.

Maybe she was right; she had told me things that could never be unsaid – things like how, twenty years ago, my mother had come to her for help, how the baby that she wanted to rid herself of was me, and how it was only Sadie's word that had stopped my mother going through with it. She had told me a lot and there was still more to be said, yet it was Sadie's last words that had lingered: 'There was something not right with her mind.'

Sadie had cleared away the cooled mugs of tea, as if signalling that the conversation was over and, when I did not get up from my chair, she commanded me to return to the cottage hospital with a list of orders that I found hard to stomach. I did exactly what she asked of me, because the tasks she had given me involved someone who I had failed; someone to whom I needed to make amends.

I tried to forget about what Sadie had said. I left the nurses' house and walked back down the path to the hospital, where I went straight to the little back room. First, I changed the bloodied dressings between Daisy's legs. Then I sat with her until she woke and waited with her until the ambulance arrived to take her to Oxworth General. Daisy said very little – I suppose it was too late for words – but I remember thinking that her face had changed – all colour had gone from her skin and her overbite no longer seemed childish and only added to her gauntness. She seemed to have aged years in that day, the youth driven from her.

It was gone seven o'clock when I finally waved off the ambulance. I watched the narrow beams of its masked headlights disappear down the driveway, carrying Daisy into a great pool of darkness and I tried to remember what it had been like to see a row of flickering streetlights or the glow from behind a curtain in the nights long before Missensham had become suffocated by the blackout.

Bridget had slept for most of the afternoon and I passed her on the garden path as we changed shifts. We did not speak or exchange a greeting, but our eyes locked together in an expressionless way, as if there was no life within us. I fell into bed.

I woke in the dull light of the dawn to the scrape of ivy on the windowpane. A dark figure stood at the end of my bed – the silhouette of a woman almost as wide as she was tall. I sat up and rubbed my eyes, the sheets disturbed from a fitful sleep. Her clothes were dark, the only colour the pale yellow of a leather coat draped over her arm.

'It seems that we are not done talking, after all,' said Sadie, and then she was gone.

When I made it downstairs, I found the stove in the kitchen already lit and the kettle boiling. I had not bothered to dress but thrown on my housecoat and I sat down wearily in the armchair by the stove. Sadie was busying herself at the sink, clattering with pots and pans and muttering to herself about how nurses of all people should know about cleanliness. Mrs Cuthbertson's pale leather coat now hung on a hook at the back of the door and I remembered my mother ripping it from my arm and trampling it into her doormat before she forced me from her house into the rain.

Sadie stomped over to the table with a plate of burnt toast and a mug of tea and slapped them down in front of me, the tea slopping into the plate. 'I went to see your mother after our little chat yesterday afternoon,' she said. 'It seems you had a long day yesterday and I was not the only one you quarrelled with.'

I thought again of my row with Sadie in the kitchen and then of Bridget's accusations as she folded Daisy's bloodied sheets into the bucket. I had left Daisy alone when she visited the nurses' house, I had visited Elmridge House against my mother's will and I had not been at the hospital at a time when I was needed. I was already blaming myself for so much that I could not face a scolding from my mother, even if it did come from Sadie's lips.

'I don't want to talk about this now,' I said. 'I have to be on shift, Bridget is already angry with me, she will be waiting for me to relieve her.' I got up to go.

'Bridget is asleep upstairs,' she said, pulling me back down again. 'I got Violet in to cover your shift. She has no training, but she is a perfectly capable girl and can phone the house if there is an emergency. We will both be here – we are not leaving this room.'

'Oh,' I said glumly.

'You left this coat at your mother's house,' she said, pointing to where the leather coat hung from the door. 'It does not seem your usual style, so I wondered how you came by it.'

'I borrowed it,' I said.

'I know,' she replied. 'Although I would guess that Mrs Cuthbertson does not know you have it.'

'How did you know it was hers?' I asked.

'Like I told you,' she said. 'I spoke to your mother yesterday' – she reached into the folds of the coat and handed me a small piece of card – 'and I found this in the coat pocket.' It was the postcard I had looked at with Hugo – the group of dancers – and I thought that I must have put it back in the pocket where I had found it, although I could not remember doing so.

My temple started to throb. 'Look,' I said impatiently. 'You told me some pretty terrible things yesterday, yet you won't say any more about those. You would rather scold me for visiting the house of some woman my mother holds a petty grudge against. Mrs Cuthbertson cannot be all bad; in fact, some say she used to be good natured. It was only the isolation of bringing up her child at Elmridge House that made her the way she is. She might be a shrew of a woman now, but that does not make her so different to my own mother who—' But the words stalled on my lips when she glared at me sternly.

'It is a grudge – you are right about that,' she said, 'but it is so much more than you think.' She pulled up a chair opposite me.

'No,' I said. 'I know my mother. She has grudges about everything. She hates the women who wear the gowns she fixes because she sees the memories they hold – memories of tea dances, balls and garden parties – memories that she begrudges because she never had any fun of her own. She gets jealous of people like that and it makes her bitter.'

'Why would she be jealous of Mrs Cuthbertson then?' she said calmly.

'Well, it must be the same kind of thing,' I said. 'She saw me holding this coat. It's one of those ones that people who could afford cars used to wear for driving. My mother has never been in a motor car, but Mrs Cuthbertson is driven everywhere. My mother must have seen Mrs Cuthbertson wearing it one day as she drove past.' I looked at the postcard again. 'Mrs Cuthbertson is rich and married, with a big house – things my mother does not have. Look!' I said, pointing to the woman in the photograph. 'Mrs Cuthbertson is tall, thin and graceful, she used to be a ballerina. My mother resents things like that. People who had what she never did.'

'You should not think well of Mrs Cuthbertson,' said Sadie quickly.

'Why ever not?' I said. 'There are worse things one can be than objectionable.'

She paused and put her head on one side. 'Did you take her Luminal?' she asked slowly.

'Luminal?' I echoed. 'No, I...' But it was a question I had not expected and one which showed that Mrs Cuthbertson was not just some bureaucrat to Sadie – she was more than some name on the hospital committee who had tried to shut the cottage hospital down. Somehow Sadie knew that Mrs Cuthbertson lived at Elmridge House, owned a leather driving coat and she had not even been surprised when I had told her about her time as a dancer. She also knew that Mrs Cuthbertson was addicted to Luminal.

'Well that is odd, then,' Sadie said. 'You see, Dr Crawford asked me to fetch some Luminal for one of the soldiers on the ward to help him sleep. I noticed some was missing from the medicine cabinet. Things have been pretty slipshod since the war started and we lost the matron and the pharmacist to the military hospitals, but I am sure that some bottles were missing. I am not sure if Dr Crawford has noticed himself, but I think that he will, given time.'

'I did take one bottle from the cabinet for her,' I said, my face warming. 'She came to the nurses' house asking for some, but I made it clear to her that she could not have any without a prescription and she did not have one so I sent her away. Then, when she telephoned the next week, she told me to bring her medicine so I assumed that she had got a prescription somehow and so I put a bottle in my bag when I set off for the house, but she never asked me for it when I was there, and it was the same the week after that, In fact, she always left pretty quickly after I arrived. I can return it. I will give it to you now.'

She nodded curtly and said no more, so I got up and retrieved my nursing bag from the hallway. I opened it on the table in front of her but could not see the bottle inside. I looked through the compartments in turn, taking out the tubing, instruments and bottles in case it had fallen to the bottom, but I still could not find it.

'I can't think where it has gone!' I said, but in fact I could. I remembered my second visit to Elmridge House when I had left my bag unattended on the driveway as I ran inside to help Hugo on the stairs. I had been inside the hallway for only a few minutes, but it had been long enough for Mrs Cuthbertson to open the bag, find the Luminal and take it. I thought of her face again as she thrust the roll of banknotes into my hand: 'Go and help Hugo down the stairs, go on!' and about how when I found Hugo he was already on the bottom step and not in need of my help. 'Maybe it has got tangled up in the instrument towel,' I said weakly, starting to undo the neat folds of cloth.

'There is no point looking any more,' said Sadie. 'It will not be there. She has approached many of the district nurses asking for Luminal, it is all she wants, no matter what services she pretends to require. You have seen that Bridget is out of favour with Dr Crawford, did you not think why? You would both lose your jobs if it were not for the war stretching things.'

'Why did nobody warn me about her?' I said, but they had of course – my mother and Sadie had told me to stay away from Elmridge House, even Bridget in her own way had not wanted me there, but I had not listened.

'Don't worry,' said Sadie. 'You are still young, and will make many more mistakes. At least some good might have come from this one.'

'Whatever can that be?' I said glumly.

'Well, I hope that you will now listen to me,' she said, 'when I tell you what you need to know about Mrs Cuthbertson.'

'It is too late,' I said. 'There is nothing you can tell me now that will help because she has already fooled me.'

'Well, you are not alone,' said Sadie. 'There is something in that woman's nature. In fact, your mother has been fooled by her herself,' but then her voice trailed off a little as if she was unsure how to continue.

'Oh!' I gasped. 'My mother? How can that be?'

Sadie spoke slowly, as if choosing her words carefully: 'Your mother met Mrs Cuthbertson a long time before she tried to close down the hospital. In fact they had been friends for years, even before the Great War.'

'I don't believe it!' I cried. They were women who could not be more different from one another in nature and their lives were so contrasting that I could not imagine their paths ever crossing.

Then she said: 'Show me the postcard again.'

I held it out to her.

'Yes,' she said. 'This is a photograph of Mrs Cuthbertson and, indeed, Clive Cuthbertson is in it too. How young they all look! But there is someone else you know here, another dancer.' Then she paused and handed the postcard back to me. 'Your mother.'

'My mother!' I repeated. 'I don't understand.' I looked at the dancers again, to the features of each face, to the contours of every limb, but I could not see the hunched, scowling woman that I knew among them, and as I searched, the faces started to blur and shimmer and I had to wipe my tears on my sleeve. 'Is the woman I have grown up with not my mother?' I said shakily. I thought about how I had always felt distant from my mother, about the difference in our natures, our features. 'Is my mother someone—'

'The woman you grew up with is your mother,' said Sadie, interrupting my thoughts, 'but there is a lot she has not told you about her life.'

I looked at the postcard again, but it was a grainy image on paper that was creased and aged. Every woman's hair was dressed identically and all their features were masked by greasepaint, the eyes no more than dark pools. 'It can't be,' I whispered. 'Nobody here looks like my mother. She has not been able to walk properly since childhood, she could never have danced!'

'She is not lying about being your mother,' said Sadie, 'but there are some lies that she has told you, yet all of them have been for your own good. There is a lot she has kept from you about her early life; the life of a dancer in London twenty years ago.'

Her words seemed so strange to me that I thought I must be mistaken. 'My mother was a dancer?' I said slowly.

Sadie nodded but I still could not accept what she was telling me about the frail and irritable woman that I knew.

'So she was like Mrs Cuthbertson?' I said, 'but you said they were friends, what happened?'

'I told you yesterday that you need to talk to your mother,' she said. 'I would urge again that you do so.' She pushed the postcard towards me. 'This might help.'

I looked at the photograph again, but I still could feel no connection with my mother. All I thought of was my mother's little sitting room. Then I imagined the questions leaving my lips and my mother's furious cry as she heaved herself from her chair and hobbled over to the kitchen, slamming the door behind her. I could already hear the silence that would follow as I sat alone with only the shudder of the water pipe and the clatter of dishes in the sink.

'I cannot,' I said. 'You know very well that she will not talk to me. You know what she is like.'

'I think she will,' said Sadie. 'She is just not ready.' Then she took my hand and squeezed it. 'You will just have to keep trying until she is.'

16

It seemed to take forever for Sunday to come round again. I worked a week of long shifts, dressing in my uniform before the dawn light and only taking off my cap and kicking off my shoes once the sky had become dark again. I had a break of two hours each afternoon in which the patients would rest and Violet would watch the wards. It was long enough to return to the nurses' house and try to settle my mind with a novel or some sewing, but somehow those stretches of the afternoon never seemed long enough to walk to Drover's Hill and visit my mother. I could have tried of course, Drover's Hill was only half an hour by bicycle from the nurses' house and the remaining time would have been enough for our usual topics of conversation – my mother's grumbles about her aching fingers and aged sewing machine, and my responses that amounted to no more than grunts and gentle agreements. Yet this time did not seem long enough for a cheery 'hello', followed by a discussion about why my mother had lied to me about her past: the childhood illness that never was; the youth as a dancer she had covered up; and the unborn baby she had tried to rid herself of.

It was a conversation that I could never imagine happening and, even when I tried to picture myself confronting her or plan what I would say, all that came into my mind was an image of my fist hammering against the blue paintwork of her front door, a door that would never open.

It was during those afternoon breaks that I would get the postcard out again and turn it over in my hands, looking for clues – faded postmarks, the significance of the single word written on the back – *memories* – and the hand that it was written in, the dent of words that could have been left behind by an erased pencil, or a detail in the background of the picture, but, no matter how hard I looked, the postcard told me nothing more. I whispered the inscription to myself over and over again: 'Leonid Postov's Ballets Spectaculaire, The Crown Theatre, Covent Garden'. I searched for my mother's face among the group and every dancer seemed to stare back at me from her darkened eyes, teasing me with her expressionless features.

When Sunday finally came, I got up and joined Bridget on the usual doctor's rounds, then I hurried back to the nurses' house and changed out of my uniform. At ten o'clock, I ignored the drone of the telephone bell in the hallway and, when Bridget looked at me questioningly, I told her to inform Mrs Cuthbertson that I was busy and that I did not mind her going to Elmridge House in my place as long as I could have the rest of the day free and away from the hospital once she had returned. She jumped up with glee and ran for the phone. Only a few minutes later, I watched her disappearing into the clump of trees at the bottom of the garden.

When Bridget returned an hour later, I was already mounted on a bicycle and ready to go. We met in the hospital driveway and she stopped open mouthed as I pedalled past her, with little more than a 'goodbye' as I set off in the direction of Missensham town.

The early autumn rain had sunk amber puddles into the potholes on Drover's Hill and, as I caught sight of the little blue door at the top of the road, my heart started to sink. A week had passed since my mother had spoken with Sadie and my questions would be expected. With every step that I heaved the bicycle over the cobbles, I became more convinced that my journey would be wasted, the image from my dream becoming a reality when I hammered my fist on the little blue door to no avail. At least my mother had the grace to keep working – the sound of the machine clattering behind closed curtains and the chimney cheerily puffing smoke. I thought it her way of telling me that she was alive and well, yet would not open the door to me.

I feared another week passing before I could stand in the cold again, knocking on a door that would not open – another week of my mother's silence and my own dark thoughts. It was not something that I could endure, so I got back on the bicycle and free wheeled down the potholed road and through the maze of narrow terraced streets until I found myself back in the bustle of the high street. I turned on to the Oxworth Road and followed it through the housing estate and away from town. My thoughts did not linger long enough to make sense. Sadie and my mother would tell me nothing more, so there was one thing left to me – the postcard that had been in my handbag for all of my journey. When I finally reached Missensham station, I purchased a ticket for Covent Garden.

I barely saw Missensham from the window of the train nor felt the jerking of the carriages or the jostle of passengers around me. It was not until the big houses and neat lawns opened up to fields and marshland that I gazed out the window and saw the toll that the war was taking on the areas closer to the city. The common land had been carved up into allotments, the reeds and flowers mown and the earth left barren where the last of the harvest had been pulled from the soil. The banks of the canal were littered with coils of wire, concrete pillboxes lining the brown stretch of water like tombstones. When the houses returned, they were smaller and tightly packed, and when the train slowed at Oxworth, there was a gap in the skyline – a place where a house was not, the walls of its neighbours shored up by scaffolding and a patch of patterned wallpaper left on the only brickwork that remained.

There had been a bomb in Missensham the previous year. It had fallen in the car park of the old lido, shattering the glass in the pavilion. Another had landed on the village green but had failed to detonate and another had ignited a container of silage in Evesbridge. I had heard of what was happening in London, but it was something I could not have imagined.

The train slowed at the platform of Oxworth Station, but a grim faced stationmaster waved it through and it continued towards the city. Then came more gaps in the skyline and more skeletal scaffolding poles and piles of rubble that had not been cleared when the priority had been to save life and limb. There were old saucepans among the piles of bricks and beams, odd shoes and the twisted metal of a baby's pram. I felt as if the train was travelling through time, hurtling forward through the years of war, signalling what was to come. Then everything went black as the train began its slow descent underground.

I got off the train at King's Cross and then was swept along with a crowd of people as I battled towards the Piccadilly Line platform, the hot underground winds gusting clouds of soot and the stench of sweat and grease. When I next saw daylight, it was in the streets of the city. I had only been to Covent Garden once before, on a school trip as a child, but little remained of the place that I recognised. The once grand buildings now stood behind sandbags and every window was missing, taped or boarded. The sky that was once squeezed into a small ceiling of grey now stretched to a jagged horizon of resilient old buildings and stark gaps in the cityscape filled only by memory.

An ARP warden in dull blue overalls and a tin hat waved me in the direction of the Crown Theatre, but despite my pleas would not direct me further, unable to spare any words as he swept broken glass into the gutter.

As I came to the spot he had pointed to, I realised I had arrived too late. I sat down on the kerb and stared at the grand entrance opposite me – wide steps and an elaborate archway that led to nowhere, and a section of brick façade that teetered defiantly from the pavement, its glass-less windows framing the view of the bomb site beyond. A collection of gaudy advertisements pasted on to the brickwork were the only things to suggest that not long ago this place had been a theatre.

I stared into the void that the bomb had left, trying to imagine an applauding audience, a stage, lavish scenery and dancers in sparking costumes, but I could not imagine the ballet here, not when the posters on the crumbling wall showed only bold colourful typefaces, square jawed matinee idols and lines of grinning girls in camisoles raising their stockinged legs at a winking man in a dinner jacket who held a gas mask aloft as if he was raising a top hat.

'Did you know someone here, dear?' the warden with the broom now stood in front of me.

'No,' I said, then realising that he thought me bereaved, I added: 'It was just a place that was dear to my mother.'

'A pity,' he said. 'We lost the old theatre last year, but some more of the walls collapsed last night before they could be stabilised. We must look on the bright side, though. I have not heard of anyone who died in this one, although James Street were not so lucky.'

'I should go,' I said, suddenly realising that the past of one woman was of little concern when so many now had no future.

'Here!' The warden picked up something from the gutter and handed it to me. 'For your mother.'

It was a small piece of plaster with a tiny rose on it, like grand buildings would have around a light fitting or archway and I remembered the glamorous dancers I had imagined performing in the theatre. 'Actually, I was looking for a ballet company,' I said. 'This was the theatre they performed in,' I pointed to the steps where the building had once risen.

The warden shook his head. 'I remember those days, but the ballet has not been here for many a year. The Crown couldn't really compete with the Russian ballets in the Opera House, so it turned to variety shows, the kind of thing that brought in the money.' He started sweeping the gutter again, glass tinkling from the end of his broom.

'Do you remember Leonid Postov's Ballets Spectaculaire?' I asked.

He shook his head, but then he stopped brushing. 'Oh, you mean Len!' and he pointed to the poster on the fragment of wall with the man raising the gas mask and the scantily clad dancing girls.

'No!' I said. 'I don't think…' But this time I looked at the poster and read the words spelt out above the heads of the girls in large red letters: *Len Post's Blackout Spectacular*. 'I'm not sure…' I began, but there was something about the poster that reminded me of the postcard I carried – the way the women were clustered around the man in the centre and the similarity of the words, and I felt as if I was looking at dancers from twenty years ago who had never stopped performing even though time had moved on around them.

'Look, either way, Len has been here since the Great War, so he will know a thing or two,' said the warden, 'but it looks like this war has done for him at last and he's shipping out. He's round the back of the Lamb and Flag at the moment. If you run, you might still catch him.'

I hurried in the direction that the warden pointed, the other side of the expanse of rubble. An old van was parked close to the cordon, a poster identical to the one I had seen at the front of the theatre pasted on to its side. An old filing cabinet waited on the pavement while a man loaded a rail of dusty costumes into the back of the van. When the man reappeared from the van, he sat on the kerb and winced with pain as he wound a tea towel round his hand, gripping it in place with his thumb. He was a man in middle age, his hair was greying and there were dark circles under his eyes, but I recognised him as the man who held the gas mask in the poster.

'Mr Leonid Postov?' I said, and when he did not hear me: 'Len Post?'

'I'm what's left of him,' he said, looking me up and down. 'If you are searching for dancing work, dear, you'll need to head out to Brighton. There are shows and dances going on there. Troops to entertain. I'm done with London now.' Then he glanced up at me. 'Is there something wrong, dear?'

'I am trying to find out more about my mother's life before I was born,' I said quickly. 'She was a dancer with Leonid Postov's Ballets Spectaculaire in about 1920.' I held the photograph out to him and he took it with his good hand but did not get up from the kerb. 'She is one of the dancers in this photograph, but I don't know which, her name back then was—'

'No,' he said, glancing at the postcard quickly. 'We were only a small company, so dancers would come for a season or so and move on when we could not cast them. We had a lot from Paris who returned there and I never saw again. I have lost touch with most of these people, I don't think I can tell you what happened to any of them…' But then his brow furrowed and his eyes darted from the postcard, to my face and then back again. 'Unless you are the Cuthbertsons' baby.'

'No,' I said. 'I am not.'

He held the postcard at arm's length in front of him and looked again from the picture to my face. 'But you look so like her,' he said. 'You must be Lily's child!'

17

I sat down on the kerb next to the man as he gazed across the skeletal remains of the old Crown Theatre. He seemed weary and the tea towel that bound his hand told me that he must have been sifting through the rubble for the things that were dear to him. There was a fragment of plaster in his hair. He had thought me the Cuthbertsons' baby and I realised that he must be confused – he did not remember the dancers in the postcard, at least not as clearly as I had hoped.

'I am Lily's child,' I said gently. 'My mother is called Lily, but she is not a Cuthbertson. My mother knew another dancer who became Mrs Cuthbertson and they had a child, a son called Hugo, you must be confusing them as they both danced here and were friends.'

'But you said that your mother's name is Lily?' he persisted, jabbing his finger at the postcard.

'Yes,' I said. 'Before she married my father, her maiden name was…' But then I looked to the poster on the side of the van with its block lettering and bright colours and remembered the name that the man had answered to when I had tried to get his attention. 'Her name was Post,' I said quietly. 'Just like yours.'

'Post,' he repeated, staring at the postcard, and when he looked up, for just a second, I saw my mother looking back at me. His face had the same cluster of freckles as my mother's and he shared her small nose and wide forehead, but the arrangement of features seemed to suit female better than male and there was something strange about his face that I could not put my finger on.

'You look like her too,' I said.

'I am Lily's brother,' he said, completing the thought for me.

'She never mentioned any...' I began, but then I realised that I could not finish the sentence because there was so much that my mother had not told me.

He held the postcard between us. 'This is me.' He pointed to the male dancer in the black tunic with the puffed sleeves. 'Of course, I was Leonid back then, but I go by Len these days.' He ran a hand through his hair. 'Oh, how I must have changed!' he said dramatically. 'You must not even think me the same man!'

'I can see the resemblance now,' I said, although in reality my brain could not settle long enough to see anything.

'... And my sister' – Len looked fondly at the postcard – 'she looks so happy.' He took some boxes from the back of the van and wiped the dust from the metal floor. 'I can still be hospitable to my niece, can't I? Even if all I have to my name is an old van and a few rails of fire damaged costumes.' He spoke cheerily as if gossiping with a neighbour, yet I felt a knot in my stomach which seemed to tighten with his every word.

'Niece,' I repeated the word that he had used so casually. 'So you are my uncle?' He had already told me as much but it was difficult for me to take in. I had come to London to find out about my mother's past but I had not considered what I might actually discover.

He nodded and patted the space next to him and I sat among the clothes rails and boxes, beside this man who was family but also a stranger.

'Well, look at you!' he said. He stared at me as if I was something remarkable, yet his eyes did not meet mine. I thought him taking in every feature and I fancied that he saw a family resemblance, or at least was searching for one. 'No wonder I thought you were looking for dancing work when I first saw you,' he said at last. 'You have your mother's figure.'

'I just thought myself scrawny,' I said. 'It is what they called me at school.'

'You have the body,' he said. 'It is just untrained, I...' He looked at me again as if meeting me for the first time, not as a woman but as a newborn.

'I'm sorry,' I said, 'but my mother did not tell me about you. She did not even tell me that she had a brother. I came looking for the Ballets Spectaculaire because I heard that she used to dance.'

'Ah,' said Len, turning to look at the postcard again. 'The Ballets Spectaculaire – those were the days! Does Lily still dance?'

'No!' I gasped. I thought of my frail and crippled mother and how little her own brother must know of her life. 'No,' I repeated. 'She...' But, from the seriousness of his expression, I realised he thought such a thing possible. 'She does not dance,' I said flatly.

'That is a shame,' he said. 'I know she must be well past her performing days, but I always thought she might go back to it and open up one of those dancing schools for posh little girls in church halls.'

For a long while he said nothing more, just stared at the postcard and hung his head and I began to realise that dancing had been more than just a job to brother and sister – it had held a special meaning, but one that I could not understand.

'Something happened to her,' I said, feeling that I owed him an explanation. 'But I don't really know what. She has problems with her hips.'

'That sort of thing is not uncommon among dancers,' he said sadly.

'Yes,' I said. 'I suppose it must be,' but my words seemed insincere as I knew so little about what we spoke of.

'It was such a loss to the ballet when she left,' he said. 'Things were not the same afterwards. We went on tour to Paris for the summer, but when we returned everything started to go downhill. We tried other principals, but none of them had Lily's talent. There has not been a ballet in this theatre for ten years now.' With these few words Len had told me so much more than the postcard had shown me. I should have had so much more to ask him but my head felt numb and I heard his words as if he was speaking about someone else – a stranger to whom I had no connection.

'But you are still here,' I said but regretted it when I remembered that both the ballet and the theatre were not.

His expression did not change. 'You can see the kind of thing that passes for dancing now!' He jabbed his thumb towards the gaudy poster on the side of the van – the lines of dancing girls kicking up their stockinged legs. 'These days there are no stars, only chorus girls. They need a good figure and a wide smile and little more. The punters have changed too. *Giselle* is a ballet about a peasant girl who dies of a broken heart after discovering the man she loves is betrothed to another – people do not want that kind of gloom nowadays' – he waved his hand in the direction of the old bomb site – 'not when there is death all around them. No, these days all the money to be had is in entertaining troops and in the big shelters. The crowds want nothing more than a few dirty jokes and jazzy dance numbers. All the girls have to do is wiggle their hips and kick their legs up, but I still train them all myself. There is less stress on the joints, I suppose, but they cannot dance properly in these heeled shoes.' He shook his head wearily. 'Ballet dancers are as strong as any athlete. They are true artists and they suffer for it.'

'Are you sure you cannot remember any of them?' I said, pushing the postcard towards him again.

He rubbed the grimy tea towel over his eyes. 'Well, like I said, a lot of the dancers came and went, but the man in the centre is Clive Cuthbertson.'

'He is not a dancer,' I said. 'Why is he in the photograph?'

He chuckled to himself. 'Yes, Clive had two left feet. He was an old friend and a benefactor of the company for a while. This must have been taken on the last night of the season and he had financed the production. I think he was in the picture for that reason. I lost touch with him when I lost touch with your mother.' He turned to me. 'You look puzzled.'

'I understood that Dr Cuthbertson is an ordered, religious sort of man, it is just a shock to see him among these naked limbs and tight costumes.'

'He does look a little stiff.' He laughed. 'I met Clive Cuthbertson in Ypres during the Great War. I was a stretcher bearer and he was a medic in a field hospital. We were thrown together, I suppose. We must have shared some fags or something and exchanged addresses. Then one night I carried a wounded Tommy for half a mile back to the field station. There were bullets flying all over the place, but I was never sure if they were aiming at me. Anyway, when I got the chap back, it turns out it was Clive's brother. Clive always felt he owed me after that. I guess that was just his way. He was a very religious man, one of those pious sorts who always feels that he has never done enough reparations. I suppose that is why he became involved with the Ballets Spectaculaire – he felt indebted to me. I did not ask for his help, but I was not going to turn it down.'

I looked at the figure of Dr Cuthbertson again. I had thought that this stiff man in his smart jacket looked quite ridiculous among the youthful and naked dancers, but now I saw that his presence did give the picture an air of grandeur and respectability.

'Is this how they met?' I said. 'Dr and Mrs Cuthbertson – was it on one of his visits to the ballet to see his investment?'

'Yes,' he said. 'I suppose it was, but I am glad you have this photo of them together, your mother looks so happy.'

I looked again at the faces in the photograph. The darkened eyes obscured any emotion and, like so many photographs of the time, most faces were glum, lest a smile should blur the image. There was only one woman who had smiled and held it long enough for it to be captured. Then I saw Len's finger pointing at this woman – the one in the centre, the ballerina.

'But that is not my mother,' I said. 'That is surely Mrs Cuthbertson.'

'It is your mother,' he said. 'Her stage name was Liliana Postova, back then, it was one of the names she used before she was married.' He tapped his finger on the central ballerina again. 'This woman is my sister,' he said, 'and your mother.'

I looked at the woman again. She stood almost as tall as the man on either side of her and the face of every dancer was turned in her direction. Her head was held high and her gaze was direct, as if she was looking out to the thousands of people who would see the postcard over the years and admire her. When I had first seen the photograph at Elmridge House, I had admired this woman's stature, her confidence and elegance – things that I recognised in Mrs Cuthbertson. I had been so sure that the woman was her, and I think that Hugo had been too, but the heavy stage make-up, the fading print and the passing of the years had hidden the truth from both of us. The woman in the centre was not Mrs Cuthbertson, but could she be my mother?

'Liliana Postova,' I repeated. 'But she is really Lilian Post – my mother's name before she was married.'

'That's right,' he said. 'Your mother was plain old Lil Post, but that is the name of a carpenter's daughter from Hackney not the name of a ballerina, so she was known as Liliana Postova. I was a dancer once too, but I was not as good, so I turned my hand to managing the company. It was fitting that I changed my name to Leonid Postov, but I was only really living off my sister's talent – Liliana Postova was the real star, but I suppose she dropped the surname completely when she married Clive and became a Cuthbertson.'

'No,' I said. 'You must be mistaken, my mother...' but it was not the first time he had connected me to the Cuthbertsons; he had done so when we first met and he had called me the Cuthbertson's baby. 'Even if my mother was the ballerina in the centre, she is just standing next to Dr Cuthbertson,' I said. 'It does not mean that they were married. In fact, Dr Cuthbertson married another of the dancers. She lives in the Cuthbertson family home and goes by the name of Mrs Cuthbertson. I know this woman because I got this photograph from her house, from an old cardboard box of her things.'

'I don't think this woman you speak of can have married Clive,' he said, shaking his head. 'For your mother and Dr Cuthbertson were definitely married in the early twenties, if he had married again after her, the second wedding would not be valid, and if there had been a divorce I would have heard about it, for if a man of his standing were to divorce, it would be all over the newspapers.' His voice was clear and steady and his gaze was direct and suddenly I no longer saw the man from the poster, the one who raised a gas mask like a top hat and winked his eye. He was an entertainer after all and that was just part of his act. He was younger than I had thought too, the grey in his hair was actually just dust from the rubble and he had wiped the dark circles from his eyes with the tea towel that bandaged his hand.

'When we met you called me the Cuthbertsons' baby,' I said shakily. 'Do you think Clive Cuthbertson is my father?'

'Well, your mother and Clive were married, so one would assume it,' he said. 'I see a lot of girls your age, you must have been born around 1920, not long after their wedding.' He spoke plainly, as if stating facts to a child, but his words were ones that I was not ready to accept.

'But she told me that my father was another man!' I cried. 'At least, I think she did, for when I ask her she always seems too upset to talk about it. I only ever knew my father from a wedding photograph on her mantelpiece.' I tried to remember the face of the groom in the photograph, but despite the hours of my childhood that I had spent scrutinising the photograph, I was now unable to recall the man's face.

'You said that Clive married another dancer from the company,' said Len. 'Who do you think him married to?'

'I only know her as Mrs Cuthbertson,' I said, 'but she is tall and thin, and elegant.' I looked at the photograph again, I knew now that Mrs Cuthbertson was not the ballerina, yet I found it hard to think of her as anyone else. 'She was a woman who was supposed to be nice and sweet in those days,' I said, remembering what Hugo had told me about his mother. I thought hard and then remembered Sadie's words: 'My mother and Mrs Cuthbertson were friends,' I said. 'Best friends.'

'Grace Mitchell,' he said without hesitation. 'For I know that she visited your mother at the Cuthbertsons' place out in Missensham. In fact, she left the company not long after your mother did. Grace came with us when we toured in Paris, but she had no commitment and returned home early. She cannot have been with us for many more years after that.'

So the woman who I knew as Mrs Cuthbertson had once been called Grace Mitchell. The name sounded so plain and suddenly my doubt returned: 'I think you are mistaken,' I said. 'It was all very long ago and your memory might be confused. It is such a long time since you have seen my mother, and I think that she must have changed so much. You see, someone like my mother could never have been the principal dancer, she could never have married...' But I lost my train of thought when I realised that he was not looking at me but the photograph, his finger tracing the woman in the centre. From the way he looked at her, I realised that there had been a bond between them, a family connection that he was now feeling again. He had grown up with my mother and worked with her day in, day out. He would have known her moods, her thoughts and her feelings. When he looked at the photograph, he saw his own flesh and blood. It was more than a picture to him, it was a memory, and I realised that he could not be mistaken.

I too knew this woman but she had become so different from the young dancer that he had known, and somewhere in between the young dancer and the bitter mother had been another woman, another Lily. She was a woman who had given up a successful career to live in Elmridge House and had been married to Dr Cuthbertson. She was a woman who one day had left her house and her marriage. The things that had once been hers – the headdress that she wore in the photograph and the bouquet that she held – had been put in a cardboard box and hidden in the top of a wardrobe. This woman had been Mrs Cuthbertson, but she was not the Mrs Cuthbertson that I had come to know, this woman had been Lily, my mother. The woman that now lived at Elmridge House had moved in with Dr Cuthbertson and married him later. It was my mother who had been the first Mrs Cuthbertson, and, in the eyes of the law, she might still be the only one.

18

Len boiled a kettle on an old army stove and we sat in the back of the van among the rails of costumes drinking tea that tasted like autumn leaves from metal mugs which were almost too hot to hold.

'I am sorry,' he said. 'I thought you knew who your father was.'

'I don't think I know anything at all,' I said. 'It feels like there are so many things that my mother has not told me; a whole life's worth, it seems. I suppose I should have expected to find out something like this.'

'You should have told me how little you knew about Lil's past,' he said. 'I think I gave you quite a shock, you seemed so pale there for a minute.'

'I'm all right now,' I said, yet when I lifted my mug I saw a tremor across the surface of the liquid and I put it back down quickly. I thought of telling him about my mother, the woman who was so different from the one that he had known, but I felt that I could not as I would be just repeating her lies to him – fanciful claims that she had been crippled in childhood and widowed during the Great War.

He began to talk earnestly about the past of a woman who seemed a stranger to me: a childhood spent in a small terraced house in Hackney with a privy at the end of the street and a rabbit hutch in the yard; a ballet school run by an aunt in an old pumping station which smelled of grease; a holiday at a boarding house in Brighton where the whole family had shared a bed; Sunday school and bible study, parents who were devout, miserly and strict.

I nodded and tried to smile but felt as if he was not talking about my mother but someone who I had never met. This woman who came from a slum yet became a ballerina was someone that I did not know. She had a family that I had never known – parents, aunts, uncles and grandparents – that would have aged and died before I could have met them. Then there was Len, my uncle that I had never known existed, and Dr Cuthbertson – a man who could be my father. His son, Hugo, could be my half-brother, a relative who, only by coincidence, I had already met.

'Dear?' And then I realised that Len was waving a hand slowly in front of my face. 'I am sorry, you looked miles away and I do not even know your name.'

'Ivy,' I said quietly, barely sure of anything any more.

'But not Ivy Cuthbertson?'

'No,' I said. 'I did not even know that I had anything to do with the Cuthbertsons. My name is Ivy Watts.'

He laughed. 'She has given you Alexander's name!'

'Alexander,' I echoed. 'Who is…'

But he was already reaching in the box of papers on the pavement. He took a photograph from the top and held it between us. It was a picture of a lone dancer, a man this time, dressed in the same dark tunic with puffed sleeves that the young Len had worn in the promotional postcard, but this man was not posing but dancing – his arm extended above his head as if reaching heavenward and his toes pointed. It was a picture unlike any other I had seen before and I realised that few dancers would have the strength and energy to hold such a position long enough to avoid blurring the exposure. It was a classical position that I had seen before in old paintings, but there was something about this man, the bulge of his muscle and the tightness of his body, that made me imagine that he might fly.

Len looked at the photograph with an intense emotion that I could not quite read and I expected him to say more about this man, who he was and what became of him, but instead he cleared his throat and said: 'Alexander was a good dancer. We were a tight little group, the four of us.'

'My mother may have given me Alexander's name,' I said, 'but she has never spoken a word about him, but then she has never mentioned her own brother either. If you were such a tight group, what could have possibly happened that now she will not even speak of you? Getting married and moving away is one thing, but losing contact with your friends and family is quite another, especially if you never even admit their existence.'

'Well,' he sighed. 'I am not proud of that. We fell out, you see.' He held up the photograph of Alexander again, but then said nothing for a while and I sensed not to press him. Then at last he said, 'Alexander and I...' But he paused again as if searching for the words. 'Well, I suppose that you could say she came between us. Life can be difficult for men like me, it can be hard to find another who understands.'

I did not know what he meant, but he looked at me as if willing me to spare him from saying any more, and then I felt as if I did understand, if only a little. I realised that he was not the kind of man to whom I had become accustomed – the family men and the bank clerks of Missensham town, nor the farm labourers of Evesbridge. I had thought his face strange when I first saw it, there was the resemblance to my mother, but there had been something else and now I saw that his eyebrows had been plucked to fine lines and there was a line of greasepaint around his jaw. I remembered things that I had read about in the newspapers, they were mainly to do with court cases but they were never more than outline details and were worded with a veil of shame. They were articles that I felt difficult to connect to this man, my uncle.

I smiled and put a hand on his, for I did not know what to say, and I was relieved when he smiled back and continued: 'Men like me can surround ourselves with arty people – the adventurous and the open minded – but when so many of us are hiding, well, it can be difficult to find a kindred spirit.' He looked back at the photograph, 'When you do, it can be something special.'

I nodded. 'I understand,' and I thought that at last I really did. He had loved this man.

'Alexander was handsome, but he had no eye for the ladies, only for me.' Len sighed. 'Or so I thought. Lil had me believe otherwise, she said that he had got drunk and bedded her. He denied it. She was my sister, but I believed Alexander over her. I guess that was the last straw for Lil. On the night before the final performance, a couple of constables came to the box office asking for Alexander. I was sure that she had called them in a fit of jealousy. I don't know if she understood that we could have been jailed for gross indecency if they had believed her. When Alexander heard that they were in the theatre, he left through the stage door, not even waiting for the curtain call. When I enquired at his lodgings the next day, his landlady said that he had not returned. The last that I heard from him was a letter I received a month or so later in which he said that he had been in prison before and to return would be the death of him. I suppose that he could not really bring himself to trust me because I was Lil's brother, but whatever his reasons,' – he sighed – 'the letter contained no return address.'

'I'm sorry,' I said, although I was not sure why I was apologising for something that my mother might have done before I was even born.

'Well, I should not really blame Lil for anything that happened,' he said. 'It had been a rough season, it would make or break us, we were only a small company, and we were struggling to make our name, but it was foolish for me to think that our English dancers could ever compete with the big Russian ballets in the Opera House.' He pointed back in the direction of the bomb site, the place where the events he described must have taken place. 'The Crown was really only a small theatre,' he said. 'We had some devotees, but most people came across it thinking it was a pub. Lil was under a lot of pressure to carry the performance, her nerves became frayed and I suppose I could have been more understanding, but at the time I was glad to see the back of her when the season ended, even if that meant we had to find another principal. After what had happened with Alexander, I found it too painful to contact her again and then the years passed, and then I suppose it was too late.'

'When did you last see her?' I asked.

'Well that would be when I went with her to Missensham, to Elmridge House.'

'You've seen it?' I said. 'You've seen the Cuthbertson House!'

'Yes, Clive said that he had a place in Hertfordshire. He offered to take Lil out of London, somewhere with peace and calm and clean air where she could rest before the next season. It was only the day after Alexander had fled and I was still so angry with her. I made sure that Clive's motor car was waiting for us at the stage door right after Lil's final performance. I went with them, Clive said that was the proper thing to do. I started to feel bad about it during the journey, but I was happier when I saw the place. It seemed lovely – a romantic old house with beautiful gardens and views in every direction. It seemed a place that she could really recover and rest,' he said. 'Is the old place still there?'

'It is,' I replied. 'It is still as you describe it.'

'She had a lovely bright room at the front corner of the house,' he said, 'with windows on two sides – views of the valley and the village from one and she looked out on to a shrubbery from the other. I am just a simple boy from Hackney and I had never seen the like of it!'

'I have been there,' I said, remembering the room that was now Hugo's. 'In that room.' I thought it strange that I had stood where my mother had and looked upon the same views. The chaise longue and the fine carpets were the type of finery that must have been preserved through the generations and I realised how little must have changed since she was there. Yet, her dark, cramped terrace on Drover's hill was very different from Elmridge House. 'It is indeed a lovely room,' I said bitterly.

'Well, despite all that, Clive would not take any money for her stay,' said Len. 'He had some strange kind of religious morality, as if me following orders and stretchering out his brother was something that he could never fully repay.' He paused for just a moment and I saw an expression on his face which I recognised, a look that I had seen so many times on the face of my mother, his lowered brows and pursed lips coming together in a way which made him look uncannily like her, and I suddenly suspected that even he was not telling me everything.

'Len,' I said, putting my hand on his. 'Is there something else?'

'I just hoped that she would return one day,' he said, shrugging his shoulders, 'but that was not to be.'

So Len's last memory of my mother had been at Elmridge House when she had stood in the large white room and gazed from the windows just as I had done, yet the woman that he described was one who had been lost long ago.

'Did you not contact each other after that?' I said. 'When was the last time you heard from her?'

He took a couple of long breaths and I saw that he still held the postcard of the group of dancers in his trembling hand and I thought him uneasy about something. 'I suppose that was not long after the photograph in this postcard was taken,' he said. 'For we left for Elmridge House that very evening.'

'This postcard?' I said. 'But this must be over twenty years old!'

'Well, there was another postcard,' he said. 'It was sent from Elmridge House, I remember, because it had a picture of the house on the front. It was from your mother and it said that she was with child and was to be married to Clive. That was a long time ago too, it can only have arrived a few months after she went to Elmridge House.'

'But you did not think about contacting her, even after that?' But my words had come quickly and I realised too late that my voice was hard and tinged with accusation.

'No, I suppose not,' he said quietly, a slight tremble on his lip.

I regretted being hard on him. He was a man who had lost his livelihood. He had lost touch with his family and was still mourning a love he lost twenty years ago. Our whole conversation had opened old wounds when he had plenty that were still fresh. I could no longer see the man who winked cheerily from the poster, Leonid Postov was now just someone small and grey among the rubble.

'You are my uncle,' I said gently. 'We should keep in touch. Let me look at your hand.' I took the hand he had bandaged with the tea towel and held it in mine. 'I always carry a bit of antiseptic and a tin of dressings just in case,' I said.

He nodded. 'Thank you.'

I took my small first-aid kit from my bag. I unwound the tea towel and rubbed a little surgical spirit over the wound. It was a large burn across the back of his hand and still quite fresh. I imagined him ignoring the wardens and venturing into the rubble to rescue the rail of precious costumes from a bombed dressing room in the basement, or maybe he had returned just for the photograph of his lover, but I did not ask him how he had got injured and he did not tell me.

I opened the tin of dressings and unwound a roll of bandage.

'You have come prepared,' he said.

'Actually, I am used to carrying more than this,' I said. 'I have not been into this part of London since I was a child, so I did not know what to expect. I just took a few things from my nursing bag in case.'

'A nurse!' he said. 'I would not have thought any relative of mine to be clever enough for that.'

'Oh, nurses are ten a penny with the war on,' I said. 'I have only just qualified and I work in a pretty quiet cottage hospital. Actually, it is in Missensham, not too far from Elmridge House.'

'Well, I will have to write to you once I am settled,' he said. 'I suppose that my life here is over. Having your livelihood bombed is a pretty strong sign that things have come to an end.'

'But there are also beginnings,' I said quickly. 'You have a family again now; you have me and your sister.'

He was silent and I suspected that, despite all his reminiscing, the connection I hoped for between brother and sister was not wanted.

'You have asked me if she still dances, but do you not want to know any more of her. You do not even ask how she is,' I said.

'Well, I...' But then he hesitated and looked at the photograph of the dancers again, shaking his head slowly. 'I was scared to. I was always worried for her, she is my sister after all, but she had her troubles, so I thought the postcard would be a nice way to think of her, I wanted that to be her happy ending. I was content to think of her as the mistress of Elmridge House. I suppose I did not want to know any more.'

'Things do change,' I said, 'and not always for the better, but sometimes we can start afresh.' I realised that I was repeating something that Sadie had often said to me as a child and wondered if she had been more of a confidante to me than my own mother– a woman who had done nothing but lie to me.

I looked across the bomb site with its piles of bricks and planks. Beyond the rubble was a street of terraced housing, the house in the centre was gone, just a skeleton of scaffolding where it had once stood, yet the houses either side of it seemed untouched, the windows still glazed and bright curtains flapping in the breeze. People hurried through the streets as if they did not notice the destruction around them, shops were still open and stallholders shouted their wares and I marvelled at how life could favour some people and not others.

'Is she dead?' said Len suddenly.

'Dead?' I echoed. 'Why would you assume that my mother is dead?'

'Well, you are here and not her,' he said. 'You only said that she did not dance and that something had happened to her hips. You wanted to find out about her past and you told me that Clive Cuthbertson had married again.'

'Yes,' I said. 'All that is true...' But then I stopped because he had handed the postcard back to me and I realised now that he still wanted nothing more to do with my mother.

'The way she lived her life could be quite precarious,' he said bitterly. 'I just thought that Clive would not have got a divorce, for his career would not survive the scandal, so the only way for Clive to remarry would be if Lily were dead.'

I thought of my mother's hatred of Mrs Cuthbertson, the bolts on her front door, her reluctance to go outside, and the change of her name. Grace Mitchell might need a legal wedding to have any claim on Clive Cuthbertson's fortune, yet my mother had got there before her. At last I understood the reason for my mother's fear and hatred and why she felt she needed to hide away – hide from a woman who had taken her life away, a woman who would make sure that she never got it back.

'No,' I said. 'My mother is not dead.' But I said no more than this, for I did not want to tell him of a woman who was poor, bitter and in hiding – a woman who did not dance.

19

I beat the heavy base of my torch against the little wooden door, then I stepped back into the dark street. The curtains were drawn, but there was a thin vein of light escaping the bottom of the blackout blind and smoke billowed from the chimney as if the fire was newly lit.

'I know you are in there, Mum!' I called, but my voice trailed off, the final word now sounding strange and insincere on my lips.

Somewhere down the street came the clatter of a dustbin lid and a dog started barking, but there was still nothing from behind the little blue door.

I sighed and took the postcard from my bag. I looked at it once more under the dim circle of torchlight, but the white ballet costumes now just seemed ghostly in the weak beam that escaped the regulation mask of tissue paper.

I pushed the postcard through the letter box. The word written on the back – *memories* – disappearing into the silent void.

The journey back from London had exhausted me. The service on the underground was slow on Sundays and

I had caught one of the last trains out of the city and spent most of the journey standing in the aisle, jostled by soldiers and drunks. I had also twisted my ankle in the well of darkness at the bottom of Drover's Hill and regretted not going straight home to the nurses' house.

I shook the torch to revive the fading batteries and stepped back into the gutter, wondering which of the narrow streets would catch the most moonlight, but then came the snap of a latch and the clunk of bolts and a chink of light cut across the cobbles.

My mother stood in the doorway, the postcard in her hand. 'Come in,' she said and nothing more.

I pushed past her into the little front room and sat on the stool by the fireplace. She stared at me and then very slowly she shut the door and hobbled over to the armchair and sat down opposite me, the postcard still in her hand.

'How did you get this?' she directed the question to me, but her eyes did not leave the postcard, her pupils moving constantly as if she was looking at every dancer and taking in every face. Her eyes were moist and a smile quivered on her lips. 'I told you not to go back to the Cuthbertsons' place.'

'I did not,' I said. 'I got it when I was there a week ago, the same time that I got the coat. The postcard was in the pocket all along, it was even in there when you trampled the coat on to the floor.' Then I added: 'I was due to go back to Elmridge House this morning, but after I had spoken with Sadie I decided not to and I came here instead, but you would not let me in.'

She grunted. 'What made you come back, and at this hour?'

'I spent the afternoon in London,' I said. 'You would not talk to me, so I decided to visit the Crown Theatre, to see if I could find anything out there.'

She sniffed. 'Did you?'

I reached into my bag and took out the tiny plaster rose that the warden had picked from the street. I threw it in to her lap. 'I was too late,' I said.

She held the rose between her fingers and I thought that at last I saw a little bit of recognition on her face.

'I did meet someone there though – a man called Leonard Post.'

'Len?' There was a hint of surprise in her voice and I thought I saw a smile on her lips, but it was no more than a flicker and then it was gone.

'His name is on this postcard,' I said by way of explanation. 'Leonid Postov's Ballets Spectaculaire.'

She turned away from me and looked into the fire as if watching the flames.

'How is he?' she said after a while.

'He's in better nick than the theatre.'

She smiled. 'Bombproof old sod!'

'He seems well,' I said, 'although now he looks quite different from the photograph. He runs a troupe of girls who dance in their undies and high heels. He says there is more money in that kind of thing these days, yet now that he does not have a theatre any more he is thinking of moving to Brighton.'

I hoped that she would want to hear more details of the meeting, tell me about her brother and their time growing up and working together in the ballet, reminisce or even gossip, but she just nodded and turned back to the fire.

'Please,' I said. 'Why won't you talk to me? I think that as your daughter there are things I deserve to know. I have an uncle that you never told me about; that is not just forgetfulness! How could you not have told me something like that, Mum? What else do I not know?'

But her smile had long faded and she did not turn back to me, the flames flickering over a face that was expressionless.

'Is Dr Cuthbertson my father?' I asked.

She did not speak or move, just kept looking into the fire.

'Is Hugo my half-brother?' I pushed.

But she was still silent.

'Well,' I said. 'I will find these things out anyway. Do you not even want to tell me your side of what happened before I hear it from someone else?' But as I spoke the words, I knew that I was wasting my time. I had learned over the years that everything had to be on my mother's terms and that I would get nothing from her this way.

I looked into her eyes for some understanding of what I had said, an acknowledgement even, but there was none.

I waved my hand around the room at the patched-up party dresses which hung from the picture rail, hoping to catch her eye. 'It has always infuriated me how you hate the women whose gowns you fix, but now I see why you do; you were once so much more than a tea dance in Missensham village hall or a reception at the lido. There was a time when you were young, and partied with an arty set in London, it must have been a shock when all that changed. Maybe one day I will find out about Lilian Post or even Liliana Postova, because that would be the only way that I can truly understand Lil Watts.'

'I cannot tell you about these women, Ivy,' she said bitterly. 'They are no more than memory, they are no longer a part of me.'

I looked at the photograph again, at the woman in the centre, the one with the bouquet and the smile, the one that my mother claimed was just a memory to her, then I looked to the men – Dr Cuthbertson in his fine jacket and cravat and Leonard Post in the velvet tunic and puffed sleeves and somehow I felt that Liliana Postova would be more than just a memory to either of them.

'Which of the dancers is Mrs Cuthbertson?' I said, holding the postcard in front of her. 'At least tell me that.'

She raised her head slightly and, after some hesitation, pointed to the picture. 'She is next to me; the one sunk at my feet.'

I looked at the woman in the white bodice and billowing skirt but recognised nothing but the hair scraped into a tight bun. 'Who was she?' I asked.

'She went by the name of Grace Mitchell back then.' She paused as if the words came with difficulty. 'We were friends.'

It was what I had heard from Sadie and from Len, but they were words that I never thought I would hear from the lips of my mother – she and Mrs Cuthbertson had been friends. There was something about the way that she said the words that made me think that the friendship had been the greatest loss in whatever had happened back then, and that the loss of her husband and home had been a mere consequence.

'Can you tell me what happened,' I said, 'between you and Dr Cuthbertson and between you and this Grace Mitchell? You had a successful career, you lived in a grand house and had a child. What went wrong?'

But she was silent again.

'Please,' I said. 'I do not believe it was polio that crippled you. I do not believe that the wedding photograph on the mantelpiece is of my father, a man who you told me died in the war. I am fed up of your lies. The people on this postcard, with their grey faces and old-fashioned clothes are in the past, but there are things which I have a right to know – I have an uncle, maybe a father and a half-brother – this all matters to me.'

Still she said nothing and I started to lose my temper.

'Do you know what?' I snapped. 'I think I will go back to Elmridge House after all, and see Hugo. He might know more about all this. His family may be strange, but I would bet that he knows more about his parents than I do of mine.'

'No!' she said suddenly, turning from the fire at last and I realised that her eyes were moist. 'Why do you think I never leave the house?' she said simply.

'Well, I...' But I didn't know. I had always accepted her little excuses about the effect of the cold weather on her joints, or the strain that the loose cobbles put on her muscles, and I had never had the will to question her about it.

'Did you never wonder why I did not buy a wheelchair and go out in to town?' she said. 'Or why I have the curtains closed on to the street even in daylight? Or why I talk of moving away from here, but cannot afford to leave Sadie's charity?'

'No,' I began, 'I—'

'My name has changed since those times, but my body has too. Nobody would ever recognise this hunched, bitter woman as the ballerina, the woman in the photograph, yet still I choose to hide myself just in case she finds me one day. One day she—'

'She?' I repeated. 'Mrs Cuthbertson?'

'Promise me to stay away from her,' she said.

'I can't,' I said. 'I like Hugo, he has been through a lot. He needs me right now. He has had some terrible experiences. It is my duty as a nurse.' Yet I did not admit the closeness that I felt to Hugo as we had talked about our troubled families – the fact that we might be related was the one piece of information that I wanted her to confirm.

She was still for a moment and looked quite pale. Then she stood shakily and hobbled to the kitchen, breathing hard. I sat down and looked into the fire, the flames now no more than glowing coals. There was so much about her that I did not know and now I felt that I never would.

Then a sound came from the kitchen. The faint breath of the kettle musing on a boil, followed by the chink of metal on china and I realised that the slam of the kitchen door that I was so used to had not come.

I looked to the kitchen, the door was ajar, and there was a shaft of light from the gas lamp striping the carpet. Then the door opened fully and my mother appeared again, looking weary, with two mugs in her hands.

'All right,' she said. 'Let's talk.'

LILY

20

It was not until the lilies under my window were in full bloom that I saw the woman in the shrubbery again. She sat alone on the bench, staring up in the direction of my room, in exactly the same way that she had done three months previously. She still wore the postwoman's uniform and clutched the postbag on her lap and, from the wool trailing from the leather, I guessed that her knitting was still not finished. She did not move when I tapped on the glass, nor miss a note from her tuneless song, and I fancied that, although her eyes were upon me, she saw and heard nothing.

This time there was something about her presence which unsettled me. I had seen nothing of her for three months, but her return brought back memories of a time when I had found myself pregnant by a man I barely knew and was living away from my friends, family and the life I had once known. It was also a time when, one night, Clive had discovered me on the bathroom floor, my body doubled over with the pain of pennyroyal in my stomach.

Yet things had changed in the months that followed. My body had recovered and the baby I carried had lived and was now a growing bump under my blouse. Clive and I had talked about the future and he had repeated his promise to provide for me and the baby, even after he was gone.

I looked at the photograph in the little silver frame which sat on my nightstand and the eyes in the picture stared back at me – a man and a woman, a smart suit and a white dress with a veil, flowers and smiles, the happy day on which Clive had made good on his promise. Yet, when I looked back to the woman on the bench, there was still something that troubled me – Clive must surely know of this woman and yet he did not mention her.

I tapped on the glass again and then waved at the woman, but she still did not respond and I withdrew behind the folds of the curtain, my hand instinctively protecting my swollen belly and the life that it contained.

I walked slowly to the chaise longue and sat back down heavily. I could no longer stand for more than a few minutes and the few steps that I had taken between my bed and the window had caused a pain in my hips so severe that I fancied my bones must be grinding each other apart. It was a condition that I had been suffering for over a fortnight. Dr Marks from the surgery on the village green had called the previous week. He had done little more than listen to my complaints and then tell me that I was suffering from a softening of the pelvis that was common in pregnancy. He seemed to take pride in reciting the long Latin name of the condition to me, but they were words that meant little and they did nothing to describe the stabs of agony which would cause my knees to buckle if I did so much as attempt to climb the stairs. It was something common among country women who had worked hard all their lives, Dr Marks had said, so it was likely that my career as a dancer would have put undue stress on my joints. It was also possible that I had suffered from small fractures in my pelvis due to what he called 'high kicks and daring leaps'.

I did not care much for his explanation, nor his assertion that there was nothing that could be done but get plenty of bed rest and wait a few weeks for the pains to pass. As a medical man himself, Clive had agreed with Dr Marks and instructed Hannah to make sure that I ventured no further than along the corridor to the bathroom, lest I risk permanent damage. Hannah had become my lady's maid but also my jailor, as she would often return me to my bed and deny me the Luminal that I needed to help me sleep, offering only the small amounts of Chlorodyne that Clive had permitted.

I shuffled towards the bell pull and tugged hard, only to feel the material slacken in my grip and I thought that it must have been disconnected by the builders who were renovating the rooms downstairs. Their constant footsteps and the thuds from the furniture had kept me from my naps over the last few days and I still had no idea how close they were to finishing. I prayed that they would complete their work before the baby arrived. Then

I heard the tinkle of piano music – the opening bars to 'Clair de Lune' and I realised that Clive must be down the corridor in his study. He would still spend many hours each evening listening to the gramophone as he worked towards his specialism, but when I heard the music, I was always reminded of how close he was, even if we could not be together all the time.

I called out to him, the echo of my voice along the corridor followed by the creak of floorboards and his footsteps.

'Oh, Clive!' I cried, grabbing his arm as soon as he entered. 'The woman is here again, the one in the postwoman's uniform who watches me from the shrubbery.'

'The woman?' He helped me back to the chaise longue and then went to the window. 'Well, whoever she is, she is gone now!'

'Gone!' I echoed. 'Well, surely she must still be around somewhere. She could be hiding in the trees, or gone round the back of the house. I can't see any further than the dovecote from this room.'

'I wouldn't worry yourself about it,' he said, kneeling down next to me. 'It is not good for you, especially in your condition. Anyway, she is probably just one of the builders' wives bringing over his lunch or maybe a rambler who has strayed off the path. You know my priority has been fixing up the house and garden. I have just not had the time nor the money to see that the fence is secure, some parts blew down in the storm last winter and the gate at the back has never had a lock on it.'

'There is something strange about her,' I said. 'She does not look like a builder's wife, nor a rambler, and that gate at the back does not lead from anywhere, she—'

But he held up his hands as if the details weren't important. 'I will go and ask the builders about her and if none of them know anything, then I will ask one of them to go and check the fence.'

'All right,' I said, for I knew that there was little more he could do, 'but I would feel better if you went to look for her yourself while you are down there.'

He nodded and turned to go, but then stopped at the door. 'Your hip pain seems a little worse today,' he said. 'Have you taken anything for it?'

'Not since this morning,' I said. 'Hannah will not let me have any more Chlorodyne and I miss the Luminal – it was the only thing that really helped me to sleep properly in the afternoon with all the racket from the builders.'

He nodded, but it was an acknowledgement not an agreement and I knew that there was no way that I would be allowed any stronger medicine. I felt he was in control of my pain – a pain he did not understand.

'Why don't you have Grace over for a visit?' he said. 'You haven't seen your friends in such a long time and you will be busy once the baby is born.'

'I'm not in the mood to see her,' I said, remembering the kiss she had blown towards the house for *Mon Chérie*. And her comments about how attractive she found Clive, or at least his money.

'Have Hannah up for a game of cribbage, then.'

'She has work to do,' I said, but really I found trying to make conversation with Hannah quite exhausting and I could not face her. 'Why can't it be you that I gossip with or play cribbage with?'

'We've discussed this,' he said. 'Let's not go over old ground.'

'Please, Clive. I feel like no more than a visitor sometimes. Your study is all the way down the corridor and it is as if you are miles away. I have to content myself with nothing more than your gramophone music and even that is always the same tune.'

'Well, it cannot be this afternoon,' he said. 'Edgar is driving me over to St Catherine's in half an hour, I must be on the ward by three.'

'Oh,' I said, downhearted.

'Do not worry.' He smiled. 'If you see the trespasser again, you can ask her to take my letter with her, it will save me a trip to the postbox.'

'I'll do that.' I laughed, although I did not feel like laughing inside.

'I'm sorry, Lily,' he said. 'Dr Clive Cuthbertson is becoming a well-known name in the field and I have to work hard to maintain that.'

'Liliana Postova was once well known,' I said. 'Yet I had to return to being plain old Lily Post and I cannot imagine a ballerina called Lily Cuthbertson. I feel quite anonymous.'

He stood up quickly. 'Just stop this, Lily,' he said sharply. 'You know I think you should be using your real name. You were her once and you can be again, you just have to find a way. It will be easier once the baby is born.'

'Look at me,' I said, clutching the bump under my blouse. 'I can't even feel Liliana inside me any more; that part of me has gone.'

The doctors had told me that pregnancy would come easily to someone as young and fit as myself, but the reality had been different. I had hoped for the baby to come in a tight contained package like a neat football under my girdle, but things had not worked out that way and my ankles had swollen to resemble trotters and my face had padded out. The bump bulged out to the sides, and my rear seemed to grow to balance it out. Once, the theatre critics had called me elegant and willowy, but now I just felt ungainly. Yet I could have suffered it all if it had not been for the crippling pain when I walked.

'Soon all this will pass,' he said in the way that men do when they explain things they know little of.

'Not soon enough,' I said. 'For a dancer, every year counts. I could not continue as a principal into my thirties. My career has already suffered, the Great War denied me so many opportunities.' I realised that I was repeating the words that Grace often used when she was trying to excuse her reckless lifestyle.

'You know I don't like it when you talk like this,' said Clive. 'It is only a few months since you tried to...' and I realised that all the composure he seemed to have at the time was no more than a stiff upper lip. He could not even bring himself to utter the words which described what

I had done when he had found me on the floor of the bathroom that night three months ago.

'Oh, no!' I cried. 'I don't mean it this time. I am much better now.' I grabbed his hand. 'Please believe me. I would never do that again. I want this baby.'

He removed my hand from his but held it gently for a moment before placing it on the bump in my blouse. 'The most important thing now is that you do what is best for the baby,' he said. 'You have all that you need here. There is nothing to worry about.'

'I know,' I smiled. 'So you keep telling me.'

The engine of the motor car clattered outside the front window, a swish of gravel as it pulled up by the fountain.

'I should go,' he said. 'Edgar has brought the car round, but first I must—'

'What?' I said. 'You can't keep him waiting.'

'The woman you saw on the bench,' he replied. 'You wanted me to…'

'Oh,' I said. 'Yes, of course,' and I realised that his touch and his reassurance had made me forget all about the strange woman.

When he left, I struggled to the front window and watched him as he got into the car. Then I watched it circle the flower bed and begin its slow crawl down the driveway, its brown paintwork flashing through the cedars and hollies.

I walked slowly back to the bed and took the silver frame with the happy couple from my nightstand. The memory of that day was still fresh in my mind and I wondered if it always would be. Clive and I had our differences, but we were in love and soon I fancied there would be more photographs, with someone else in them – a baby and then a child. I imagined a little girl with reddish hair who would cherish my keepsakes – the bouquet of silk lilies that Clive had sent me on my last performance and the bits of costume I had kept from the shows. I could darn her dancing shoes and show her how to point her toes. I could teach her friends to dance too and hold a class for little girls in the village hall. Just like Clive has said, I would find a way, and maybe one day, I too would dance again.

21

September 1920

'Madam, are you awake?' The heavy bedroom door creaked open and Hannah's head appeared round the gap. 'Is it a good time to make your fire?'

'Yes, come in,' I said. 'I was not asleep, just reading.'

She shuffled quietly across the rug in the direction of the grate.

I turned carefully on to my side and watched her from my bed. Over a month had passed since Clive had first stood at my bedside and told me that the pain in my hips would pass, and since then it had not only stayed with me but got worse and I could only bear to leave my bed for a trip to the bathroom or to call from the top of the stairs when Hannah did not hear me.

I pulled myself up on the pillows, trying to keep my legs as still as possible. 'Wait,' I said, pointing to the brown paper packages that rested on the top of her coal scuttle. 'Are those parcels for me?'

'Yes, Madam,' she said. 'The postman has just been.'

I raised myself up on to my elbow.

'Don't trouble yourself, Madam,' she said, casting her eyes downward. 'Dr Cuthbertson would not want to hear that you were out of bed.'

'I suppose not,' I said grumpily and lay back down again.

'I will bring them over when I have made up your fire.' She placed the parcels on the hearth and the coal scuttle next to them, then knelt on the rug.

'Has it always been the same man?' I asked, but she did not answer and I wondered if she had heard me. 'The postman who comes here?'

'Oh, you mean Mr Robson?' she said. 'Yes, for the last twenty years or so. He escaped the draft as he was already too old to serve.'

'Never another?' I said. 'I mean, if he was ill or had a holiday perhaps...'

She sat back on her heels. 'Never missed a day,' she said.

I said no more because I did not want her questions. Clive had already denied ever seeing the strange postwoman and I began to wonder if the woman would go to the bench at times when she knew that only I would see her. I thought that she must need a reason to be at Elmridge House – perhaps she was waiting for someone, Edgar perhaps, for she must be nearer his age, or even Clive. I tried to get the thought out of my head, but when I closed my eyes I saw only the woman's face and heard the click of her knitting needles.

'Can I have some more Chlorodyne?' I said.

Hannah opened her mouth, but when no words came she turned back to the fireplace as if the clattering of the poker would drown out my voice and I realised that my request went against Clive's orders. It was not until the flames were crackling that she wiped her hands on her apron, stood up and came over to my bed. 'Your parcels, Madam,' she said, handing me the packages.

'Please stay with me while I open them,' I said. 'I don't get much excitement these days and it will feel strange if I am alone.'

She glanced nervously at the door but nodded her head. 'Yes, Madam,' but she did not fetch me the paperknife.

She propped up my pillows and helped me to sit and I took the first parcel, recognising the Missensham postmark and the stamp of Partridge's Department Store from the high street.

'I wrote to Partridge's last week,' I said. 'You see, I wanted to order something for myself. After all, there will be so much for the baby.'

When I tore away the brown paper and opened the little box inside, Hannah let out a little cry. 'You ordered a ring, Madam?'

'Yes,' I said, 'I know it is an extravagance, but my fingers have become too swollen for the other and it just didn't feel right not wearing one, so I have ordered this larger one to wear for just a few months until the swelling goes down.'

'Does Dr Cuthbertson know?' she said, the question coming automatically.

'There was no need to tell him,' I said, a little annoyed that she felt I needed Clive's approval for everything. 'I paid for it myself, Partridge's actually do some very cheap ones.

It is brass rather than gold, but I do not need it to last.' I put the ring on, it slid on nicely and I fanned my hand at her, spreading my fingers so that it glinted in the light.

Hannah did not smile and I thought she must be somehow bitter at my relationship with Clive when she had served him for so long.

'Maybe I should have got something more expensive,' I said, a little deflated, 'but it will make do for now, until Clive is really established in his new field.'

'I'm sure it will do fine, Madam,' she said, although I could see uncertainty in her eyes, and I knew that she would run and tell Clive the moment I dismissed her.

'I'm hot,' I said to cover my embarrassment. 'I just need a bit of air until the fire dies down. Are the windows still jammed shut?'

'They are, Madam,' she said.

'Well, can you get those builders to come and fix them?'

'I will have to ask Dr Cuthbertson about that,' she said and I fancied that she lacked the courage or intellect to make any decisions without Clive.

'Will you at least draw the curtains for me, then,' I said. 'The ones to the side of the house. The sunlight from the window is falling directly on to the bed.'

She nodded and went to the window and I watched the stripes of sunlight move across the counterpane as she adjusted the curtains. Then the grate of the curtain rail stopped suddenly and I looked up to see her silhouette motionless in the glare of the sun, her face angled downwards as if she was looking out of the window towards the bench.

'What is it?' I queried.

'Oh, nothing,' she said quickly and drew the curtain fully. 'It's nothing to bother you with, Madam.'

'Is there a woman there?' I said.

'A woman?' she echoed. 'No, Madam.'

'Clive must have mentioned to you that there has been a woman watching my room,' I said. 'I thought he would be concerned for your safety as well as mine.'

She shook her head.

'I saw someone in the shrubbery last month, outside the window,' I said. 'It is not the first time that I have seen her, but I have become so worried about it recently. I expect that Clive says that I am just being silly with my nerves.'

'No, Madam,' she said, looking away from me quickly. 'I have heard nothing of it.'

I sat up. 'She is there, isn't she? She is there now!' I bent my knees and tried to slide my feet off the bed, wincing with the pain.

'Madam!' she cried, running over to me.

'I need to see for myself,' I said, grabbing her arm.

She pulled free, a look of astonishment on her face. 'There is nobody there,' she repeated.

'Well then, you won't mind me seeing for myself, because I have seen a woman three times now and I will see what you saw just then.'

'Was she a postwoman?' she said quickly.

'Yes!' I cried, trying to stand. 'Now I know that she is on the bench again and that another person has seen her!'

'No, Madam,' she said. 'I told you that I have seen nobody.'

'But how can you have known that—'

'There is nobody out there,' she said. 'I just thought of a postwoman as you had been asking if Mr Robson had ever missed a day, and one of those big leather postbags has been left on the bench.'

'Oh,' I said. 'She has left her bag.'

'Please, Madam, do not injure yourself for this – there is nobody to see.' She wrung her hands and suddenly I realised how much my behaviour had frightened her.

'I'm sorry,' I said, relaxing back on to the bed, 'but now I might find out who she is at last. Could you go down and get the bag and bring it back up to me?'

'Yes, Madam,' she said. She left the room quickly without even mentioning Clive and the permission that he would probably not give.

I took the other parcel from the nightstand. The brown paper bore a London postmark and I recognised the handwriting on the front immediately – Grace. She must have returned from Paris earlier than planned.

My fingers sank into the soft brown paper and I hoped that Grace had brought me some clothes back from Paris – a dress maybe, or some more pyjamas to replace the ugly grey nightdress that Hannah always set out for me since my pyjamas went missing. Grace had always had a good eye for fashion and I remembered how elegant she had looked in my yellow leather coat with the fur trim.

I tore the paper away excitedly, but it was not clothes for the baby, nor myself – it was a ragdoll, made from old woollen stockings and bedsheets, held together with clumsy stitches of twine. The doll's face and hands were a dull orange rather than pink or white and the thick woollen strands of hair were tied with a knot of white yarn in which a length of felt had been curled into an approximation of a white lily. It wore a white, ankle length dress, the waist pinched tightly with string to force the skirt out into the billow of a long ballet skirt. The eyes were buttons and the mouth just a few stitches of red yarn, pulled into a gormless smile – the same expression that a clown might pull on the delivery of a joke. There was a note among the torn brown paper, scrawled in Grace's uneven hand: *I am sorry about everything. Here's to a new future for you both.*

There was something about the surprise of the gift and the expression on the doll's face that made me laugh. Whether it was my condition or the days that I spent within the same four walls, I don't know, but I couldn't help it. I laughed until the heave in my chest turned to a dull ache and only tears remained. I hugged the doll to me. I thought of Grace, with no mother to teach her how to use a needle and no money for fabric, taking the time to sit in the dressing room and stitch together a doll for my baby, using nothing but the needle she used to darn her pointe shoes.

'I am sorry, Madam.' Hannah stood in the doorway, with the postwoman's bag over her shoulder. 'Is something wrong?'

'No,' I said, wiping my tears across the back of my hand. 'I do not think I am even sad.' It was true, I was not sure what I felt, but the doll was not like the little outfits or blankets that I had been ordering from Partridge's – it was an embodiment of a child that I would soon have and at last I finally accepted that I was going to have a baby.

Hannah walked slowly to the bed, shuffling her feet as if embarrassed by my tears.

I cleared my throat. 'Please – the bag?' I said.

She held it out to me.

It was a postbag, just as Hannah had said, but the leather was quite faded. I put my hand inside but felt no letters or parcels, only the cold knitting needles and the softness of the wool. I pulled out the knitting – it was a long piece of dull green with close stitches and, as I pulled out more loops of the knitted wool, I realised that it must be a scarf, yet one that would stretch the length of the room. At one end, the knitting needles were still looped with wool as if the scarf was not finished and the knitter had no intention of stopping.

It was not yet the weather for scarves and I thought that I must first have seen the woman back in April when winter would have been a distant thought.

Hannah gazed at the scarf, open mouthed.

'I don't know why this woman is here,' I said shakily. 'There is nothing I can do about her from this bed and no one will listen to me.'

'Calm yourself, Madam,' said Hannah, bundling the knitting back into the postbag and tucking it quickly under the chaise longue. 'Perhaps I can go to Dr Cuthbertson's study and put the gramophone back on again, you know how he says all that gentle piano music calms him.'

'No,' I said. 'I have had enough of that. I am due a nap and I would like some Chlorodyne.'

'Madam, I'm not sure—'

'The pain is bad today,' I said. 'I can barely turn over in the bed and I need to be rested because another doctor is visiting me this afternoon,' I added, suddenly remembering the only appointment that was in my diary.

'Dr Cuthbertson has not mentioned it,' she said. 'Is it Dr Marks from the surgery on the green?'

'Oh no,' I said. 'Clive won't have all that provincial stuff; it is one of his colleagues from Oxworth. He thinks this pregnancy has thrown up too many problems.' I sighed.

'Very well,' she said, 'but Dr Cuthbertson would not want you taking too much.' She took a teaspoon and the small blue bottle from the pocket of her apron, broke the seal and uncorked it. She poured the thick brown liquid in to the teaspoon until it was level and handed it to me.

I took it without hesitation, my whole body warming before it had even hit my throat, the pain in my hips fading to a dull ache.

Hannah fussed with the counterpane and, as she reached across me to plump my pillows, I took the bottle of Chlorodyne from the nightstand and pushed it down the side of the mattress.

When Hannah had finished with the bed, she glanced at the nightstand and then to the windowsill and the floor, her eyes searching frantically.

'Is something wrong?' I said.

'No,' she said quietly.

After had Hannah left, I lay back on the mattress with the doll next to me. Gentle piano notes drifted along the corridor and the ceiling above me started to blur. The things that had been troubling me for so long – my worries about Clive's lack of affection and fears for my body and the birth, my homesickness and regrets – seemed to slowly fade with the dimming of the light, but somewhere deep inside my head, I could still hear the click of the postwoman's knitting needles and hear her tuneless song.

22

I dreamt that I was at the Crown Theatre again, lying on the floor of my dressing room on that cold evening in February. The sounds of the tinkling piano and the muffled laughter from the corridor raced round my mind and I raised my hand to catch the flickers of green light which danced across the wall. I felt the softness of the blanket beneath me and the warmth of the man whose body pressed down upon mine. Then I saw his face again, his eyes large in the darkness and I felt the warmth of his breath as he whispered in my ear.

'Lilian?' A man perched on the chaise longue which had been pulled up to the side of my bed.

I blinked away the memory – the tinkling piano and the dancing green light fading away but somehow the feeling remaining. My bedroom was flooded with daylight, but I had no idea of the time and the hands of the clock on my nightstand pointed to numbers which made little sense. My head was heavy with the fug of Chlorodyne and I remembered that I had taken another dose on top of the one that Hannah had measured out for me. Then I remembered my appointment with the doctor, the one that Clive had arranged for me – the man who sat at my bedside.

He was a man a little older than Clive in a fashionable suit, his hair neat and greying at the temples and a notebook resting on his knee.

I propped myself up on my elbow and blinked at his silhouette. The light from the window threw his features into shadow, but when he leant forward, I realised that his face was one that I recognised.

'Walter!' I cried. 'It is good to see you again,' but my throat closed round the words and he handed me a glass of water which he had poured from my bedside jug.

'Hello, Lilian,' he said, with a smile.

'Clive told me that one of his colleagues would be coming to see me, but he did not tell me that it would be you!'

'It's good to see you,' said Walter, 'and I am glad you remember me because it has been such a long time since I dined at Elmridge House. It must have been when you first arrived here.'

'It was,' I said, 'and you should not be surprised that I remember you. You see, you have been Clive's only visitor since I arrived. Clive often talks about what his colleagues are up to, but with St Catherine's so far away in Oxworth, I get to meet so few of you.'

A shadow moved at the foot of the bed and I saw that Clive had brought in a chair and was watching us. I smiled at him, but I could not see if he returned it.

'How long ago is that now?' said Walter.

'It must be about seven months,' I said, patting my swollen belly. 'You see, I have a constant reminder inside me.' I tried to prop myself up on my pillow, but the bones of my hips seemed to grate together painfully and I thought better of it.

'Don't get up,' said Walter. 'Clive tells me that you have a softening of your pelvic bones and that it is causing you some discomfort. In fact, we were unsure whether to wake you. I hear that sleep is not coming easily.'

'It is not,' I said, 'but I do not mind to be woken if it is by you. Clive always says that obstetrics is not his area, but really I think he is afraid that I will scold him if he cannot help. As his department director, is there anything you can do?'

'Well, unfortunately, it is not really my area of expertise either,' said Walter, 'There is not a known cure for this condition, but I am sure that things will improve after the birth, if not before. For now, I'm afraid it is just a case of making you comfortable.'

'Oh,' I said, disappointed.

'You have been using this?' He took up the little blue bottle of Chlorodyne from the nightstand and I noticed that it was empty.

'Yes,' I said. 'Clive has allowed me to—'

'She is taking it within the guidelines,' said Clive quickly, 'and Hannah knows that she is not to bring her any more than that, isn't that right?' But his head was not turned to me and I saw that Hannah stood silently by the door.

'I only really take it when the pain is unbearable,' I said. Then I added: 'And Hannah is very strict.' I thought that Hannah looked relieved and I suspected that Clive had already scolded her for the bottle that he must have found pushed down the side of the mattress. 'I have such trouble sleeping,' I continued, 'and sometimes even the Chlorodyne cannot help.'

'Would you like a stronger painkiller?' said Walter.

'Luminal was the only thing that helped when I first arrived here,' I said. 'Clive prescribed it to help me sleep, but he stopped me from taking it when he realised that I was pregnant. You see, it is not just the pain that keeps me awake – sometimes my body is tired but my mind will not let me sleep.'

Walter took a little notebook from his pocket and opened it on his lap. 'What kind of thoughts keep you awake?'

'Oh, well, things like...' But I had not expected the question. I had always seen the medication as something to switch the thoughts off, it had not occurred to me that it might matter what the thoughts actually were.

The truth was that the pain in my hips had only increased my isolation and now I barely saw anyone in the house, let alone spoke with them. I would sometimes look down on to the driveway and watch Edgar prepare the motor car and, even though he would often look up at my window, the expression in his eyes told me his mind was elsewhere. I would only see Hannah when she brought me my meals or came up to light the fire, and when I called for her, she always seemed as if she had more important matters to attend to. The staff that Clive hired from the domestic agency seemed to come and go at all hours, and the only thing that reminded me of their presence was when I heard a raised voice from downstairs or saw a figure hurrying down the driveway. But these were things that I could not say while Clive was in the room – I had complained of boredom and loneliness to him before and never received anything more than reassurances.

'I suppose that I miss my old life as a dancer,' I said after a while. 'Like a kind of homesickness.' I looked to Clive, but his face was still in shadow. 'Of course, it is just because things are so different from how they used to be,' I added quickly. 'I do not have such thoughts during the day. When I am fully awake I realise how fortunate I am to be here, and to have Clive.'

'How do you think you will feel once you have the baby?' asked Walter.

'I suppose things will be different again,' I said. 'I don't know.'

Walter scratched a word in his notebook with the stub of a pencil. 'Having a baby in the house can keep you awake, no matter how far you are from the nursery. The nanny may not always...'

'It won't compare to the pain I have now,' I said. 'It can't do. I think that once my hips have returned to normal then the sleep will come and I will feel much better.'

'And the thoughts that you have been having?'

I noticed that the doll Grace had sent me was propped against the foot of the bed, staring at me from its button eyes. 'The thoughts?'

'The life that you miss. Do you think that these thoughts of homesickness, as you describe them, will go away?'

'No,' I said simply. 'They will not, they cannot. Not as long as...' But then I realised that I could not see an end to my torment – the pain would go, but then there would be a baby and the thoughts that disturbed me would be a reality.

'Do not distress yourself,' said Walter.

'But I'm not upset, I just—' But my hands were twisting round the counterpane.

'Do you take more Chlorodyne when you worry about the future?' he asked. 'When you can't sleep? Do you think that taking something like Chlorodyne or Luminal will make the baby go away, just for a little while?'

'Go away?' I replied.

Walter took a long breath. 'Well, Clive tells me that you ordered corsets as if you aimed to hide the pregnancy, yet it was no secret. There was nobody to hide it from.'

I looked to Clive, but he stared at the window and I was angry that he must have been through my belongings. 'I barely wore them,' I said, 'and, anyway, it's not as if I could get away with that now.' I pointed to the hump in the blankets. 'I am past that point – I am reminded of this baby every minute of the day, at every glance in the mirror, or when I can no longer look down and see my feet. I feel it in every painful step or every time that I cannot even turn over in the bed.'

Walter looked at me, his eyebrows raised, I realised that I must have sounded dramatic.

'I suppose you are right,' he said. 'There is little use in pretending now.' He paused. 'But was there a time not so long ago when you wished the baby to be gone forever?'

'I don't know what you mean,' I said.

'Have you ever done anything to harm your unborn child?' He looked at me sternly, his words slow and firm.

'No!' I said. 'I have not.' I looked to Clive, but his eyes would not meet mine and I knew that he must be the reason for such a question.

I had not thought of taking the pennyroyal as harming the baby, merely as a way of getting my life back, and suddenly I could taste the mint in my mouth again. 'I have not,' I repeated, but this time I heard a catch in my voice.

'You should not worry yourself over it,' said Walter. 'We can't have you agitated in your condition.'

'I am not agitated,' I said, but they looked to one another and some shared knowledge passed between them. I worried that they thought the baby harmed by what I had done.

Walter glanced at Clive. 'I think the worst of it was many months ago and things seem better now,' he said quietly.

Clive nodded.

'Perhaps the most important thing is to make sure that you are happy. You have no more than a couple of months to go, think of it like that and do not worry yourself. Think of what is best for the baby, for worry can bring on a premature birth. You should relax and put your feet up.'

They were words that I had heard before and they were words which came from the lips of a man. Walter spoke with authority but had not experienced what I was about to, and never would. I imagined him outside the delivery room, his ears plugged to his wife's screams, then being presented with the baby only once it was born and washed – such was the experience of a father.

The rag doll stared at me from the foot of the bed and I realised that I had not seen Grace in over four months, even Hannah's visits to my room were brief and she would only come when I called for her. I had visits from Clive of course, and now Walter, but they were men – men of science and ones who saw me only as a specimen to be studied. I no longer felt like a lover or a wife, nor even a woman – one who was about to become a mother. Suddenly I longed for the support of a woman, one who really understood me, and I remembered the stocky nurse who had listened to my woes as we sat and drank tea by the warmth of a stove. It had been a meeting that had brought me comfort, if only for an hour or so.

'There is something that would put my mind at rest,' I said. 'I was hoping to have a midwife for the birth.'

'A midwife,' Walter repeated as if his lips were trying out the word for the first time. 'A handywoman?'

I heard a long intake of breath from the foot of my bed and saw Clive lean back in his chair.

'We are in a new decade,' said Walter. 'This is the modern age. Doctors are much better qualified than these women, who are little more than birth attendants; they are men with the latest scientific knowledge at their fingertips. With Clive's medical background, I hope that he won't object to such folklore.'

'Just for comfort then,' I said. 'My mother always spoke highly of hers.'

Clive leant forward as he spoke, a slight crease on his brow. 'All right, but I am only allowing this as it will calm your nerves. We will find some local woman when the time comes. I believe there are some connected to the cottage hospital.'

Walter nodded. 'Well, that seems like a good solution. Hopefully it will be something that will stop your worrying and you will have less need for Chlorodyne.'

'Yes, it is best to keep the Chlorodyne locked away.' Clive looked sternly at Hannah.

'I think that concludes things here for now,' said Walter briskly. 'It was lovely to see you again, Lilian, and I do wish you the best.' It was only then that I realised how his voice had changed over the course of the appointment, the pleasantness of his greeting only now returning.

'Thank you,' I said.

He put away the notebook as if to signal the end of the conversation and I was glad for it. Walter was a doctor but he was also a friend of Clive's and I felt that I owed it to him to be hospitable.

'Will you be staying for dinner?' I said. 'Edgar went out with his rifle this morning and I think we have a brace of pheasant as well as a rabbit.'

'I am sorry, Lilian,' he said, 'but I have other patients.'

'You and Clive both work so hard,' I said. 'It is a shame.'

'You are right,' he replied. 'I cannot stay for supper, but I suppose that it would not hurt to have a stroll in the grounds.'

'You would be welcome,' I said, 'but, as you know, I won't be able to join you. Hannah tells me that some of the lilies are still holding on to their blooms this late in the year. You will find them in most places in the garden now.'

'Thank you.' He stood up and turned to go. 'Oh, Clive says you saw a stranger in the shrubbery,' he said matter-of-factly. 'Could that have got you worried?'

I glanced at Clive but his eyes were fixed on the window, and I suspected that the woman I had seen in the garden was a subject that he did not want to discuss.

'Yes,' I said. 'There is a woman who I have seen three times sitting on the bench outside my window, but she is not sinister. What troubles me is why she is here and how she gets in. She has a bag full of knitting, which Hannah brought up to me and put under the chaise longue, but there is little more I can tell you other than that.'

Walter went to the window and glanced through the glass. 'Well, I cannot see her now. I doubt she will return.' His words were stated slowly and firmly and I felt embarrassed that Clive had told him about the woman in a way that must have made me sound like a child fussing. Clive had not seen the woman, so it was no wonder that he dismissed her as a lost rambler or a builder's wife.

'You are right, it is probably nothing.' I said. 'In fact, it has been a while since I have seen her.'

Walter returned to the bed and took up the photograph from the nightstand; the little rectangle of silver that framed the smiling faces of Clive and me.

'That's lovely,' he said. 'A happy memory.'

'Yes,' I said. 'I suppose that day was the start of my new life.'

'Indeed,' he said. 'Just remember that feeling, for it will come again one day and you won't need Chlorodyne for it. It will happen as soon as the baby is born. Your body will settle down again and you will see things differently.'

'Differently?' I enquired.

'How you once saw them,' he said, 'long before you came here.' I thought it was a strange thing to say, but Clive nodded, so I smiled and did likewise.

The men left, Hannah following them closely and closing the door behind her. I heard their footsteps along the corridor to the front of the house and then the creak of the stairs. I sat back on the pillows and drank a little more water. I heard the gentle hiss of a breeze blowing through the shrubbery but I could not feel it through the jammed windows and had to content myself with watching the dapple of the light on my counterpane. Then came the shriek of a blackbird as it was startled from the trees and the gravel path crunched with the men's footsteps.

Their mood seemed light and their voices animated and I felt glad that Clive might at last have a friend who understood his work and whom he could invite to the house. The sound of their footsteps grew louder as they passed under my window and went on towards the dovecote cottage and I could hear the rhythm of their conversation but only make out odd words. Then the silence returned and suddenly I remembered that I had not seen the late bloom of lilies that Hannah had told me of. I bent my legs and slowly dangled them over the side of the bed, twisting my body painfully but moving inch by inch until my feet were flat on the floor. I hobbled slowly to the window and slumped onto the window seat.

I rested my forehead on the windowpane, the coldness of the glass on my skin waking me from the fug of Chlorodyne and I realised that my mind was clear at last.

Down by the shrubbery, a lady in a postwoman's uniform sat on the bench. It was a place next to the gravel path that Clive and Walter had walked on just moments before and talked as if nothing was unusual. They must have walked right past the woman, they must have seen her. The woman wrung her hands in her lap. Then she looked up at me.

23

Clive did not return to me after Walter had left and I took my supper alone in bed that night. The pheasant stew which would have easily made a sociable supper for three was divided between all that remained in the household, and each congealed portion was eaten alone. Hannah had left my nightly dose of Chlorodyne on my supper tray. The medicine no longer in its little blue bottle but a glass tumbler, the amount carefully measured – a thin brown film of medicine coating the bottom of the glass. I drained the sticky liquid into my mouth, scraping the last remnants out with my knife.

As I lay down for the night, I felt the pain fade to little more than a tingle, yet my thoughts would not be numbed and I found myself in a strange middle place where I was neither asleep nor awake. Memories of the day fleeted through my mind but never lingered long enough to make sense: a raised eyebrow; an accusation; a look of understanding that I was not part of; the stare of a doll with button eyes; and an empty blue glass bottle – and then the woman sitting on the bench in her long postwoman's coat. It was this final thought that stayed with me the longest. I pictured the woman with her knitting on her lap – the scarf which seemed to go on and on forever, the click of her needles echoing in my head. I imagined her looking up at my window with unblinking eyes which saw all and nothing.

Then a pain in my hip jolted me awake and I realised that the Chlorodyne must be wearing off. The carpet was striped with a pale shaft of moonlight – morning was still far away and I feared returning to the torments of my half-sleep.

There was a thin line of light coming from under the door and somewhere the creak of a floorboard and I knew that Clive must still be up and working in his study. I sat up slowly and pulled my legs over the side of the bed so that my feet were on the floor. The empty Chlorodyne bottle was still on my nightstand and I thought of taking it to Clive to remind him that I had no more that I could take. I took a few deep breaths, then stood up gingerly, gasping until the pain dulled a little, and then I walked slowly to the door and into the corridor with the empty bottle in my hand.

When I reached Clive's study, I pushed the door open just a crack so as not to startle him and peered into the room. A long shadow fell on the wall opposite me – the blurred outline of a man caught in the light of the oil lamp, his shoulders hunched and his head bowed. Then came another creak, deep in the floorboards, but the shadow on the wall did not move. I stood still and listened to the silence. Then came another sound, faint, yet somehow familiar; the hiss of a record as it spun on the gramophone and the gentle crackle of the recording. The silhouette on the wall moved, the outline Clive's long distinguished face and the flat surface of his half-moon spectacles outlined on the wall for just a second as he turned his head towards the sound.

Then came the grate of his chair on the floorboards and the shadow became no more than a blur on the wall before reforming into the crisp outline of Clive, now standing, facing the sound from the gramophone, his head shaking and his finger to his lips.

As if in response to this gesture, the hiss of the recording became muffled and I heard the pad of feet – a step much lighter than Clive's – and another shadow appeared on the wall.

The silhouettes moved slowly together and blurred into one, then broke apart and came into focus again, bulging and stretching until I felt as if what I was watching was somehow unreal, like a magic lantern show.

Then the floorboards creaked again, this time in rhythm, as if a slow dance was beginning, and the shadows on the wall merged and swayed gently together as the first delicate notes of 'Clair de Lune' floated into the corridor. The shadows danced slowly as if time itself was idling and I watched them, entranced by the movements. I no longer heard the gentle flow of the music nor felt the pain in my hips, my body numb as if I no longer inhabited it.

Then the rhythm left the dancers and they moved together as one, the curve of a back or the swell of a breast coming into focus for a moment before blurring back into shade. The music was left to play, forgotten until the faint piano notes died down to nothing more than the hiss of the needle on shellac. The shadows remained together, moving only in time with the slow breaths which rose over the silence.

At last a voice: 'We shall have to be quiet, *Mon Chérie*, for we cannot wake her.'

24

'Stop it! How dare you? In my house! My husband! My friend!'

They were words which echoed in my head, words which came from deep inside me, words which I felt with all my being – but they were words which never left my lips.

My lungs should have screamed those words, my hands should have flung open the door and my legs should have carried me into the room where the shadows danced together – but I did none of those things. I did nothing because I knew that as I stood in front of them, in the middle of that room, with the hiss of the gramophone and the flickering oil lamp, Clive would see my bloated body in the dull grey nightdress and he would put his arm round Grace's thin waist.

He would tell me to calm down and be reasonable. He would tell me that I must not upset myself, lest I harm the baby. He would say that it did not matter so much because, after all, he and I had been forced together and the baby was all that mattered. No matter who he bedded, he would always provide for the baby, for all of its life, even after he was gone. He would think that it would be what I wanted to hear and that I would be grateful. I would not be grateful, but I would not force him to make such a choice because I knew that he would choose Grace over me, and that was something that I was not ready to hear.

I did not stay at the door to watch them. I did not have to because, as I lay in my little bed, I imagined that I could hear sounds from far down the corridor – every shudder of floorboards, every creak of a bed frame and every gasp of joy, telling me of their lust. The glow of the oil lamp in Clive's study lit the corridor and cast a narrow strip of light under my door. I watched it flicker, the lovers' movements somehow travelling with the light, reminding me of Grace's energy and Clive's passion.

I thought that I could hear the gramophone again, the hesitant notes of 'Clair de Lune' in the silence of the night. The music was so faint, though, that I wondered if it was inside my head, my mind repeating a tune that my ears could not hear. Somehow I heard the rise and fall of every note before it was played, each bar returning to an earlier one as if the music was an endless torment.

As the tears ran down into my ears, I felt that I could see in the dark. I imagined his lips on hers, the arch of her back and the bud of her breasts, the heave of his chest and the force of him inside her. Every sigh and every groan cut deep inside me, even when the air was silent.

I remembered a night not so long ago when I had also felt such passion. I remembered the smell of him on my body and the bulge of his muscles, the weight of his body on top of mine as he pressed himself into me, and his words, now meaningless: 'I love you, Lily.'

They were snatched memories, few and fleeting, but to remember any more than this would be too painful.

Then one muted cry rang out into the night, and the silence became thick and suffocating. The narrow strip of light that flickered under the door went out, and I was left in darkness.

25

It was not until dawn that I heard the heavy crunch of Edgar's boots on the path outside and the clatter of the engine as he struggled to start the motor car in the cold of the morning air. Then there were more footsteps at the front of the house, the gentle laugh of a woman and a hushed voice. The rooks called out, woken by the headlights that cut through the dull morning light. There was a swish of tyres on gravel as the motor car spun a wide circle on the driveway, the chug of the engine dying away into silence and I realised that Grace had gone.

At nine o'clock that morning, Clive came into my room, holding my empty Chlorodyne bottle.

'I found this,' he said, 'outside the door to the study.' Then he paused. 'Did you perhaps drop it there?'

'Hannah gave me the last of it,' I said, 'but I still could not sleep. I came to your study to ask for more, but I suppose it must have slipped out of my hands.'

'When was this?' he said, his voice suddenly faltering.

'I don't know what time it was,' I said, 'but it was dark, your oil lamp was lit.'

'Why did you not come in?' he asked, but I knew that he did not need an answer.

'I heard the music,' I said quietly, 'and I could see shadows moving on the wall. I could see that you were...' But I did not feel that I could explain what I had seen, not when it was Clive that owed me the explanation.

He sat down heavily on the chaise longue, his face a little pale, and turned to the window, his eyes not moving for several minutes. I fancied that he did not even see the shrubbery, the fading lilies that surrounded the bench, nor even his reflection in the glass. He was thinking of what to say to me, he was thinking of what he had done; things so shameful that he could not even look at me.

'I'm sorry,' he said at last. 'None of this is your fault, but you should know that I have an attachment with Grace and have had so for months.' It was a funny turn of phrase and I could not work out what he meant, but I thought it was his pious, religious way of not admitting what he was actually doing.

'An attachment?' I asked. 'Most people would call it an affair.'

He paused. 'I think your condition is making you emotional.'

'My condition!' I cried. 'How can you blame my condition? I did not want this baby any more than you, but things have changed. I have to make the best of it. I have no choice.' I picked up the photograph from the nightstand. 'Does this mean nothing to you?' I said. 'You cannot leave me for her!'

He paused as if the wind had been taken from him. He had an expression on his face that I couldn't quite read and I dreaded the decision that he seemed to be making in his head. He stared at the photograph and the ring on the finger that held the frame.

'You have to stay with me,' but then my voice weakened, 'don't you?'

He was silent for a while but would not look at me, and I feared the words which would follow. But the words I had dreaded did not come and instead he said: 'I cannot risk anyone hearing you talk like this, I have my career to consider.'

'Your career?' I said. 'Is that all you can think of?'

'I have to do what is best for you,' he said, but then added: 'but I have my own life too, and I have to do what is best for Grace.'

'Well, I cannot leave here,' I said, 'not now; I have a baby to consider. I can barely walk. I cannot get downstairs.'

But he did not respond.

'Clive?'

'I cannot do this,' he said. 'I cannot talk about this now. I have made a mistake.'

He stood up quickly and walked to the door, shutting it behind him.

'What mistake?' I screamed after him. 'Of all the things you are responsible for, what is this one thing you feel you should not have done?'

Then I heard a peculiar sound. I could not work out what it was at first, like the clunk of metal and the scrape of wood and the door frame seemed to shudder, then there was the creak of a floorboard far down the corridor and I knew that he was gone. I got up slowly and clutched at my belly as I hobbled to the door. I grasped the door handle and tried to turn it, but it just twisted in my fingers and would not open. I tried again, this time with my foot against the bottom of the door, but then I realised that the door must be shut tight and locked from the outside.

I limped back to the bed and sat down slowly. Suddenly the room seemed different to me. The door was not just shut, it was locked and somehow this knowledge made it seem small and suffocating.

Hannah had always told me that the windows were jammed, and the builders had not come to fix them, but two jammed windows was too much of a coincidence and I realised that neither of them had ever been opened during my stay at Elmridge House. I wondered if they were jammed, or if they were actually just locked, and I found that deep down I knew the answer.

I thought of the other things that had happened since I had stayed here in this room: the bell pull that had been permanently disconnected; the paperknife that Hannah did not bring me when I opened Grace's parcel; the poker that she always took with her once she had made the fire; and the scarves and silk stockings that I could no longer find. Even the heavy silver candlesticks had been taken from the mantelpiece. Yet other things had made their way into the room – the chamber pot that was under my bed even though I could still hobble along the corridor to the bathroom, and the grey flannel nightdress that had replaced my silk pyjamas.

I got up and walked slowly to the window, but my steps faltered when I saw that the woman had returned to the bench in front of the shrubbery. I raised my arm but let it fall back to my side when I realised that I did not know whether to shoo her away or signal to her for help, and I felt my heart start to race. The woman still wore her heavy postwoman's uniform and wide brimmed hat, yet I had not returned her bag to her and she clutched at her heavy coat and looked anxiously about her. She sang as she often had before, but this time her voice was slower and at last the notes seemed to fall into place and I recognised the tune – 'Clair de Lune' – the same one that played constantly on the gramophone and floated into every room of the house.

I knocked on the window with my knuckles, and this time the woman jumped at the sound and looked up at me, her eyes squinting under the large brim of her hat. Her stiff coat was not buttoned and I saw a flash of grey underneath it. I clutched at my own nightdress, the one that had appeared after I had taken the pennyroyal, then I looked back at the woman on the bench and saw that she wore the same.

Around her the trees were starting to rust with autumn colours, some already no more than bare twisted twigs. The sky was washed with milky white and I felt a wave of cold coming from the glass.

Down by the postwoman's feet, the lilies in the flower bed were dead.

26

'That woman,' I said. 'The one who sits on the bench knitting, who is she?'

Clive leant back in his chair and took a deep breath but said nothing.

It was mid-morning, the day after we had rowed about his affair with Grace and he had walked away from my screams, locking my bedroom door behind him. I had spent most of that day in anguish and confusion, made worse by the hours of solitude that Clive had enforced. It was only now, over twenty-four hours later that he had returned to my bedside with nothing to say for himself except that I had needed some time alone for rest and reflection, and he was glad to find me in a calmer state.

'Clive?' I persisted. 'Who is she?'

'Her name is Maureen Tuttle,' he said eventually. 'She is staying in one of the rooms downstairs. She is the wife of a decorator who lives in the town.' He spoke softly and I thought him somehow different to the man I had rowed with the previous day. Something between us had changed and I sensed that now he was willing to talk.

'I have her bag,' I said. 'I thought that if I got hold of it I might find out who she was, but there was nothing in it, no purse or identity, just a scarf. It is far too long already, it would easily stretch from here to the fireplace, but the needles are still attached as if she has not finished it.'

'She will never finish it,' said Clive. 'She is knitting it for her son. There was a lot of hypothermia in the trenches. If she knits him a scarf that is long enough, it will keep him warm. It is for when she next sees him.' He paused. 'She has been knitting it since she heard of his death back in 1915.'

I got up slowly from the bed and took a few painful steps towards the window seat. I lowered myself on to the cushions carefully and looked down at the shrubbery. The woman was sitting on the bench again. I watched her – Maureen Tuttle, a woman who had once been a wife and a mother but seemed to me like neither. I laid my hand on the bump under my nightdress and thought of her son – the baby she had once had, the man that he had become, and his death that had torn her apart. It was then that I realised I had a bond with my own unborn child, and I thought that I understood something of her loss. Mrs Tuttle looked about anxiously as if something were lost and I wondered whether it was the bag she sought, or some ghost of her son.

'Why is she here?' I said. 'Here in my home, at Elmridge House?'

Clive turned his chair to the window. 'The war was like no other,' he said slowly as if searching for the right words. 'You will know of the casualties in the newspapers and seen the veterans begging on the streets, but it is not just bodies that were wounded. It was minds too, many of them in ways never seen before. Places like St Catherine's and the London asylums are full of the shell shocked.' Then he paused. 'The women are referred to doctors like me. I have been treating a few women here, but when I am fully qualified, I hope to grow my practice at Elmridge House.'

'There are others here?' I said.

'Only a couple and they do not always stay here. This is private therapy for local women and those whose families can afford a little payment. These ladies suffer from mild nervous conditions. They do not need straitjackets or cells. They just need a little refuge, somewhere that they feel safe.' He paused. 'And a little confinement, perhaps.'

'You told me that the women I had seen were hired from a domestic agency,' I said.

'They are,' he said. 'Hannah needs help sometimes, although some of the ones you have seen will have been patients.'

'There are no workmen downstairs, are there?' I said. 'There was banging, but I never heard the sound of a drill or saw.'

'No,' he said. 'The ladies can be difficult to handle sometimes, they will bang, or stray beyond the dovecote and into the view of the main house when they know they should not. Maureen tends to stray when she is distressed, she forgets the rules – those are the times that you have seen her.'

'Why did you not tell me?' I said.

'I thought that having them here in the house would worry you,' he said. 'So I wanted to hide them for as long as possible. I wanted to make sure that your stay here was relaxing. You see, you were always more than my patient, because you are Leonard's sister and I will always be indebted to him.'

I looked down at the woman on the bench once more. 'Am I like her?' I said. 'Have I become like those women you speak of, like Maureen Tuttle?'

'You are fragile at the moment,' he said, 'that is all.'

'Fragile?' I repeated.

'Yes, all it means is that I will put you on some special care for a bit. Think of it as when we were preparing you to return to your dancing, but it will be your mind that we need to strengthen.'

'So this is your *special care*!' I said, waving my hands around the room. 'The locks on the windows and doors, the paperknife gone from the desk and the poker gone from the fireplace, all scarves and stockings confiscated as if I was a child!'

'I am sorry,' he said. 'I did not plan for you to find out this way. I aim to renovate all the rooms in this way, in case they are needed. I never know what the demand from the asylums will be. You must think nothing of it.'

I looked down at the bump under the grey flannel nightdress and I felt the baby kick a little as if it knew of the world it would be born into and I blinked back tears.

'You seem so different from how you were a couple of days ago,' he said. 'I fear that these discoveries will do your nerves no good.'

But I could not face talking about what I had seen that night nor about Grace, not while the images of the dancing shadows were still so fresh in my mind. 'You cannot keep me in just one room of the house forever,' I said.

'I don't mean to,' he said, 'just until you have recovered and—'

'But that time will be soon upon us!' I said. 'The child will be born in less than two months, my bones will harden again and the pain will go. I will be fit again. I may even dance. I—'

But the look on his face stopped the words in my mouth. 'I do not mean that,' he said sternly. 'You must know that I do not mean that.'

'Well, what happens when I recover from my *other* illness?' I said, my voice faltering. 'When I recover from being fragile, as you call it?'

'I intend to live here with Grace,' he said, 'and I want to marry her.'

'You can't!' I cried. 'I will not allow it!'

'You know that Grace has had a hard life,' he said. 'She grew up looking after her brothers and sisters in a room no bigger than this. By marrying her and bringing her here to Elmridge House I will be helping her escape from that life.' He nodded his head earnestly as if in agreement with his own sentiment and I realised that he saw himself as the hero, someone who was doing the right thing in the eyes of his precious God.

'Well, thank goodness you will be saving *her*,' I said bitterly.

'You have nothing to worry about, Lilian,' he said. 'Leonard entrusted me to care for you and I will not let either of you down. Remember what I have always said to you – I will always provide for you and the child, even after I am gone.'

'But that is just money,' I said. 'I will have nowhere to go and no help looking after the baby. My parents threw me out when I became a dancer and I have fallen out with Leonard—'

'You don't need to worry,' he said. 'I can provide for you here, at Elmridge House.'

'But you said Grace will live here!' I cried.

'You will have this room,' he said simply, 'for as long as you need it.'

'This room,' I echoed and my eyes returned to the locked door and windows. 'You mean to keep me as a patient!'

'At the moment, it would be the right thing to do,' he said.

'What do you mean?' I persisted.

'Well, you were assessed by a qualified psychiatrist only a couple of days ago.'

'What?' I cried, but as soon as the word left my mouth I thought of Walter's visit – the little notebook that had rested on his knee, the questions he had asked me and the way that he had studied my face with his eyebrows raised.

Clive sighed deeply as if my misfortune was his own. 'I have done all that I can for you,' he said. 'In fact, if Grace had her way you would be in St Catherine's by now.'

'This is nothing to do with her,' I screamed. 'She cannot just barge in here and take my life from me!'

'No,' he said. 'Of course she can't, but it does make her uneasy that you were once friends and I want her to be happy here.'

His words did little to soothe me because the way in which he spoke, the tenderness with which he said her name, told me more than his words ever could and I knew from that moment that one word from Grace's lips, spoken softly into his ear, would see me locked up in an asylum forever. The doll which sat on the end of my bed and watched with its button eyes now seemed to stare into my soul, as if Grace was watching my every move and judging me for it.

'You have to see her point of view,' Clive continued. 'You came here physically and emotionally exhausted, you tried to harm the child...' He continued to talk of other things, trifling moments and silly acts that were supposed to be evidence of my madness – the corsets I had ordered to hide the pregnancy and my fondness for alcohol, cigarettes and sleeping draughts – yet he had already mentioned the one thing that would mark me as mad to any religious man. I had tried to harm the baby as it grew inside me; a baby that he had, only moments ago, promised to care for. My actions had been an insult to him as a man – I must indeed be mad.

'I am better now.' I said desperately. 'I want the baby now. I have changed,' but as I spoke my voice began to weaken and Clive stood up from his chair.

'You will get well again,' he said. 'Sometimes it just takes time. Your illness may die down with the passing of the years.'

I pictured myself sitting on the bench by the shrubbery, just as Maureen Tuttle did, staring but not seeing. I imagined a place to the front of the house, far beyond the dovecote that was used by visitors and house guests – a place that I was forbidden to enter. It was the place with the long sloping lawn and the neatly trimmed hollies, the place with a view over the town. I imagined hearing laughter from this place and maybe catching a glimpse of Grace running playfully through the hollies, followed by a little girl with reddish hair in a white ballet skirt. This was the future that Clive wanted for me – a future in which I was a patient and Grace was his lover and stepmother to a child that I could not care for.

Clive nodded to himself, as if satisfied that he had reassured me, and turned to go.

'Wait!' I cried. There was so much more that I wanted to say to him, but every scream, every emotion, every tear would only convince him that I deserved to be here in this room with its locked windows and doors. I held it all back, yet there was one thing I could do: 'Mrs Tuttle,' I said calmly. 'The woman on the bench – will you give her bag back to her for me, for I think that she must be missing it?' I pointed to the bag that Hannah had tucked under the chaise longue.

'Of course,' he said and took it with him to the door.

'And please pass on my apologies to her,' I said weakly.

He nodded and shut the door behind him, the grate of the key in the lock echoing round the silent room.

27

October 1920

My recovery would take time, Clive had said. He told me that it was time during which I could do nothing but wait, and that is exactly what I did, day in and day out, until I realised that another month had passed and all that I had done for thirty days was lie in bed and watch the change in the landscape from the windows of my locked room.

As autumn drew in, the leaves in the shrubbery started to rust and flutter to the ground and the wind rattled the windows in their frames and flung rain against the glass. Mrs Tuttle seldom returned to the bench and I told myself she was just keeping out of the rain or had been sent home because the alternative did not bear thinking of. I watched as the fields beyond Missensham faded to brown and the town sank under a cloud of chimney smoke. The lilies which grew by the shrubbery died back, leaving just dagger like leaves, and only a few blooms remained at the front of the house, sheltered from the cold winds by its high walls. Yet with all the coldness and death in the world outside, inside me there was life as the baby grew stronger.

I tried to write to Leonard many times, but when I came to put pen to paper I could never find the words. I wanted to apologise for what had happened with Alexander, but when I read back what I had written, the words always sounded like I was the only one to blame and I would cross them out only to reproduce the same words again just seconds later. I longed to ask Leonard to come to Elmridge House, to help me, but somehow it felt ungrateful, after all Clive had always been so generous and would give the child a life that would be better than any I could have hoped for. I also realised that the bond that had once existed between brother and sister had been broken by jealousy and I wondered if Leonard actually cared what became of me. In the end I did write, but with only a brief explanation of my situation – that I was married and with child – and I squeezed the words onto the back of a postcard so that I did not have empty space to fill.

Everything changed when Grace moved in. Clive would not admit anything to me, but I know that they took a room together somewhere at the back of the house. Grace kept herself away from me and made no attempt at an apology or reconciliation. The fact that my one time friend was now a stranger was what I found hardest to bear and, despite all that Grace had done to me, I felt her evasiveness to be her cruellest act. I was never sure when Grace was at home, after all, I now knew that she was just one person among several. Yet there were times when I knew that my suspicions could not be due to the patients downstairs or the movements of the servants. It was at these times that I felt as if she was all around me: the gust of her French perfume in the corridor; the hairbrush in the bathroom, matted with bottle blonde tresses; the flash of yellow leather from the back window of the motor car as it turned in the driveway; the lightness of her footsteps echoing along the creaking floorboards; the rhythmic thud of the bedstead in the silence of the night; her voice as she sang along to the music of the gramophone; a word caught in the corridor; a giggle; a hush.

Then one day, a shout. It was early one October morning and the sound woke me from my sleep. It was the anger in her voice that I heard and not the words themselves. I rose slowly from my bed and limped over to the front window where the shout had come from. I lowered myself slowly on to the window seat and looked out onto the driveway to see Grace standing on the gravel in my yellow driving coat, her hands on her hips and her face turned to Clive who had his finger to his lips in an attempt to silence her.

But now I could hear her words clearly: 'Damn your reputation!'

Edgar rushed towards her, but she slammed the car door before he could get to it.

'And damn your piety!'

Clive mumbled something that I could not hear and put his hand on her arm, but she shook him off as if he was dirt. She marched towards the house but Clive followed her, grabbing her arm and spinning her round to face him.

He held her shoulders, but she tried to wriggle free. Then, for the first time, Clive raised his voice: 'I have made mistakes and I must rectify them. It is my duty to God. I must make sure that Lily and the child are provided for, even after I am gone.'

It was the words that he had spoken to me after I first told him of my pregnancy, the words that he had used to comfort me after he found me twisted with pain on the cold bathroom floor, and the words that he had used to placate me when I found out about his affair. Now he repeated those words to Grace and I understood the reason for her rage.

I shrank back behind the curtain, but they had now forgotten all those that might be listening, their eyes locked together as if no other existed.

'I think of you too,' said Clive, 'but I must not forget what has gone before.' Then his voice fell again and Grace leant her head close to his and I saw her bring her hand to her cheek as she gently patted the skin under her eyes with the tips of her fingers. It was a gentle movement, something that we used to do in the theatre when we feared that tears from the glare of the arc lights would smudge our greasepaint, and I realised that she was crying.

Clive pulled her towards him gently and she laid her head on his shoulder and whispered something in his ear. I could not hear what she said, but I could feel the bite of her words. Clive pushed her away quickly and took a step back. He stared at her for just a moment, then with a final shake of his head, he walked shakily to the house, Edgar trotting after him.

Grace stood alone, tapping her foot in frustration, her hands on her hips. Then she raised her head slowly and looked up to my window. She took a few steps closer to the house and craned her neck upwards until she was so close that I could see the fur trim on my coat and each perfectly arched eyebrow. I retreated further behind the curtain, but our eyes had already met and she knew what I had witnessed.

She bent down by the flower bed and picked every lily whose flower had lasted the season. Then she carefully arranged the flowers into a small bouquet and held the stems with both hands, twisting them together until they weakened and snapped. I watched as her hands gripped the stems, her knuckles white with the force of the grip, the diamond of a large engagement ring glinting in the sunlight. Then she looked back up at me once more and slammed the flowers down on to the driveway, grinding them into the gravel with the heel of her boot.

I got up quickly and hurried to the bed, wincing with every painful step, my heart pounding. I sat back down heavily and tried to slow my breathing. I was living in a world that I struggled to make sense of – Clive no longer loved me and my home was now my prison. Grace had been my best friend since childhood, but what was she to me now? I could not bear to think of it. Outside, I heard the crunch of her feet on the gravel, the jangle of her bracelets and her slow, twisted laughter.

28

From the moment that I saw Grace in the driveway, wearing the leather driving coat and diamond ring, I knew that she would hide from me no more. That evening there were no more hushed voices or softly closed doors. I sat alone in my room, alert and listening, the air darkening around me, and I realised that the row on the driveway must have left Hannah too anxious to leave her room and light the mantles.

The first sound I heard was that of Grace's footsteps, the heel of her expensive boots falling heavily on the stairs. It was the first time that she had not taken the back staircase and I thought it a message to all – there was a new lady of the house and she was entitled to use her grand entranceway. I listened as her footsteps headed past the door to my room and along the corridor to Clive's study. From there I heard the music of the gramophone – the peppy notes of a ragtime tune replacing the gentle waver of the piano.

Some time later I heard Clive follow her upstairs. There were no more cross words between them, in fact I fancied that I heard the chink of glasses united in a toast and soon after that came a laugh. It was not Grace's usual laugh; it was louder and shriller and I thought her to be laughing in defiance of the rules that Clive had set for her – rules which no longer mattered. Something had changed after the row in the driveway. Grace's presence at Elmridge House was not a secret any more, and she knew it; she was now something to be seen and heard, something to be flaunted.

But neither Clive nor Grace would stay at Elmridge House that evening. The clunk of the pipes in the bathroom was followed by the scent of French perfume in the corridor. The sound of the grandfather clock striking four times from down in the hallway was accompanied by Clive's voice, gruff with annoyance as he reminded her that they were running late.

Then came the creak of floorboards, followed by the light tread of Grace's slippers in the corridor. The footsteps stopped outside my door and I saw a waver in the crack of light under the door as if she was shuffling her feet as she contemplated whether to knock. In the end she did not, nor did she speak, instead she pushed something under the door, papers of some sort, but I dared not collect them until I heard the retreat of her footsteps.

I limped slowly to the door, supporting the weight of my belly on my arm and took the papers back to my bed. There were only a few pages and on top was a postcard. On the front was a photograph of dancers with billowing white skirts, each gracefully stretching a limb towards a smiling woman holding a bouquet; the triumphant ballerina, with a man on each arm. It was the photograph that had been taken after my last performance as Giselle; a time when Grace and I had been true friends. The words:

Leonid Postov's Ballets Spectaculaire, The Crown Theatre, Covent Garden

were printed across the bottom in a swirling typeface, but when I turned the postcard over, there was no message, just a single word handwritten in fresh ink: *Memories.*

Under the postcard was a small booklet – a gold edged theatre programme with embossed letters sunk into the thin paper. It was for a single performance of *Giselle* by the Ballets Spectaculaire at the Crown Theatre, Covent Garden. The date was printed under the title, yet it was not one of the dates that I had danced over eight months ago. I glanced at the little calendar on my nightstand and only then did I realise that Grace and Clive would head into London that evening, to the Crown Theatre. It was a reminder of a life that I had known and a life that was continuing without me and I felt pride but also a hint of sadness – despite Len's best efforts, he had been forced to stage *Giselle* again because he could not afford new costumes, and the thinness of the paper that the programme was printed on only reminded me that the company was still struggling and would never make it to the Opera House.

Dancing the part of Giselle, in the place that I was so used to seeing the words *Liliana Postova*, was the name of another – a dancer named Grace. Yet Grace had not used a Russian name, she had taken the name of Cuthbertson – Giselle was now danced by Grace Cuthbertson. I told myself that Grace could not have married Clive – stage names were common enough among dancers and surely this was no more than that. After all, Clive had not mentioned anything of the sort when we had spoken, and a wedding would not have been possible while I still lived. Grace may not have married Clive, but, by taking his name as hers, she was making her intentions very clear.

I had waited for Grace's big moment for so long, yet now I could not feel happy for her. I knew that she was not a good enough dancer to have won the role on her own merits and I suspected that it was Clive's influence as a company benefactor that had swayed Len to give her the part. Grace had got what she wanted and she had gone about it the only way she knew how. She was to dance a part that had once been mine and live in a house that would have become my home, but now with just two words – Grace Cuthbertson – she had taken away everything that I had left.

There were more footsteps along the corridor, followed by the creak of the floorboards. Then the slam of a door from downstairs in the hallway and the crunch of gravel on the driveway. There were voices too, shouts and laughter that were no longer hushed.

I looked at the postcard again, and the photograph of the ballerina that I no longer recognised. I thought of the leaps, the lifts and the holds that Grace would perform that night and of the applause of the audience, and I thought of my swollen aching body and the silence of the locked room.

Outside, a car door slammed and the engine clattered as it sprang to life. The light from its headlamps spun across the ceiling as the car turned in the driveway, then, with a swish of gravel, the engine faded away into silence.

I used to dance, but now it was Grace's turn.

29

I held the theatre programme and postcard in my hand. I could not bear to look at them any longer, yet I could not put them down. They were my connection to a life that I had once lived; a life that was continuing without me, a life now lived by another.

I walked slowly back to my bed and lay down, placing each leg carefully on the mattress, and held the small rectangles of card to my chest. The smell of ink that rose from the paper and the feel of the embossed letters under my fingertips was enough to turn my thoughts to dancing again, yet this time the memories which returned were not of my performance but what had happened after. I shut my eyes and felt it all again: the musty smell of the dressing room carpet and the rub of the wool against my shoulder blades; the green glow of the bottle caught in the glare of the lamp; the muffled notes of the piano and the distant laughter; and the warmth of the man that lay next to me. Then I felt as if I had left my body and was watching the scene from the eyes of another looking down on the naked tangle of limbs nestled together on the blanket, the tightness of the embrace and the passion of the kiss, but when the lovers broke apart, it was Grace's face that I saw looking up at me from the blanket.

I woke with a start, from down in the hallway the grandfather clock was chiming the hour. It was eight o' clock already. Grace's moment had come, the audience would be seated and the curtain rising.

It was then that it started. I thought it a twinge at first or a shift of the ache in my pelvis when I had moved in my sleep, yet this pain was different; it was duller, like a pulse of heat low in my girdle, and then it faded as soon as it had come. It was not until I felt it again some minutes later that I really noticed it. This time it was more than a gentle cramp but something that was quite unmistakable, as if my insides below the bump were being gently twisted.

It was too early, wasn't it? The baby was not due tonight, I still had at least three weeks to go. I watched the clock on the nightstand, glad for every minute that passed without the sensation returning, but then, when it did, I realised that it could not be ignored.

I lay on my side watching the minute hand of the clock jerk its way around the dial, yet my mind was too fraught to remember when the cramps had come and how long they lasted and I spent the minutes dreading their return. This was what Dr Marks had spoken of, I was experiencing contractions – they were just the beginning and there was nothing that I could do to prevent them or what they would lead to. Whatever situation I was in now, whether wife, patient or captive, did not matter because soon it would not just be me to consider – there would be another.

I screamed for Hannah, glad when I heard her footsteps in the corridor and the rattle of the lock, and I asked her to send for the midwife.

'Does Dr Cuthbertson...' she began, but her face changed as she saw me clawing the bed frame, biting my lip and clutching at my groin as another wave of pain took the breath from me. Only then did she realise that the visit I was requesting was not a check-up that could be postponed until her master was back from the ballet. 'I am on my own tonight,' she said. 'There is no one in the house who can help now. I should...' But she seemed unable to finish either her thought or her sentence and turned away from me, her brow furrowed.

I listened to her footsteps fading on the stairs, but then heard nothing more. I wondered if Clive had left instructions for her – if he had forbidden her from calling a midwife or whether her only call would be to the theatre. Even if she did manage to get a message to him, Edgar would have to drive thirty miles from Covent Garden and it would be hours before their return. I was left in Hannah's hands – a woman whose every thought was dictated by Clive.

I watched the room fade further into darkness and now every time that I looked at the clock the hands seemed to point at random numbers and I realised that I was losing track of time as well as my senses. The only things that I could depend on were the contractions. They were no longer the strange warming sensations that they had once been. They felt as if my insides were being squeezed in a vice, a pain that was so intense I could neither think nor breathe, leaving my mind and body helpless until they passed. The gaps between them were increasingly brief, giving me time only to draw breath and brace myself for their return.

Downstairs, some banging started and I realised that there must be a patient that was keeping Hannah busy and that she would not return for some time. Then the light that had been coming from the corridor went out and I was left alone in the darkness.

The clock in the hallway struck nine – only an hour had passed, yet the pain was unbearable and I realised that I could not face any more time alone. I waited for a contraction to ease and then I rolled over and got up slowly and hobbled to the door to shout for Hannah, but as I was about to hammer on the thick wood, I heard the clunk of the bolts and the rattle of the key in the lock and the door swung open. A woman stood in the corridor; a short stocky woman, with a round face, one that seemed familiar, but I could not think how.

'You're not Hannah!' I cried.

'I bloody well hope not,' she said. 'If she was the girl who let me in, you would not want her around at a time like this, for she clearly has no sense.'

I gasped with relief, but then realised that there were tears in my eyes and that the heaving of my chest was sobs and not laughter.

'Come on,' the woman said briskly. 'Let's get you on the bed.' She took my arm, but when I stumbled and screamed in agony, she leant the weight of my body against her own and said: 'Ah, your hips have softened, that's a bugger!

Not to worry. I have seen this before and we can work around it.'

She took my weight as I stumbled to the bed, then she helped me on to the mattress, piling the pillows behind my back.

'This room has no air,' she said. 'I can't have you overheating. Bear with me while I open these windows.'

'No!' I said quickly. 'I am feeling hot, but the windows are—' But the pain returned in a huge wave, taking the breath from me, and I could not force the words out.

She took my hand in her own and I grasped her fingers, twisting them inside my fist, but she did not flinch.

When the contraction had passed, she straightened me out on the bed and plumped the pillows behind me. 'Now,' she said, 'let's get this room straight, we've got a long night ahead, so we need to get things prepared. First things first, you need air.'

She marched to the windows and threw open the curtains, but when she found that she could open neither window, she stood still as if faced with the unexpected, the moon casting pale light on the carpet.

'Oh well,' she said, recovering herself. 'I'm afraid that my skills end at your body. I know little of conditions of the mind. That silly girl muttered something about locking up the room, but she did not say that you were a—'

'I'm not,' I said desperately. 'I am Mrs Cuthbertson, Dr Cuthbertson's wife. This is our home, but he took a lover, she runs the house now as if they were married. I tried to abort the baby... so he...' I was talking quickly, my words confused and my voice shaky and I stopped because suddenly I saw what she did – a woman in a grey nightdress with locked windows and a locked door – a woman who was babbling and emotional.

She put her arms around me. 'No more,' she said. 'There is new life tonight. A future – we will not think on the past. We must make this a new start for you both.'

I nodded, but the agony welled up inside me once more. I trembled in the knowledge of what would follow and I grabbed her arm. 'Help me,' I said, but I knew there was only so much she could do.

'Take deep breaths,' she said, 'and remember that it will pass. Now, look at me.'

I looked into her face. She wore a slight frown and her lips were pursed, and I realised that she felt none of the panic that I did, and then the pain was gone.

'There you are,' she said gently and she started to stand, but I grabbed her arm.

'Something will be wrong with it,' I said. 'It should not hurt this much. I tried to abort it, I must have harmed it, and it will be twisted inside me.'

'When did you last feel the baby move?' she asked.

'It still does,' I said, 'even now.'

'There is little to worry about then. Just take some deep breaths.'

I looked to the clock, but it held no meaning any more and, whatever I did, I knew that time would march forward relentlessly. I watched the blur of the midwife's silhouette as she moved around the room, gathering towels from the airer, laying out sheets and rummaging in her bag. Only once she was satisfied with the room did she remove her boots and cape.

'Where is that silly girl with the hot water?' she said. She disappeared out of the door to call for Hannah and when she returned she came straight back to my bedside. 'Your fingers are swollen,' she said, taking my hand in hers, 'but you still wear your ring.' Then she looked at my face, pulling the hair back from my brow. 'No,' she said. 'You are not one of those kept here, for I have seen your face before – you came to me because you wanted rid of it, but you thought about your situation, you changed your mind and you did what you felt was right for you and the child. You had your moment of difficulty and you lost yourself for a little, but that time has passed. It does not make you insane – we see many like you.'

Then she took the silver frame from my bedside table. 'This is you in this photograph, isn't it?' She held it up to my face. 'I do not know this Dr Cuthbertson by sight, only by name, but this indeed shows that you are wedded, and to a gentleman, and at one time at least you were happy.'

I tried to thank her, but the words caught in my throat, so I just nodded and managed a weak smile. I had doubted myself for so long, but this woman had come in from the outside, from a world I had not seen for ages, and she had seen for herself what had happened to me and she believed me.

'Well, I don't know what this lover thinks she is doing,' she said, 'but there cannot be two Mrs Cuthbertsons, not while you still live. Now, Mrs Cuthbertson,' she said, 'I'll need to take a look at you and see what we are dealing with.'

I nodded.

She put a hand on my swollen middle and started pressing my bump firmly with both hands. 'Before we do that, I will just need to...' But she did not finish her thought, and I noticed that her face had become quite serious.

'What is it?' I said. 'What's wrong?'

'When did you last see a doctor?' she said.

'I have seen Dr Marks,' I said, 'but it was a few months ago. I haven't really felt the need as Clive is a doctor and has told me what I should be doing.'

'Dr Cuthbertson has other specialities,' she said, 'and they are not of women's bodies. You should have seen a doctor in the last few weeks because this baby has not turned.'

'Not turned,' I echoed.

'It will be coming out arse first,' she said, 'but it will be coming out. Where is the telephone? I must ring for an ambulance.'

'No!' I cried.

'It's nothing to worry about,' she said. 'There should not be any problem, it is just best to have help close by, in case we need it. We are just a bit stuck out here in all this countryside.'

'No,' I said. 'It is not that, it is just...' But despite everything that had happened to me that evening, I was still ashamed of my situation and the words came with difficulty: 'If I am taken to Oxworth General, they will call Clive and in the end I will have to come back here to this room.' I realised that whatever happened to me, I could not return to Elmridge House. I could not return to this room and I could not keep a baby here – a child that would be raised by Grace, one that would be told that her mother was incarcerated as a lunatic because she did not want her. 'They will take the baby from me,' I said. 'They will give it to Grace.'

It was what I meant to say, but I do not even know if the words had left my lips or if they were just in my head. The exhaustion had left me senseless, with only the pain of the contractions breaking through the blur of consciousness. I tried to say the words again, but then another contraction seized me and tore them from my mouth.

I cannot have said what I had wanted to, for the midwife did not listen to me. She left the room and did not say where she was going and through the pain I saw only jumbled images – the minute hand of the clock, the trailing light from the gas mantles, the sheets twisted in my hands, the little blue bottle now empty and the rise of my belly as my body writhed underneath it.

And then the midwife's face again: 'It is sorted, help is here now.'

And then another face, this time Hannah: 'You cannot leave before I can ask Dr Cuthbertson about it!' She snatched the key from the midwife's hand, then they both stopped to listen to a sound outside; the crunch of gravel under tyres and the clatter of an engine as the beam of headlights spun across the ceiling. The performance must be over, Clive had returned. I would have the baby in this room or in Oxworth General – either way, the child would never be mine.

Hannah put the key to the lock, I looked about me frantically but the midwife was gone.

'No!' I screamed. 'You cannot keep me here.' I forced myself from the bed, but instead of the sensation of my feet on the floor, there was nothing – no carpet underfoot, no tense of muscle – and time seemed to slow as I fell from the bed. I know only that I landed heavily on my hip. There was a jolt of pain deep within me, sending shivers of agony through my body – the flash of a light, the sound of my scream. Then only darkness.

30

The midwife had made a phone call that night, but it had not been to the Crown Theatre for Clive, nor to Oxworth General Hospital for an ambulance. The vehicle that arrived on the driveway of Elmridge House that night was a taxi cab.

I do not remember much more about it, but I know that I must have passed out from the pain of my fall because I remember the midwife's face looking down at me as I lay on the floor, the ceiling above her spinning a slow circle. Somehow she lifted me from the floor and put my arm around her shoulders, bearing my weight while I screamed and stumbled; the agonies of labour mingling with those that came with every step. Hannah followed us closely, fretting to herself about what Dr Cuthbertson did or did not know.

The midwife bundled me into the back seat of the taxi cab and bunched a clean bedsheet between my legs, then she squeezed in after me. She leant forward and spoke quietly to the driver.

I screamed at her. Despite all my suffering, one thought broke through my pain and confusion – I could not go to

Oxworth General because I would lose the baby to Grace and I would end up in a locked room at Elmridge House or a padded cell at St Catherine's.

'It will not be a hospital' she said. 'I promise. We would not make it to Oxworth in time anyway.'

The cab pulled off down the long sloping driveway, the dark domes of holly flashing past the windows, and turned slowly onto the Oxworth Road. The tall hedges lining the road sped through the circular beam from the headlights, but I shut my eyes and saw little else of the journey, feeling only the shudder of the engine through my exhausted body. After some time I opened my eyes again and saw the oak tree of the village green and then the engine slowed to a growl as the taxi bumped over a long, rough driveway, a low white fence caught in the beam of its headlights, then it turned sharply and I saw a clump of trees, dark against the sky.

Just as the midwife had promised, we had not come to a hospital. It was an old detached house and, when she helped me through the door, I saw that it was one so clean and uncluttered I knew that it could not just be a home. She took me through the back door and into a little kitchen, pulling me to my feet when another wave of pain caused me to collapse onto the cold floor tiles. She put me in a chair by a warm stove and pulled a large table away from the wall. Soon I heard the hiss of the boiling kettle and smelt carbolic soap, the glare of the gas lamp ghosting purple when I shut my eyes.

It was in this place that my baby was born on the kitchen table. It was a difficult birth, just as the midwife had feared. She had neither the medical assistance nor the hospital equipment that she desired, but she assured me that a mother who was distressed by her surroundings would have been harder for her to bear. The baby's position caused her many problems but, after several hours my daughter was delivered, as the midwife put it, 'the old-fashioned way.'

After the birth, the midwife cut the cord, delivered the afterbirth and put the baby to my breast. Then, with neither rest nor reflection, she mopped up the blood and took the dirtied linen into the scullery to soak in bleach.

Once the baby's head had lolled away from my breast, she took her from me and placed her in an old tin hip bath she had lined with blankets, and carried the bath up the stairs to a room she had prepared. It was only when I tried to follow that the pain in my hips worsened, and this time it was different. It was no longer the grinding sensation of my softened hips, but a stabbing pain, an agony that shot through my hip to every part of my body – the same feeling I had felt when I had fallen from the bed. It was only the grate of the infant's cry that forced me to crawl up the stairs to the landing and to a little room at the back of the house that had barely enough space for a bed and the hip bath that the midwife had placed next to it. I lay on the bed doubled in agony while the baby slept beside me.

The midwife fetched a mug of hot tea and a plate of burnt buttered toast and put them carefully on the bedside table. She told me that my pelvis must have fractured when I fell from the bed at Elmridge House. I may have already had a fracture from an old dancing injury, but the softening of my pelvis that the pregnancy had caused had not helped matters. It was a rare thing to happen, but she had been a midwife for twenty years and had seen it before. I was to rest as best as I could, but I should accept that I might never dance again.

When I cried, she said: 'Oh, none of that. You are fortunate. You must be thankful for what you have.' She took the baby from its makeshift bed and handed it to me. I looked at it properly for the first time. It was as tiny as a rat, with a mop of matted red hair and a swollen face and I did not think that I could ever love it. Then, just for a second, the baby opened its eyes – they were eyes which were practically blind, but they were still shiny wet pools that gave some character to its face and at last I saw some humanity in the tiny warm creature.

'Get some sleep,' the midwife said, 'and just remember that you still have so much more than many of us women have right now.'

They were the same words that the midwife had used on our first meeting over six months ago. It was only now that I remembered she had told me that her name was Sadie, and that we had sat together and drunk cold tea at the very table the baby was born on. Somehow I trusted her and knew that she would always be there for me and the baby.

I looked at the little nest at the side of the bed and the small hump in the blankets; the baby's face, creased and red. She was tiny and she was perfect and she was loved. My daughter was with me at last, and for the moment, we were safe. Now I felt that we would have a future together

and I decided to name her – I chose 'Ivy' after the green
tendrils that scraped the frost patterns on the window.

I was woken early by a sound, although in my drowsy
state I could not make out what had made it or where it
had come from. I looked to Ivy in her little tin bath, but
her eyes were closed, the tiny hump of blanket pulsing
with her breaths. It was early morning – the daylight was
no more than a dull glow under the curtain, a gust of
cold air wafting from the frosty window. Sadie had visited
while I slept – Ivy's bed had been moved on to a low,
sturdy table, making it level with my mattress and her
swaddling had been tightened.

A photograph in a little silver frame was on my bedside
table. It was the photograph of me and Clive on our happy
day, yet now when I looked at the photograph I did not see
Clive – I saw me alone in my white dress, my eyes staring
out from the glass and my face framed by my veil. I had
always kept the photograph close to me while I was at
Elmridge House, yet I had taken nothing with me when I
left and I wondered how it came to be on my nightstand;
something so familiar in a room that seemed so strange.
Then I remembered the night of my labour – how I had
lain on my bed in Elmridge House and watched Sadie as
she squinted at the photograph. She had recognised me in
the picture and knew that I spoke the truth. I realised that
she must have taken the photograph with her as we left. I
don't know why she took it, but she must have known that
it had once been important to me, and could be so again.

I heard the noise that had woken me repeated downstairs – it had come from the kitchen and I realised that my bedroom door had been left ajar to let in the warmth from the stove.

It was not the cry of a baby but the grate of a chair, followed by a mumbled voice and the chink of china and I thought that the midwife must be taking tea with a woman, as she had done with me all those months ago. I imagined them sat at the table opposite each other, their polite introductions before the weight of the conversation that was to come.

Then came the breathy whistle of the kettle, followed by the latch of the cupboard under the stairs, the scrape of chairs on the floor tiles and the thud of the leather book opening on the table and I thought of the fountain pen recording dates, symptoms and life stories, but never a name.

The kettle built up to a shrill whistle, only to waver as it was taken from the flame. Then the midwife spoke: 'Prevention or cure?'

There was a silence as if the woman was drawing upon all her courage, but at last there was an answer. It was a voice that I had known for many years. It was the voice that had shared gossip after my final performance as Giselle, spoken words of encouragement when I came to Elmridge House and had lifted my spirits when I heard it.

It was also a voice that had whispered sweet nothings in Clive's ear, urged me to kill my unborn baby with pennyroyal and cursed at Clive for his commitment to me and the child.

'I am looking for a baby,' said Grace.

31

'I am looking for a baby,' said Grace, and when I heard those words I knew that there was only one baby which would do.

I felt a stab of ice deep inside me and I looked at Ivy's puffy little face and watched the gentle swell of her breaths under the blanket. I knew that every childless woman who came to a place such as this would be able to give a good home to a baby. These women had husbands who were rich and dependable and the baby would live in a big house and be well fed. The mothers who came to places like this were destitute and desperate, their babies born into bad circumstances, endangered and unwanted. As I looked at little Ivy asleep in her makeshift cot, I felt pity for her – she was a baby born in bad circumstances, yet she was not alone – she was wanted and she had me, her mother. I vowed that I would protect her from Grace if it was the last thing I did.

I lay in that little room with the bathtub cot and the frost on the window and listened to the women talking downstairs. I imagined them sat across the table from one another, Sadie's elbow resting on the crease of the big leather book and Grace, who would be turned out perfectly despite the early hour.

I would know Grace's voice anywhere, but now I realised that it had changed so much over the past few months, the vowels had become slow and drawn out and every word that she uttered had a crispness to it as if she was giving a lesson to a child, and I fancied that Elmridge House itself was moulding her into shape to fit its grandeur.

'I am looking for a baby,' Grace repeated, and the world around me seemed to fall into silence.

Sadie must have said something, but I did not hear it, so I imagined one of her little nods as her pen scraped across the page in the leather bound book.

'I was told this was the place to come,' said Grace. 'Do you know of any?'

'I can take your details,' said Sadie, 'and let you know when something suitable turns up. If you would be so kind as to leave your name and address with me. I do not have to record all your details, but you must give me a way by which I can contact you—'

'I was hoping for something soon,' said Grace quickly. 'I hear that the nurses here often help out with bad situations – a mother who might want to give up a newborn before she is too attached, perhaps. If you do not know of any yourself, you must hear of things, things where infants are involved. The child must be newborn for I would not want it attached to the mother yet.' Then, as an afterthought, she added: 'I think that would be cruel.'

'We do hear of such things,' said Sadie, 'but these desperate mothers you imagine are rare. This is neither Victorian times nor a romantic novel. Most mothers these days would want to meet you. They cannot just leave their babies with me here and I could not keep them.'

'Oh,' she said, 'but you must—'

'Look,' said Sadie firmly, 'you are young, you have no cause to rush. The Great War has done funny things to people and they are looking for new meanings in everything. You wear a large engagement ring, so I assume that you are to be married to a wealthy man, but you should enjoy your first years of marriage. Babies are hard work, this is a new decade not shackled by war, so many your age just want to live for themselves.'

There was a silence and for the first time I could not imagine what either woman was doing or feeling and I felt a twist of fear deep inside me. Ivy stirred a little and I prayed that she would not wake and cry.

Then at last Grace said: 'I understand you pass on donations to these mothers that you help.'

'Yes,' said Sadie sharply.

There was another silence and then: 'Would this be appropriate?' said Grace. 'And a little for yourself?'

I held my breath.

'Indeed,' Sadie said at last, and for the first time I heard uneasiness in her voice. The woman who had broken me out of a house where I was held captive and dealt with a difficult and bloody birth, all without flinching, was at last tested with an offer I feared she could not refuse.

I glanced to where Ivy slept in the old tin bath and around me the world seemed to freeze, the gentle sound of the baby's breath suddenly deafening.

Then at last Sadie spoke again. 'Although I cannot take it until I have found a suitable mother who—'

'I see,' said Grace, her voice losing some of its softness.

'I hope we have an understanding,' added Sadie.

But Grace said nothing.

'Is there anything you want to tell me about yourself?' said Sadie, her voice suddenly lighter.

'About me?' said Grace.

'Yes – what kind of home you keep, your husband's line of work – anything you can tell me about the kind of life you could give a child.'

'Oh!' She laughed as if in relief, but still said nothing.

'What kind of infant you are looking for even – boy or girl?'

'That does not matter,' she said, 'but it must be a recent birth.'

'Well, if you are so set on a newborn, you will not mind waiting until I know of one,' said Sadie, 'or an expectant mother who—'

'Do you know of any born this week?' said Grace quickly.

'You know it is a Monday,' said Sadie. 'The week is still young!'

'But do you know of any?' said Grace, her voice now carrying the weight of her new social class. 'Like you said, you must hear things.'

Then came a thud, the closing of the thick leather book, just as I had heard it when I sat in the chair that Grace was now in.

But Grace was undeterred. 'Maybe you have someone desperate who wants rid of their problem quickly,' she repeated.

'Well, like I said, I don't—' Sadie's words were sharp.

But Grace continued, 'You see, I always imagined myself helping a fellow woman,' her voice now sounded confident as if at last she had settled on a story that made sense. 'I imagined her as someone in some distress, maybe she suffered circumstances that led to a traumatic labour. I suppose I imagined her cold, in the dark, in thin clothes, with no money of her own, someone so distressed that maybe she was not in her right mind.' She paused. 'Have you come across such a woman?'

IVY

32

September 1943

It was ten o'clock on a Sunday morning on a clear and crisp day in September 1943, and the phone in the nurses' house had not rung.

A year had passed since a conversation with my mother in the front room of her little house had changed everything that I knew, and since then, things were different. I sat in the kitchen by the stove, trying to read a book. It was not the usual novel that I favoured, but an old one of Sadie's that she had given me for study. It had the title of *Married Love* which made it sound like a romance, but I knew only too well that the contents did not have anything to do with marriage or love. It was the kind of book that Sadie would lend me now – part of a change of heart that had been brought on by the events of a week that had seen the girl in the daisy print dress hospitalised.

I put down the book and crept into the hallway. I bent down to look at the telephone, putting my ear close to it, but I could hear no dialling tone to suggest the receiver was off the hook and it seemed to be placed firmly in the cradle. I checked my watch and then the clock in the hallway – there was little difference between them. For every week that I had been apart from Hugo, I had needed to know that all was well at Elmridge House and the routine phone call and the request for a nurse was my only confirmation of this. The call also meant that nothing had changed up at the house and that Mrs Cuthbertson was still none the wiser as to the parentage of the nurse who had visited her house for such a short time the previous year, and was unaware that her leather driving coat was missing. It was now a minute past ten and Mrs Cuthbertson had not called.

I could hear Bridget upstairs, the shuffle of her feet on the bathroom floor as she touched up her make-up in the mirror, and then the creak of the floorboards on the landing as she stood at the top of the stairs and listened for the phone call that had not come.

Since my mother had told me what had happened to her at Elmridge House all those years ago, I had refused to return there. For the last year, Bridget had made the journey along the Oxworth Road, carrying with her my excuses of sprained ankles, influenza and, eventually, other nursing duties which I claimed prevented me from visiting ever again. Bridget had never questioned my reluctance to return. I suppose she assumed that Hugo had tired of me when he finally realised my lack of breeding or spirit. She did, however, pass on Hugo's requests to see me, all of which I declined politely. Whatever Bridget thought, she was more than happy to return to the job where she was paid well for doing little and had the sole attention of a handsome and rich young war hero.

I went back into the kitchen and tried to concentrate on my studies, but soon my eyes began reading the same line over and over again with no comprehension of what it said. Thoughts came into my head but they were incomplete and repetitive as if my mind had become a broken record player, the needle constantly skipping.

Then came a cascade of footsteps on the stairs and Bridget's head appeared round the doorway. 'I can't wait around like this. I'm going to check how Violet is doing on the wards. I'll be no more than an hour. I'm going to finish early tonight – you can cover for me then,' she puffed impatiently. 'Just come and get me if that bitch calls.'

I nodded, but I could already hear her footsteps in the hallway and the latch of the front door.

'Bitch' was a word seldom uttered in a place like Missensham, but it did not shock me as I knew now that it had its uses.

I thought of what my mother had said as we sat by the fire in her tiny sitting room with the faded party dresses lining the walls like ghosts of times passed. As she spoke, she had held a postcard in her hands – a picture of the life she had left behind. She had talked of the things which had marked the end of her youth: a yellow leather driving coat, now drab and outdated; a photograph, now faded; and a grand house, now falling into decay. Then there was a husband who became an adulterer and a friend who became an enemy, and there was my mother – a woman who became crippled and fearful. Grace Cuthbertson was a woman who had encouraged my mother to abort her baby, had an affair with her husband and took over her house and career. She had also visited the nurses' house when I was a newborn, trying to track my mother down.

Yet there had always been something that Grace could not take from my mother – the title of Mrs Cuthbertson. My mother had married Clive Cuthbertson first and they had not divorced. With one word from my mother, Grace's marriage would be exposed as a sham, she would face the shame of having borne a child outside proper wedlock, and have a weakened claim to her husband's estate and fortune. My mother also knew that Grace was aware of the promise that Clive Cuthbertson had made to her – a promise in which he vowed to provide for my mother and me financially, even after he was gone.

They were secrets which bound Grace and my mother together. Grace had too much to lose if my mother spoke out about what had happened and she would do anything to silence her. I finally understood that this was the reason that my mother feared Grace Cuthbertson, and it was the reason that I did too.

Yet, although my mother had spoken of fear and heartbreak, she had also spoken of joy – a baby who had not been wanted until she was born but was then cherished, and I realised that, while I had never guessed the rest of the story, this part I had known all along.

She had talked until the oil ran out.

I looked at the clock again now, watching the minute hand creep further round the dial. Then I opened the book again.

When I next looked up, I saw a movement in the garden, I thought it Bridget returning at first, but then I saw it was her – the woman, the bitch, who I had not seen in over a year, and I knew that I was not safe.

Her hair had become quite grey and she seemed even thinner, but just the sight of her was enough to send shivers of ice down my spine. Mrs Cuthbertson had returned, but she was not welcome.

She stood at the bottom of the lawn, her hands on her hips, and gazed across the grass, her hand shielding her eyes from the low autumn sun as she looked first to the back of the cottage hospital and then up to the nurses' home and I feared she could see right in through the little window where I sat.

I shut my book and stood up slowly, my legs quite numb and my heart throbbing. I took a deep breath, filled the kettle and put it on the burner, setting out two tin mugs with a milk bottle and the almost empty sugar bowl. The sitting room curtains were open and there would be smoke coming from the chimney – she must have known that I would be at home to receive her, and to not welcome her in would be to admit something was amiss.

I opened the cutlery drawer and rummaged round for a teaspoon, but then I stopped, my heart pounding. My eyes fell upon a small paring knife that had been pushed to the side of the drawer. I took it out and touched my trembling fingertip to the sharp blade. Then I loosened my grip and slid the handle into my sleeve so it was covered by the fabric of my housecoat, my fingers forming a loose fist around the blade. Then I twisted my arm behind my back and waited for the knock on the door.

33

I had known that the knock would come, but my blood still surged when I heard the sharp rap of Mrs Cuthbertson's knuckles on the door. I had watched her in the hospital garden for several minutes, readying myself for her visit, but my knees still trembled with every step to the door and I opened it with a shaking hand, forcing my lips into a polite smile, the knife clutched behind me in my trembling fist.

'Mrs Cuthbertson!' I said, trying to sound surprised, for I knew that it would not do to admit that I had been watching her through the little window.

'Ivy,' she said. 'It is good to see you again, it has been too long.' The words seemed forced from her lips and I remembered that pleasantries were not her way.

She frowned when I did not return the sentiment.

'May I come in?' she said, her voice returning to its usual manner which made the question seem like a command.

'Of course,' I said and ushered her in stiffly, ensuring that my back was always kept to the wall, the knife secreted behind me.

I pointed to the chair by the stove and she perched on the edge, crossing her long legs to reveal proper nylons, her scarlet lips pressed together in what she hoped was a smile.

'What a lovely kitchen,' she said, even though we both knew that it was not.

'It is the same as it was last time you called here,' I said.

But she ignored my comment and only raised a single pencilled eyebrow.

'Do you require the services of a nurse today, Mrs Cuthbertson?' I said impatiently. 'For I am very busy,' although my housecoat and slippers said otherwise.

She sniffed and shuffled her feet. 'As you know, Ivy, I am a prominent member of the Oxworth and District Hospitals Committee and have been for more than twenty years, and we are both fully aware that the services you run from this kitchen are not legitimate, although I understand that the practice of the nurses receiving troubled women into this kitchen goes back long before your time.'

'We have been here as long as the women have needed us,' I said bluntly, 'something you know personally.'

She hesitated a little, realising that it would not do to continue on the subject, so she got up and walked slowly round the kitchen, peering through the windows and running her finger along the draining board as if inspecting the premises on behalf of the hospital committee.

I watched her, the knife clenched behind my back, the only sound the hard crack of her heels on the kitchen tiles and the breathy whistle of the boiling kettle.

She took a large key from the windowsill, holding it up to her eyes with pinched fingers as if she expected it to be black with mould, and I held my breath, fearing that she would discover that the key was the one for the under stairs cupboard where the medicines for the visitors were kept, but then she turned back to me and said: 'Your mistake was not returning to us at Elmridge House, Ivy. For when you did not, I began to ask questions. After all, you know that I am a well connected woman. It was indeed a surprise when I found out who your mother was.'

'You cannot want anything more with my mother,' I said quickly. 'You have done enough, you have no business with her.'

'Of course.' She laughed lightly. 'For that was all so long ago now.'

We stared at each other, the clock ticking in the background. The kettle became a shrill whistle, but neither of us looked away.

'You know we always have tea for our lady visitors,' I said, gesturing to the door. 'I will see to it now. Maybe you would care to wait in the sitting room instead?'

She turned without a word, shutting the door behind her and I ran to the draining board, only now breathing again, the knife clattering into the basin as it slipped from my hand.

I hurried to fill the teapot. Then I steadied myself on the worktop, trying to catch my breath, my fingers fumbling as I tried to loosen the belt of my housecoat.

I poured tea into one mug with a shaking hand, the yellow liquid barely brewed, and dribbled in milk from the jug. Then I took up the knife again and held it inside my sleeve, picking up the mug in the other hand and shouldering open the door to the sitting room.

I found her looking out of the long window, across the lawn to the back of the hospital building, her coat and hat still on. She seemed quite unaware of my presence until I put the mug down on the coffee table with a loud clack.

'You will not stay for tea after all?' I asked.

She turned and I saw that her face seemed to have lost some of its haughtiness. 'I have come here today to tell you that Dr Cuthbertson is dead,' she said flatly.

'Dead?' I echoed.

'It happened yesterday,' she said bluntly, but she did not have the look of a widow about her and did not wear black. Her eyes were bright and her voice was steady. Her make-up was heavy, yet there were no smudges around the eyes.

I should have said something about being sorry for her loss, but I did not wish it. Dr Cuthbertson was a man who should have been part of my life, yet he had not been. I had expected his death and would not mourn him, yet I still found that I was shocked by the news and felt a strange weight within me, as if my dreams of having a father had died with him.

Mrs Cuthbertson took a newspaper from her bag, a rolled copy of the *Missensham Herald*, and lay it on the table, open at a page near the back. 'There is a full obituary,' she said, gesturing towards the lines of print, but I neither glanced nor moved towards it.

She looked at me searchingly again but said nothing more in the way of explanation and I did not ask for one.

She seemed a little disappointed. 'I just thought you should know,' she said.

I nodded. 'I will show you out.'

We walked back through the kitchen and to the back door. I opened it with one hand, the other still twisted behind my back where the knife was clasped. She brushed past me in the doorway. For so many months she had just been a memory but now her closeness, the smell of her perfume and the warmth of her breath reminded me that she was alive and real. Then she turned and looked me directly in the eye, her pupils small and wavering, and I felt a wobble in my knees. She looked away and stepped out on to the iron mat.

'You do not even ask about Hugo,' she said.

'I do not,' I said. 'I know that Bridget still visits Elmridge House and she always seems in a good mood when she returns, and that is all I need to know.'

She nodded to herself and, for the first time, I fancied that I saw a little wetness to her eyes. Then she leant forward to me. 'My husband died intestate,' she whispered. 'I have had Mr Crozier searching for a Will, but he assures me there was nothing.'

'Nothing?' I echoed.

'I must admit that it came as a bit of a shock to me as Clive was always so...' she hesitated as if searching for the right word, '... thorough.' She tried to smile but succeeded only in baring a row of yellowed teeth. 'I expect that your mother will have told you that many years ago my husband made a stupid little promise to her about always making sure that she and her child were provided for, even after his death. The money to do that would indeed be a sizeable sum.' She stared at me intently as if she was trying to read my expression.

'Yes,' I said stiffly. 'She did mention it.' Dr Cuthbertson's promise to my mother was something that I had not expected Mrs Cuthbertson to ever admit to, and now I fully understood the threat that this promise posed to her and her way of life.

'I always thought that he meant to keep his promise by providing for you in his Will, but unfortunately for you that does not seem to have happened.' She raised her eyebrows. 'Unless you can tell me otherwise.'

'I have heard nothing,' I said, 'and neither has my mother.'

Then her voice hardened. 'There is no Will – isn't that right, Ivy?'

'No,' I said, hearing a catch in my voice. 'Not that I know of.'

'Hugo is my only son,' she said, her words slow and clear. 'I would do anything to protect his birthright. Do you understand me? *Anything.*'

'I do,' I said, but my voice was just a croak.

'Regards to your mother.' she said, the lightness returning to her voice. 'Do get her to call on me, for it has been far too long.'

I shut the door behind her and bolted it. My back pressed against the hard wood. I took my hand from behind my back and prised apart my rigid fingers, the knife clattering as it hit the tiles. Across my palm, blood seeped from a fresh wound where the blade had cut deep into my skin.

34

Dr Cuthbertson's obituary was shorter than I had expected. In fact, it said very little. It was no more than a paragraph of newsprint squeezed on to page twelve of the *Missensham Herald*, between advertisements for soap and custard powder.

I sat down on the bench under the old oak tree on the village green, running my trembling hand down the crease in the newspaper, but my eyes seeing none of the words. My lungs were still heaving after my run from the nurses' house and I regretted leaving so hastily, without changing into my outdoor shoes. There was a streak of red at the top of the page and I looked again at the wound on my hand, beads of blood swelling from the cut in my palm, the pain only then returning.

I took a handkerchief from my pocket and wound it round my hand, pressing my palms together and taking deep breaths as I tried to read the obituary again. I had to understand what it meant, get my breath back and keep a clear head so that I could continue my journey through the town centre and on to Drover's Hill where I could deliver the news of Dr Cuthbertson's death to my mother.

I took a deep breath, held the trembling page of newsprint close to my face and started to read.

The obituary told of Dr Cuthbertson's birth in Missensham and his schooling in Harrow and Oxford. It said that he had been married in London, but gave no date for the wedding. His wife, it said, had been a famous ballerina and prominent member of various committees, although it did go into some detail about her attempt to shut down the cottage hospital. There was mention of a son, but only that. There was no mention of either the first Mrs Cuthbertson or me, his daughter.

Most of the obituary told of Dr Cuthbertson's career. First at an asylum called St Catherine's and then at a private practice, which he shut down after only a year. His interest in psychiatry had been triggered by the shell shock that his brother had suffered in the Great War, but since then he had specialised in women's problems: frayed nerves, psychoneurosis and delusions. He had gained some renown when he treated a local murderess named Millicent Bewsey in Holloway Prison. Millicent Bewsey was notorious and her name featured several times in the obituary, always in bold type. When Millicent Bewsey had committed another murder on the day of her release, Dr Cuthbertson's reputation had suffered and the newspaper seemed to take delight in this, stating that his final months were dogged by ill health brought on by his failure. He had died of tuberculosis at the age of fifty-three.

There was no photograph of Dr Cuthbertson either in youth or middle age, yet there was a photograph of Elmridge House with the motor car and driver out the front. I felt that the newspaper had chosen the photograph as some kind of testament of injustice – the riches enjoyed by one who had failed so badly.

There was so much more to the story than the words contained in the short obituary, yet only a handful of people knew the truth and none of them would want that reported in the newspapers. Besides, there was a war on and the death of one man seemed trivial in the face of so much suffering in the world. It was only Millicent Bewsey's name that gave the obituary any prominence at all, and the fact that – as Mrs Cuthbertson had told me herself – no Will had been found.

I read the lines of print dispassionately. I had visited Dr Cuthbertson's house twice, yet had never been allowed to even wander into the view of his window. I had often imagined the man who lived in the back room with a view beyond the dovecote to be frail and irritable, confined to a wheelchair with a blanket over his knees, yet I had seen Dr Cuthbertson's influence on the family he had left behind him, and on my mother – the one who had escaped him. The only person who had my sympathy was Hugo. Dr Cuthbertson was most likely my father, when I cared to acknowledge it. He was my blood and he was part of me, but in spite of all this, I was not sad that I had never met him.

I rolled up the newspaper, got up from the bench and hurried towards the high street and the maze of tiny terraces on the hill behind it. When I reached the top of Drover's Hill, I knocked on the little blue door at the end of the street, but my mother did not answer. I pushed the newspaper through the letter box, leaving it stuck halfway, the page with the obituary folded outwards so her eyes would catch the title. Before I could turn away, I heard the rattle of the locks and my mother opened the door, the folded newspaper in her hand. She hobbled back to her armchair by the fire and I followed her, watching her face as she squinted at the newspaper through her reading glasses without saying a word, her face blank.

At last she looked up.

'What will you do?' I said.

She shrugged.

'Well, you must have known this day would come. It was only a year ago that I told you of Dr Cuthbertson's failing health.'

'I expected a Will,' she said simply, 'and that would answer all doubt, so I never thought about it.'

'Don't you see,' I said. 'This is your chance – you could make a claim on the Elmridge House estate. If you came forward as the first Mrs Cuthbertson. You could prove any marriage that came after yours to be a sham. You would no longer have to live like this, you could…'

But her face was glum. 'No' she said simply. 'I could not do that.'

'You are scared,' I said. 'You are still scared of her and what she might do.'

'No,' she said, but her hand was shaking. 'There is so much I should have told you.'

'You don't need to,' I said, kneeling next to her. 'You have told me the worst, I know how hard it was for you to speak about it, you told me of the locked door and windows and how she hunted you down even after you were gone. You do not need to tell me more, I have an imagination after all. You told me enough for me to know that these people could be dangerous and that I should stay away from them. It was what I needed to know.'

Her eyes turned back to the newspaper. I watched her read, her thick glasses held close to her face and suddenly I realised how fragile she looked. To tell her of Mrs Cuthbertson's visit to the nurses' house that morning would only unsettle her, but there were things that she needed to know – for her safety and for my own.

'She knows,' I said, my voice sounding strange.

She looked up at me, but then just nodded.

'She knows who I am now,' I said, 'and she knows who you are and that you are my mother.'

She paused, and I expected her to question how Mrs Cuthbertson had found out, and then for her to rattle round the house, closing windows and securing bolts, but instead she seemed calm and a little frustrated when she could not find a place to put the newspaper down. Eventually she said: 'Well, she may have known that all along. After all, who would pay a nurse three whole pounds just to wheel her son round the garden? It is a coincidence, don't you think?'

'A coincidence!' I echoed, but she was right and suddenly I felt as if I had played a small part in a game that I did not know was being played. Mrs Cuthbertson had been dictating everything that had happened all along, maybe she already had an ending planned for my mother and me, but I would not let her win.

'You can't give up,' I said. 'It is so unfair. She took everything you had and hunted you down. Even if someone were to take away all that money from her, and the house, she still has her connections, she must have friends on the hospital committee and the charities. You only have me and my nurse's wage and a rent so low that Sadie is practically giving us charity. Mrs Cuthbertson has a son to provide for her, for when Hugo recovers—'

'Recovers?'

'When he walks again.'

Her face fell, but she did not say anything and I wondered what she knew of Hugo.

'Hugo was wounded in battle. I think that the wounds must be mostly closed and healed by now,' I said. 'He needs rest and some physiotherapy that is all. A year has passed since I last saw him. Bridget visits now and she does not speak of him to me, but he is sure to have almost recovered.'

'Hugo?' she repeated.

'You did not know this?'

'I know of Mrs Cuthbertson's son,' she said, 'but not the man you describe.'

'I don't understand,' I said.

'Grace Cuthbertson had a baby not long after she drove me from the house; a male child, but the baby that I heard of was born with legs that were withered and weak,' she said. 'That child would never have walked.'

'No, you must be mistaken,' I said. 'I…' I remembered how I had first heard about Hugo, when Bridget had referred to him as a 'wounded soldier' and how, when I met him, he had reminded me of the soldiers resting up in the cottage hospital. I had assumed that he was like them, when he was not – was it possible that Bridget had made the same mistake? I had thought his broad shoulders and strong arms due to military training, but now I wondered if his physique was due to years of heaving his body up and down the stairs and the strain of turning the wheels of his chair. I had congratulated myself on lifting his body from the stairs to the wheelchair, but if his leg muscles were wasted there would have been less weight to bear. I thought of the thick tartan blanket that was always on his lap despite the season and how he had flinched when I had tried to remove it. There had been no evidence of dressings, splints or exercise bars and I had never heard mention of him from anyone at the cottage hospital.

'I'm sorry, Ivy,' she said. 'Sadie heard it from old Nurse Pritchard, the district nurse back then. She had known about the child for a while. His parents had taken him to London and tried every doctor and specialist there, but Nurse Pritchard had visited the child, she had read his notes and she knew that he would never walk.'

'No,' I said. 'It can't be true, Hugo told me that...' but then I realised that he had not. He had never told me anything. His bookshelf was crammed with military manuals, but he had never claimed to have served in the regiments whose crests adorned the covers. He kept a souvenir of the Eiffel Tower on his desk, yet had never mentioned fighting in France. The old shell case was battered, but it had probably come from the last war and I fancied that he kept these things just to amuse himself, just as a little boy would play with a pop-gun or tin soldiers. The past that Hugo imagined for himself had never happened, and neither would the future that I had wished for him.

Hugo had never lied to me, but he had never contradicted me when I spoke of his war wounds and never corrected me when I spoke of life after his recovery. I thought of the empathy I had felt for him as we had spoken of our troubled families, yet when I had discovered that he could be my half-brother, I had felt a different kind of closeness to him, one that was stronger, and this made his deceit even harder to take.

'The bastard,' I spat. 'I didn't want to believe that he could be like his mother, but now I am sure of it!'

'No,' said my mother calmly. 'He may have avoided the truth or even been a little deluded, but that does not make him like her.'

'How can you defend him?' I cried. 'He lives a lie, just like his mother does.'

'I do not defend him,' she said. 'I just think that he needs to dream. He has had such a hard life.'

'You cannot think that!' I said. 'I have seen the men who have been crippled by the war. I know what kind of a future they face and they do not have all the good fortune that he...' But my argument was waning, and I found that I could not even convince myself of Hugo's privilege. Despite the grandness of Elmridge House, there was still something wrong and I remembered the feeling that I had when I first visited; something was not right with the place, something that I could not put my finger on.

I thought of Hugo's room on the first floor of the house. He had said that he liked a view, but even the view from the downstairs rooms must have been spectacular, and I wondered if at one point the stairs would have been enough to prevent him ever leaving the house. There were his mother's fears – how she always wanted to be at his side and felt that he needed a nurse, even if all she did was push him round the garden.

'It might be that he kept to his room willingly,' said my mother, as if reading my thoughts.

'No,' I said. 'I have met him, he is not the type!'

'He might not have had much choice,' she said.

'I don't understand.'

'When the boy was five years old he had grand mal seizures,' she said. 'Dr Cuthbertson was ashamed of him, so he kept him hidden away for a while, I do not know how long for. It might be that Hugo has only been allowed out since his father became ill. When he was a child, epileptics were still sometimes put in asylums. His father must have thought that he was doing him a kindness by keeping him at home.'

'No,' I said. 'That can't be right, he is twenty years old now. A long time has passed since his birth. Dr Cuthbertson would have had no reason to keep him there other than some outdated sense of shame. Medicines for epilepsy have been around for years, with those he would have managed to live a reasonable life and...' But then I realised that Hugo had been taking medicine – Luminal. The little tablets that Mrs Cuthbertson was always claiming she needed for Hugo to sleep were in fact often prescribed for seizures.

I knew that Bridget had been stealing Luminal for Mrs Cuthbertson. It was what Mrs Cuthbertson had demanded when she had visited the nurses' house, and it was what she had stolen from my bag when I left it on the driveway of Elmridge House to help Hugo on the stairs. I remembered that night when I had sat with her in the kitchen – the waver of her eyes, the shake of her hands and the sweat on her top lip, her irritability and rudeness. I had thought all these things due to her addiction, but now I just saw agitation – an urge to get the medicine that she needed for her son in a manner that was discreet and did not involve a visit to the local doctor where the people might gossip. That night she had been a nameless woman to me, a drug addict, and not the mother of a man with an illness that was once misunderstood and shrouded in shame. It was Hugo who needed the Luminal and whether Mrs Cuthbertson herself was addicted or not, he would have been how she came across it.

My mother sighed wearily. 'It will be a long time before Hugo can support himself, I'm afraid, let alone his mother,' she said. 'It is her that needs to provide for him and she needs her husband's money to do that.' Then I remembered Mrs Cuthbertson as she had stood on my kitchen step no more than an hour ago and said that she would do anything to protect her son's birth right – *anything*.

I did not leave my mother's house until midnight. We spoke little more, just stared into the fire, each of us lost in our thoughts. I knew now what had happened, yet my mind seemed too weary to make sense of it, and I feared that I never would. No matter how I felt about Hugo, his mother had been pursuing mine and now that her husband was dead, Mrs Cuthbertson needed to be sure that his money came her way. I still feared her and when I left that night, I looked about me and did not linger on the step.

'Be sure to lock your doors,' I whispered to my mother as I stepped into the street, 'and all the windows.'

'You know, I think I have spent too long hiding,' she replied wearily. 'All we can do now is wait.'

35

October 1943

'All we can do now is wait,' is what my mother had said, and that is what we did.

By the time October came round, my mother and I had waited a whole month without hearing from Mrs Cuthbertson, so one morning when I came across a parcel waiting for me on the kitchen table of the nurses' house, my thoughts first turned to her.

I had been trying to keep Mrs Cuthbertson out of my head for one long month. The day after she had told me of her husband's death, I had gone to work as usual, so too the day after that, and then every day for the week that followed. Then, on the Sunday, the telephone in the nurses' house had rung at ten o'clock and Bridget's visits to Elmridge House resumed their familiar pattern. I should have felt comforted by the return of my usual routine, but somehow I felt that Mrs Cuthbertson was always present, watching and waiting for me. I would see her shadow among the trees as I walked to work, and I would jump if I heard a door bang. If I could not find the key to the medicine cabinet, I would suspect only her. I would mistake the echoes of my footsteps for those of another, and when I heard a voice mingling with those on the wireless, I would turn it off, only to hear silence. I would see her face among the crowds in the high street or her shadow as she passed me in the road and I was grateful each time that Sunday came around again and I stood at my mother's door and heard her unfastening the locks, relieved to know that another week had passed and all was well.

Yet the parcel that waited for me on the kitchen table was not Mrs Cuthbertson's doing, in fact it was from someone unexpected and welcome. It was wrapped in brown paper and string and addressed to Nurse Ivy Watts at the Cottage Hospital in Missensham. It was not until I saw the Brighton postmark that I remembered my Uncle Leonard's plans to move to the town, and how I had told him my place of work when I bandaged his hand.

Bridget sat by the stove, her eyes flicking up from her novel at the rustle of the brown paper when I pulled at the strings, but, when she realised that the parcel contained only papers and not nylons and chocolate, she made her excuses and went to her room.

The parcel contained a small stack of postcards and photographs and on top was a letter – a brief note from Leonard. He had taken a place at a boarding house in Brighton. It was a small room, so he thought it better that he pass some of his 'keepsakes' on to me as the landlady did not like clutter in the rooms. Brighton was suffering little better than London, the piers had been blasted in two to prevent enemy landings, but the entertainment folk were still around and there were plenty of troops for his dancing girls to entertain. He sent regards to my mother, although he still did not enquire after her.

There was a recent photograph of Leonard with another man, standing rigidly, shoulder to shoulder. They were not touching, yet their eyes were upon each other and I wondered if the other man was Alexander, the dancer whose youthful vigour had been captured in the photograph that Len had cherished. Len had claimed that my mother had driven Alexander from him and I hoped that, whatever had happened in the past, the men had found each other once more.

I felt happy that Len had not forgotten me, but in a way the parcel had come too late as my mother had now told me about her past in great detail and whatever Len could add to this would be no more than a gentle fleshing of the bones. However, he had at least mentioned my mother and this made me curious about his other 'keepsakes' that the folds of brown paper contained.

First there was a gold edged theatre programme for a performance of *Giselle*, the lettering was ornate but the paper was thin. Leonid Postov was named as the creative director and then again as playing the part of the duke. The lead role was danced by Grace Cuthbertson. There was no mention of my mother – no Liliana Postova as the ballerina, nor even a Lilian Post in the corps de ballet. That phase of my mother's life had ended.

There was an assortment of faded photographs: a studio portrait of a little boy and girl dressed in Victorian swimwear that reached to their elbows and knees, posing with buckets and spades against a backdrop of Brighton pier, and a grainy image of a woman standing in a street of small terraced houses holding a baby in a christening robe. This was the past that Len had told me of, the history of his family and mine, yet my mind had been elsewhere when we sat in the back of his van in Covent Garden and I had only half listened to his stories. There was another studio photograph, this time in sepia – a strict looking man stood with his hand on a bible, and a plainly dressed woman sat next to him. These were the parents that Len had spoken so bitterly of – grandparents that I would never know.

Another of the photographs was the same image that I had seen on the postcard from Elmridge House – the group of dancers with stretched limbs and billowing skirts arranged around the central group of three – the ballerina with a man on each arm – my mother's final performance with the Ballets Spectaculaire. The picture was larger and clearer than the one on the postcard and this time I recognised Leonard as a handsome young man, and I fancied that his over plucked eyebrows and the thick layer of greasepaint I had seen on his skin were his way of clinging on to looks that had faded long ago. The other faces were clearer too, and I saw my mother and the Cuthbertsons again, as with fresh eyes, but their expressions gave away nothing of what was to come.

Then there was a postcard, this time a photograph of Elmridge House. The flint walls and high gables of the old building were free from the boughs of wisteria and the hollies on the front lawn were pruned into neat spheres, and I realised that the house I had visited must be ramshackle compared to what it once was. The same motor car was parked in the driveway, a much younger and more handsome Edgar standing next to it in full chauffeur's uniform as if he were a decoration.

I turned the postcard over. The ink was fading on the handwritten message but the words were still legible.

Dearest Len,

I am recovered and quite well now. I have found a new love in your dear friend Clive and we are married and I am in the family way! Things have changed and I regret my old ways. I hope in time you will forgive me.

Your loving Lil

It was the postcard Leonard had told me he had received from my mother – a story which I had once doubted. Yet Len had not been confused; here was the final contact between sister and brother and the words were unmistakable. My mother had even signed her name with a flourish that I could not imagine her using now.

As Len had told me, she was married to Clive and expecting, and I assumed the apology she included was for what had happened with Alexander. The words said exactly what Len had told me, yet there was something strange about them that I could not put my finger on, as if they had been translated from another language and some of their meaning lost.

I had felt a sense of completeness after my mother had finally spoken of what happened to her, but now that feeling was fading. What I had heard from Len and Sadie seemed to confirm my mother's story, but I was starting to realise that they were only repeating what she had told them.

The only other person who had played a part in what had happened was Mrs Cuthbertson – a woman who was rude and overbearing, a woman who had stolen medicines from me and threatened me in my own home – a woman I could not ask. At that moment I thought that I would never return to Elmridge House again.

36

December 1943

One Sunday at exactly ten o'clock, the phone in the hallway rang again.

It was now over two months since Mrs Cuthbertson had come to the nurses' house and put a copy of the *Missensham Herald* on the table, open at the page of her husband's obituary. In the weeks that had followed, winter had taken hold, changing the landscape from one of stubble fields and rusted copses to one of skeletal trees and mists sunk deep into the valleys. Christmas was barely a week away, yet the sparkle and indulgence that usually came with it was dampened by rationing and the blackout and I dreaded another Christmas lunch sharing a cheap cut of mutton with my mother in her tiny front room. The seasons had changed, but little else had and neither my mother nor I had heard a thing from Mrs Cuthbertson.

Sunday mornings had become a time that Sadie would show up at the nurses' house, letting herself in through the kitchen door with a basket of journals and textbooks.

She would stoke the stove and make buttered toast, and Bridget and I would sip tea from tin mugs while she read aloud from the books and told us of the things she had seen in her forty years of nursing. They were a strange type of lesson, but at least now I was included.

On that particular Sunday, the sky outside the kitchen window was a dull yellow, the clouds heavy with the snow that was forecast. When the phone rang, we all looked to the clock to see the minute hand click to the hour just as the first ring ended. After Mrs Cuthbertson had visited the nurses' house with the news of her husband's death, the telephone had rung every Sunday morning. I had come to expect Mrs Cuthbertson's call, yet I still felt a weight in my stomach when the ring echoed through the house. I glanced at Bridget and she caught my eye but looked away quickly, then she stood up, smoothing her hair as if the caller would see her, and walked slowly into the hallway. I listened to the click of her heels on the floor tiles and the choke of the ring as she picked up the receiver. Sadie had come to know what the phone call meant and she always kept a respectful silence until Bridget had finished the call and left the house.

After Bridget's formal greeting, Sadie and I heard nothing for several seconds. Then at last Bridget's voice: a few 'yes's and 'no's punctuated with seconds of silence and then the words 'Elmridge House, right away.'

Sadie sat down in Bridget's chair and reached across to me, taking my hand.

There were no more sounds from the hallway other than the click of the receiver, but Bridget did not return and the next thing we heard was her hurried footsteps on the stairs and the creak of the floorboards above us.

When Bridget returned, she wore a big overcoat and scarf. 'I have to go right away,' she said. 'Mrs Cuthbertson has had to leave Elmridge House at short notice and will not be able to return for several hours. I can't have the patient alone with snow forecast.' Then she added: 'The poor love will need someone to keep him warm.' She winked and gave me a knowing look. 'It's a shame you went off the place, Ivy.' She took a shiny spatula from her nursing bag and held it to her face and started smoothing her hair into place.

Sadie looked at me, her eyebrows raised.

'What?' I whispered.

'She said that Mrs Cuthbertson is not at Elmridge House, Ivy,' she said quietly. 'You should go and talk to Hugo; this might be your only chance to hear him out. Go on' – she tilted her head towards the door – 'I promise that I won't say a thing to your mother about it.'

'No!' I hissed. 'I—'

But Sadie cut in: 'Bridget, I have so much for you to do here, let Ivy go. I will pay you the money myself. You can go every weekend after, I promise, just let Ivy go this once.'

'No!' she protested.

'Well, you can't be going to Elmridge House for the money then, maybe you hope for something else there…'

'But…' she began, a blush appearing on her cheeks, 'I—'

'Well,' said Sadie. 'I am surprised that you would want to go this week, because if Mrs Cuthbertson is not there, you will not be able to sell her the Luminal that has been disappearing from the medicine cabinet.'

'I have been doing no such thing!' she said indignantly.

'Have it your way then,' said Sadie, 'but if you go to Elmridge House now, there will be no point in continuing this lesson, so I might as well busy myself with some stock taking in the medicine cabinet so that I can report back to Dr Crawford.'

Bridget sat back down heavily. 'You know, I think it better that Ivy goes this time,' she said shortly, opening her text book again. 'You had better go and change, Ivy.'

I did not manage to leave the nurses' house until nearly midday. Sadie had fussed around me so much – pointing at the sky and relaying the doom of the weather forecast – that I felt as if I was on an expedition to the Arctic. The pressure of my bicycle tyres was checked, the chain oiled and a thermos put in the basket on the handlebars. I was then wrapped in an overcoat and scarf so thick that I wondered how I would be able to pedal in them.

As I wobbled down the driveway of the cottage hospital and past the village green I felt foolish – there was snow in the air, but it was no more than a few flurries. The town was quiet, with barely a soul out to brave the cold. The Oxworth Road seemed barren – the rolling fields that rose above the hedge lined track stripped bare of all life. The breath came quickly in my lungs and clouded in the frozen air, my nose smarting with the cold.

When I reached the turning to Elmridge House and looked up at the crest of the hill, I thought the house looked somehow starker since I had last seen it. The wisteria had died back, making the flinted walls and gables look dark against the sky, yet as I approached I saw that the curtains were open and black smoke billowed from one of the chimneys.

Hannah let me in without a word and avoided my eyes, her gaze cast down to her feet, and I wondered how much she had overheard from her mistress about what had happened in these rooms. She watched me wordlessly as I took off my boots and went up the stairs. I hesitated on the landing, remembering my first visit to the house over a year ago, and the feeling that had overwhelmed me – something was not right with the place. Now I knew more of what had happened in these rooms, yet the feeling still remained.

In the corner room the door was open and a fire was crackling in the grate, yet I noticed the smell of the burning wood more than the heat it gave.

'Ivy!' Hugo swung his wheelchair round to face me, a big grin on his face as if merely a week had passed since he had last seen me and nothing at all was wrong. 'I see you have a new coat,' he said. 'It suits you much better than that ugly old leather affair.'

'Do you think so…' I began but stopped myself. 'Hugo, I did not come here to chat about fashion and to wheel you round the garden.'

'Ah,' he said. 'She has brought you here.'

'Your mother?' I said. 'No, actually... Well, I suppose that in some way she has.' I sat down on the window seat. 'Why am I here, Hugo, why was I ever here?'

'What do you mean?' he said, the grin still on his face.

I did not answer him, for I wanted to hear what he knew – the words which would come from his own lips, and not just some agreement with what I would tell him. Instead I said: 'Your mother does not need to pay me three pounds just to wheel you round the garden. You can do that yourself. You have staff – a driver and a maid. You always said you were not helpless.'

'No,' he said, nodding slowly. 'I am not.'

I glared at him, waiting for him to continue but he did not.

'Why was I brought here, Hugo?' I implored.

'I am not like you,' he said, with an edge to his voice. 'I only have this room. I did not even have the garden until my father became ill, and even then I could not go beyond the dovecote in case he saw me from his window. I could not go out and have a life, so I had to bring one to me.'

I looked again at the bookshelf stacked with military manuals, the polished case of an artillery shell used as a bookend, and a miniature Eiffel Tower on the desk – things that I had once thought were part of his past. These things, however, were no more than toys – comic books full of heroic tales and props to use on some imagined battlefield. They were things that he had used to entertain him, just as I had been.

'So you were playing with me,' I said. 'Just like you were playing at being a soldier!'

'I never told you that I had fought,' he said simply. He was telling the truth – he had never claimed anything of the kind. I had just believed what I wanted to believe. Bridget had spoken of him as a wounded soldier, Mrs Cuthbertson had said how hard the war had been for her son. Even I had talked of his recovery, and of bullet wounds that had only ever existed in my imagination. Everyone had talked of Hugo as a wounded soldier but he himself had said nothing.

'No,' I said. 'You didn't say anything at all, you put words in my mouth and you enjoyed me saying them.'

'What did you expect me to do?' he said. 'Admit that I was born imperfect and that my father kept me close for fear that I should fit. I cannot work, not the kind of work that he would have wanted for me. I was an embarrassment to him.' So it was as my mother described. Hugo was not the war hero that I had imagined; he had barely left Elmridge House, and he had been here longer than my mother ever was. 'I hoped that we would be friends,' he said, 'but you are young and adventurous, you would have not wanted to know someone who had never left this place and never would.'

'It is not too late,' I said. 'I have seen how you can use the stairs. You have medication now that will help with your fits. You can still leave.' But somehow I knew that he could not.

'Do you really think that I can just escape from here?' he said flatly. 'Just as your mother did all those years ago.' He stared at me, his face serious, and for a moment I could not find an answer for him. I had suspected that he had known about my mother, but I had never been sure, and his words still shocked me.

'When did Mrs Cuthbertson tell you?' I said shakily.

He laughed. 'You think that my mother would tell me anything?'

I shook my head because I knew that she would not.

'When my father became ill, he was often delirious. He would say the same things over and over again, most of them meaningless. He would talk about ballet and the murderess, Millicent Bewsey, and the newspapers that he always detested, but there were other things...' He paused, a slight frown on his face as if he was trying to recall his father's words. 'Well, there were some things that seemed to have nothing to do with his life that I knew of. He spoke of a woman who was about to have a baby. I thought that he was remembering my mother at first, but sometimes he would say a little more – this woman could not walk, yet left here in the middle of the night. She was in pain and screaming as if she feared for her life. She was taken by a midwife and could not be found again. He kept saying that it happened in this room.'

'This room,' I echoed, but my lips barely formed the words. Over the past year I had often been haunted by thoughts of my mother's escape, but, as I sat in the room where it had happened, it suddenly seemed more real and I fancied that I could see my mother, pale faced and screaming, her arms clutching at Sadie as she tried to walk. 'But you said that your father was delirious,' I said. 'It could have been nonsense, why did you listen to him?'

'He made me listen,' said Hugo. 'He would grab my hand and squeeze it hard. It was as if this particular memory was important to him and he would get quite distressed. He seemed to think that he had failed this woman. He said something about not being here when she fled and blaming himself for that, but there was something else, it was as if he had broken some kind of promise to her. He may have been lots of things, but my father was a man with a strong sense of duty, and to him this failure was serious.'

So Hugo knew of my mother, but not who she was to his father nor of his promise to her.

'He said nothing else?' I asked.

'The only other thing was something about a ring; a ring that was not gold, only brass. It seemed important to him, but I assumed it some kind of delirious raving as it seemed a stupid detail when compared to the other horrors he would describe.' He shrugged. 'That was it, but Hannah told me more.'

'Hannah?' I said, surprised.

'I noticed that whenever Hannah was in the room, she would try and quieten him, but only when he started talking about the pregnant woman. She would talk over him, put a thermometer in his mouth, that kind of thing. It was all around the time that Bridget started coming here. She came here to start with to nurse my father, but I think that Hannah was worried what Bridget might overhear, so she made sure that Bridget's only duties were with me.'

'What did Hannah say?'

'Well, nothing at first. She tried to reassure me that the woman he spoke of was not my mother, but this just showed me that there was some truth in my father's ravings and that there had been another woman in this house.'

'Maybe Hannah was there when it all happened,' I said. 'If she was there when your father was not, she must have seen everything.'

'She did not say anything more about that night,' he said, 'only that nothing sinister had happened to the woman and that her limping was due to an old dancing injury that was made worse by her pregnancy.'

'Did you not ask who the woman was?' I said. 'Did you not wonder what a pregnant woman was doing in this house, one who was not your mother?'

'Of course I asked her,' he said. 'I thought that this woman might have been in danger and something terrible had happened.'

'And?'

'She just said that the woman was fine and was nobody important.'

Nobody important – so that was how my mother had been seen in this house. She had been the mistress of the house if only for a short while, she had been Clive's wife, but even the servants were erasing all memory of her as if she had never existed.

I looked out of the front window over to Missensham town in the valley and to Drover's Hill. The road which I thought to be my mother's was already threatened by a thick cloud and I wondered if snow would be falling there already. At Elmridge House, snowflakes had started to fall silently on the sloping lawn and driveway, the flurries replaced by a curtain of steadily falling flakes. There was patchy snow cover on the gravel and tiny drifts were starting to collect in the hollows between the dagger shaped leaves in the flower bed. The motor car had been left out in the driveway. I had not noticed it there before, but the covering of snow suggested the long bonnet was cold and it had not been driven for some time, and somehow I thought it odd to see it there, and then slowly I began to realise why.

'But she is here after all!' I turned to Hugo. 'Your mother is always driven in the motor car. Bridget told me that Mrs Cuthbertson had to leave and would not return for several hours. Where is she?' I felt the fear that had drained away over the past few weeks seize me again.

'I don't know what she told Bridget,' he said, 'but I know little more than she does. I heard my mother quarrelling with the servants this morning and then when she came to see me she said that she was going to Crozier's, the solicitors in the high street. She took an overnight bag with her and her wellingtons, so I suppose that Edgar must have refused to drive her anywhere after the quarrel.'

'She would not need an overnight bag and her wellingtons for the high street,' I said, 'and there was no snow this morning.'

'She said she did not care for the condition of the roads on Drover's Hill.'

'She is going to Drover's Hill?' I cried. 'My mother's house is in Drover's Hill!'

I jumped to my feet, bundling up my coat and bag. 'What time is it?' I yelled.

'It's almost three,' he said, and suddenly I realised how long my journey to Elmridge House must have taken as I battled against the gusts of snow. I feared that I faced an even slower journey now that the snow was settling and I had to tackle the steep slopes on the other side of the town.

I looked out of the window again in desperation, willing the snow to stop. On the driveway I could see my footsteps, the gravel still dark with the imprint of my soles. I had not noticed the footprints already there in the thin layer of snow, the ones that were now no more than outlines in the white. The footprints circled the flower bed and made off down the driveway and I imagined Mrs Cuthbertson striding purposefully, her head bent into the wind and her face grim as she set out for the town centre, the solicitor's office and then my mother's house.

I looked back to the distant horizon, the opposite ridge, where I was so used to seeing the tiny clump of houses clinging to the hillside, but now when I looked out into the swirl of snowflakes, all I could see was a blanket of whiteness as if my mother and her house had been erased.

LILY

37

December 1943

It was almost three o'clock on a Sunday afternoon. Lunchtime had been and gone, and Ivy was late. I peered through the crack in the curtains – the snow was light and gusting, with little drifts collecting in the gutters, but there was not a soul in the street and I wondered if Ivy too, had decided to stay indoors. Drover's Hill was steep and could be slippery for a bicycle if there was ice, but Ivy was a good girl and something told me that she would still come. She was a nurse after all, and used to venturing out in all weathers.

It had been an hour since I had waved Sadie off on her wobbly bicycle, the panniers full of neatly folded finery for the townspeople of Missensham, yet the track left by her bicycle was still clear in the fine cover of snow and had not been disturbed by tyre, hoof nor footprint. It had been twenty-three years since Sadie had spirited me from Elmridge House and rented out her own little house to me and every week since that day, she had come without fail, torn and stained party dresses bursting from her panniers.

Ivy had left me the little postcard that she got from Elmridge House and I took it out and looked at the faces I had once known. There was Grace dipped in a curtsy at the front of the picture; once a friend but now an enemy. There was Len in the velvet tunic; my brother but now estranged, and there was Clive; once my lover but now dead. Alexander was not among the faces, he had already left, and I realised that it was after that moment things had started to fall apart. The scene in the photograph had once been so much more than shades of light and dark captured in chemicals and cardboard – it had been real and vibrant and suddenly I could smell the greasepaint again, the rosin and sweat. I could hear the orchestra and taste the crème de menthe.

It was a world that was now lost – the theatre was bombed, the audiences had waned, the stage hands had left to fight in a war overseas and the dancers had aged and were no longer beautiful. Yet there was a remnant of my youth that was still with me – a young woman with a hint of red in her hair, one with long, slender limbs and high arched feet, but Ivy had never known anything of my life – it had been a world from which I had kept her sheltered.

Ivy had always visited me every Sunday at lunchtime. There had been a time when I would open the door for her and she would rush past me, busying herself in the kitchen as she washed the dishes, dusted the high cupboards, put away the shopping and prepared lunch, but little over a year ago all this changed. There had been that one day we had spoken properly for the first time in our lives and since that day we were now more likely to sit down together and share the second squeeze of the tealeaves and a square of garibaldi as we talked – and I was glad of it. These days when Ivy visited me I was happy to see my daughter and I was not afraid to show her with a smile or even the occasional hug. Since I had told her about my past, I felt that she understood the events that had led to her birth and how they had changed me from a sweet young girl with a lithe and able body into the mother she knew; a woman who was hunched, crippled and suffered terribly from her moods.

Throughout Ivy's childhood I had always shied away from any affection because, while I loved her, I feared that any sentimentality would make her weak in a world that had treated me so harshly, and I dreaded her questions about the family that she did not have. Now things had changed between us and, although I was not always able to hold my tongue, she had come to understand that it was just my nature, and I felt that we were mother and daughter at last.

I drew the front curtain to keep in the heat from the fire, then I leant back in my chair. Sadie had brought a pile of new dresses with her, but I did not have the energy to start working on them. The distant church bell clanked three times, but there were no other sounds from outside as if the air itself was clenched and waiting in anticipation of snow. I felt my mind wander, but my youth had been short-lived and there were not many places that I wanted my thoughts to go.

When the knock on the door came, I noticed that the light behind the curtain had dimmed. I glanced at the clock and realised that I must have dozed. Then the knock came again and I felt relief that Ivy had made it safely through the snow.

'Hold on, I'm coming!' I called. I ran to the door and unbolted it quickly, loosening the bolts one after another and swinging the door open.

But it was not Ivy.

There was a woman standing in the darkness, a woman with a little yellow hat pulled low over her brow, and when she raised her head, I saw her face for the first time in over two decades. She had changed, of course, her face was severe and wrinkled, but her eyes held a brightness that I recognised – her aged appearance just a mask for the soul I had once known.

I saw the plane of her cheek. I saw the jut of her shoulder. I saw her arm braced against the open door and her boot jammed against the wood. I smelt the tang of her sweat and heard the quickness of her breaths, and I felt the force of her body as she pushed her way into my house.

IVY

38

I sat on the hard flagstones at the bottom of the stairs and laced my boots clumsily, my fingers numb with cold.

'Why are you leaving?' Hugo's voice echoed somewhere above me. 'I thought you wanted to talk about this. There is so much more we need to say to each other, isn't there?'

'Yes,' I shouted, pulling my laces tight, 'but my mother could be in danger. I need to go to her right now!'

'Wait for me,' he said, the staircase creaking with his weight. 'I am coming down.'

'No!' But by the time I stood up he was already halfway down, and from his expression I realised that I must have shouted.

'I don't understand,' he said. 'The snow should not be a problem for her, not if she stays indoors, and if what you say is right, she will not be alone, my mother will be visiting her soon.'

'That is exactly why she is in danger.' This time I heard the echo of my shout in the empty hallway.

'You speak as if my mother is evil!' he panted as he clung to the balustrade.

'After all that happened,' I cried, 'how can you think her blameless? All you have is some partial ravings of a dying man who was losing his mind, she has obviously told you next to nothing herself.'

'But you only have your mother's word!' He grabbed at my sleeve, his hand reaching out through the bannisters. He had hurried down the stairs after me and endangered himself in doing so. His touch on my arm was enough to make me hesitate for just a second.

'Why would my mother lie about something like that?' I said. 'Besides, I have also spoken to Sadie and Uncle Len...'

But his face said that he knew nothing of the people I spoke of.

'Your mother drove mine from this house,' I said, but I could not say any more for the words were choking me.

He hurried down the last few steps, almost falling in his haste, his legs twisting underneath his body until he sat on the flagstones, clinging to the bottom bannister, his face red from the effort.

'Don't try to stop me, Hugo.' I stood up and pulled on my coat.

'Look, you have no need to worry,' he panted. 'Hannah told me that everything was fine. She told me that the woman, your mother, was alive and well and living in Missensham. She even told me about you – she said that the woman now had a daughter who was a nurse who could care for her. Whatever you think my mother has done to yours, I don't think that it can have come to much.'

'None of you can have known what my mother suffered,' I said, wrestling with the buttons on my coat. 'How could Hannah have found out about what happened to my mother after she left Elmridge House?' But I already knew the answer – Hannah would only have repeated whatever Mrs Cuthbertson had told her. All the time my mother had spent in hiding had been in vain because Mrs Cuthbertson had known about her all along.

'You can't go,' said Hugo. 'The snow will get deeper, what if you fell from your bicycle or slipped?'

'I would get up again.'

'But if you could not, you would catch a chill. If you lie down in snow you get hypothermia and you might never get up again.'

'Don't be ridiculous!' I said, but then I realised that his view of the world came from the instructions in his army manuals – Arctic survival and expeditions to frozen lands. He had little experience of real life, only of imagined adventures and stories of tragedy. 'I'm going,' I said firmly.

'But I am not sure when my mother will return,' he cried, and from the panic in his voice, I realised that he feared being alone.

'I'm sure she won't be away for long,' I said, but my voice sounded as if I was reassuring a child, for really I did not know.

But Hugo was insistent. 'I told you that she quarrelled with the servants before she left,' he said, 'but somehow it seemed more than that, they were rowing about something important, but I could not hear what. Then she came up and said goodbye to me,' his voice cracked a little, 'but there was something strange about the way she said it.'

'Your mother will come back to you,' I said. 'I am sure of it, but I have to go to my own. I cannot be here while Mrs Cuthbertson could return. This might be goodbye.'

'It's my fault,' he said shakily. 'It's all my fault.'

I hesitated again. 'No, Hugo, you weren't born. What can you have possibly done to—'

'I made it so you could wear that coat in front of your mother,' he said, 'and I did not stop you when you put the postcard into the pocket. I hoped that one day she might see that, too.'

'Why would you do that?' I spat.

'My mother never said anything about you,' he said. 'but one day Bridget—'

'Bridget?' I cried. 'What can she have to do with this?'

'She liked to chat,' he said simply. 'It wasn't until Bridget mentioned that she had a housemate – a nurse, who was younger than her but no fun, who did little else except visit her crippled mother, and I thought of the limping woman that my father had spoken of and thought you might be the baby she gave birth to.'

'And then one day it was not Bridget any more,' I said, winding my scarf round my neck. 'One day I just happened to answer the telephone.'

'I was not sure when I met you, but when you said that your mother's wedding ring was only brass, then I remembered what my father had said. I thought if your mother saw the coat and photograph it might—'

'So this was the way you livened up the dull life you spoke of,' I said. 'Did you not think that it was none of your business?' I picked up my bag. 'Goodbye, Hugo.'

'I told my mother about you,' he said suddenly, 'and who I thought your mother was.'

'Why would you do that?' I cried.

'Well, you did not return,' he said. 'You left me no choice.'

'What did she say?' I said shakily.

'She said that she wanted to talk to your mother.'

'About what?'

'She didn't tell me, you know her way.' He paused. 'Although she said that she wanted the postcard back.'

'Is that all she said? After all that has happened, all she can think of is a postcard?'

'She said that your mother already had her own copy.'

I remembered my mother's face when she saw the postcard, how it had lit up as if she was seeing the faces in the photograph for the first time in years.

'No,' I said. 'I have never seen anything like it in her house and I am pretty sure that she had not seen it for several years, she was surprised when she saw it.'

'Well,' he said. 'I am glad. She should keep my mother's copy then.'

I opened the heavy door, snowflakes gusting on to the mat. 'Why didn't you tell me any of this before?' I said.

'I tried, I left messages with Bridget, but you would not come.'

I thought of the times Bridget had grudgingly passed on his messages – his requests for my return to Elmridge

House, and how I had declined each one with the excuse of a sprained ankle that never was.

'Look at me,' he said. 'How could I meet you if you would not come to me?' The tartan blanket had fallen from his lap when he had struggled down the stairs and I saw that his legs were bent in front of him, the jut of his knees and the curve of his bones no bigger than that of a schoolboy. Hugo was a man that could barely leave his house, he had a driver who was probably forbidden to take him past the end of the driveway and a maid who was probably instructed to take all his letters directly to his mother. Bridget's messages were all he had and I had ignored them all. I pulled the tartan blanket back over his legs and took some old coats from the stand, piling them on top of him, but it was all that I had time to do for him.

'I should have come,' I said, 'and I am sorry for staying away, but it was not you that I was avoiding. You see, at last my mother has spoken about what happened to her in this house.' I stepped out into the snow. 'Now I know everything.'

'No,' he shouted after me. 'You do not.'

But I did not stop to question him because, as I hurried across the driveway and got on my bicycle, I no longer thought about my mother's past, only her future. I had heard what Hugo said, but I did not listen.

39

I reached the top of Drover's Hill exhausted from my journey through the snow. My stockings were sodden with icy spray from the roads, my back was prickly with sweat and my leg muscles trembled with exertion, yet as I looked towards the little house at the end of the road, my body became numb. The rows of little terraced houses were in darkness, but there was a tiny chink of light escaping from the blue door of my mother's house, cutting a small shaft of brightness into the snow. I pushed the door open slowly, my heart pounding in my ears, and stepped into the front room.

The warmth of the fire wafted across the doorstep with the sound of hushed voices. The women were sitting together by the fire, my mother in the old rocking chair and Mrs Cuthbertson on the stool. Their heads were bowed as in deep conversation and when I entered, they glanced up briefly as if I was no more than a mild distraction.

'Mum?' I said shakily. 'What is she doing here?'

They fell silent and looked first to one another and then to me and I realised that there was an understanding between them, one that I did not share, and suddenly I felt as if I was the intruder in the house where I was raised.

I had thought of this moment for all of my long journey through the snow. I had imagined screaming, crying, pulling Mrs Cuthbertson from my mother and throwing her into the street, but she was not the attacker I had imagined her to be and there was no malice in her face.

There was a tea tray resting on the hearth but instead of the usual mugs there was a bottle of some sort of green liqueur. The two old sherry flutes that my mother used only at Christmas stood next to the bottle, a tinge of green lining the base of each. My mother had not fought off Mrs Cuthbertson, in fact she had received her as a guest.

'You are drinking with *her*, mother!' I said. 'You are drinking with this woman that you hate and you do not even drink!' I knew that it was a strange thing to say as soon as the words left my mouth, but drinking was the only thing that I could scold her for because she seemed quite content.

My mother looked weary. 'Please sit down, Ivy,' she said.

I looked around, but she had given my seat to Mrs Cuthbertson, so I perched on the windowsill.

Mrs Cuthbertson pulled her stool away from the fire so that she could look at us both. 'I am here for a truce,' she said. 'I no longer wish to cause harm to anyone.'

'I don't believe you,' I spat.

'Please, I have no cause to...' She rubbed her hand across her receding hairline wearily and I realised that she must have already said all that she had to say and that it hadn't come easily. 'Here,' she said, and handed me a document from under her stool. 'Please, just read it.'

The document had the name of the local solicitor, Mr Crozier, printed at the top.

'I don't understand,' I said.

'One of my husband's final instructions was that his paperwork be moved to the office of a solicitor in Devon. It unsettled him when the bomb fell in Missensham Lido and he instructed Mr Crozier to put all his documents in a locked box and to send them away to keep them safe. Mr Crozier knew that his property deeds and the documents for his private practice were being stored in Devon, but he did not recall the Will, yet he still wrote to the solicitor in Devon' – she pointed to the document which I held – 'and they replied with this.'

I tried to read the document, but my eyes were tired and I could barely focus in the dull light of the room, but there were words that stood out over any others – words which were unexpected and out of place.

I laughed. 'Is this what I think it means?'

None of us were mentioned in Dr Cuthbertson's Will; neither wife nor child. There was only one name that stood out in the text, one beneficiary of the assets and estate – Edgar Cuthbertson, the damaged and dependent brother; a man who the Cuthbertsons had always treated as a servant.

'Well it serves you right, you bitch!' I said, flinging the document back at her.

'Ivy!' said my mother sharply. 'Control yourself and apologise!'

'What?' I turned to her. 'How can you even—'

'No, no,' said Mrs Cuthbertson sharply. 'It is me that should apologise. I have behaved in a most terrible manner over the last few years.' Her voice was hard and she spoke with her usual tone, her mouth tight and her eyebrows raised like daggers, and it took me a while to realise that she was not chastising me but apologising. 'It is no justification for what I have done, but I was concerned for Lil when I first visited Elmridge House back in 1920. I knew that something wasn't right and, after we had said our goodbyes, I stopped in the hallway and asked the maid to fetch Dr Cuthbertson for me. Clive would not speak of what had happened, but he said enough to reassure me and I thought him a caring man.' She took a deep breath. 'He said if I was still concerned that we could meet again when he was next at the theatre. I agreed, but by then, I'm afraid that my concerns were no longer with Lil and, well, things happened. I knew that Lily's pregnancy was unwanted at first – I thought that I was doing the right thing in helping her to terminate it, but looking back, I suppose that I was also thinking of what I wanted for myself. The fact that we were friends, Lil, kept me away from Elmridge House for a long time, but in the end I had to be with Clive.'

My mother nodded, her brow furrowed. 'I always wondered why you returned from Paris early, Grace,' she said. 'You had your heart set on it, but I suppose that being with Clive was more important to you.'

'It wasn't easy,' said Mrs Cuthbertson. 'I could not bear to be so far away from Clive when I knew that you would be so close. I was so envious of you, Lil. Clive treated your pregnancy as a medical condition, and to his dying day he never spoke a word about it. He would say that, as a doctor, he was bound by his Hippocratic oath. He would never even admit to me that he was your father, Ivy – he always had the perfect excuse not to speak of it, and I knew that he never would. But when he spoke of leaving money to Lil and her unborn child, I knew for sure. That drove me mad and I'm afraid that is when the jealousy really got the better of me.'

She turned to my mother and leant forward, taking her hand. 'I acted badly towards you, Lil, I am truly sorry for that, and I did not consider how you must have been suffering with your illness. It was only when you left Elmridge House that night that I realised what I had done. I became so worried about you, but I could not find you to make amends, and by the time I did it was too late.'

'I suppose that you will be challenging this, then?' I said, holding the document out to her. 'After all, you have the means to do so.'

'No,' she said. 'I do not. I barely have the clothes on my back. Clive always kept his money to himself. He paid me a small allowance, but that has stopped on his death. You see, our relationship soured after what happened with Lily. We thought that marriage and then a having a child might strengthen our commitment, but, in the end, these things just forced two unhappy people to stay together. Over the years Clive came to resent me and I don't blame him because I never had a kind word for him. It does not surprise me that he did not remember me in his Will.'

It was then that I remembered the feeling I had when I entered Elmridge House for the first time; the same feeling that returned to me when I stood in the house little more than an hour ago. It was what I could sense all around me yet not identify – and now I knew that it had been the air of decay. Everything had been grand but none of it was new – the Persian rug was faded, the white paint on the walls was peeling, the chaise longue was threadbare and the silver candlesticks were tarnished. Nothing had been fixed, replaced or purchased in the last twenty years. I had thought the chill in the house had been due to the cold weather, but now I realised that the fire in Hugo's room must have been the only one that had been lit. Elmridge House itself had deceived me – I had been overawed by a grandness I mistook for wealth, but the wealth went no further than the bricks and mortar.

'I suppose you will appeal to Edgar,' I said. 'For he would see that his nephew and sister-in-law were provided for.' But then I remembered the way she had berated him on my visits to Missensham House, blaming him for her lateness, the insults that Hugo had told me of, and her row with the servants that morning.

'Edgar and I have already spoken,' she said shortly. 'Hugo is permitted to stay at Elmridge House, but it would seem that I am not.'

I thought of the threat she had made to me on the doorstep of the nurses' house, when she said that she would do anything for her son, and I realised how desperate she must have felt. Her fears for Hugo had not been the shame of an institution or even of poverty, but of separation from her son, the only family she had left and maybe the only person she had not alienated. Dr Cuthbertson must have known that Edgar would provide for his nephew, maybe they had even discussed it before his death. Even though Mrs Cuthbertson would not have to worry about Hugo's future, she would still live without him, and that was the part that she had feared the most.

'Clive told me once that he had to atone for what happened to your mother,' she said. 'How he had failed her. He told me that he would always provide for her and her child, even after his death. He was a very religious man, he believed in making amends. Clive said that he had not made a Will since we married and I worried that he was always so busy with his work that he had never got round to it. I feared this Will ever turning up, and I feared your mother inheriting everything, yet that was not to be either.'

'Well,' I sighed. 'I suppose all this is somehow fitting. You had my mother locked up in Elmridge House and you drove her from it.'

'I did suffer too,' she said. 'I know it is little consolation to you, but you should know that your mother stayed in that room for only a few months. Hugo has not left Elmridge House for twenty years. It is only since Clive died that I have been able to let him out. I had to watch him suffer for all those years. Clive was a doctor – he told me it was for the best, what did I know? – a mother's intuition against all those years of study.'

The room was quiet for a while, just the crackle of the fire and the tick of the clock.

'I did not know he was kept there,' I said. 'I just thought it difficult for him to leave, I—' I had been with Hugo barely an hour ago and had thought that he trusted me when he spoke about his past, but even then, there was so much more that he had not told me. He had not felt as close to me as I had hoped. 'He did not tell me,' I said. 'Even when we spoke today, he did not tell me.'

'So you went to him!' She smiled. 'When I told Hannah to ring the nurses' house and say that I was away, I hoped that you would go. It is right that you saw him again.'

'I saw him,' I said, 'and we spoke, but it appears we did not say what we needed to.'

'You saw him,' she said, 'and that is enough for me.'

I thought of the woman who had come to me in desperation for Luminal and stolen it from me, the woman who had threatened me when she thought that I might know of a Will, stowed secretly, which would deny her a fortune. As she herself said, she had behaved in a terrible manner towards my mother, but everything she had done to me had been driven by one thing only – her need to be with her son.

'What will you do?' I said.

'Edgar told me to leave for good this morning,' she said, 'but I went straight to Mr Crozier's office and it seems that I will be allowed to stay on the estate until all the paperwork is sorted out, so I have a bed for tonight at least. After that...' But she did not have the words to finish her thought. 'I know that Hugo will be cared for,' she continued, 'but it will not be the care of his mother. My son was once a normal boy, but Clive could not see that and treated him as he would any of his other patients. Hugo is damaged now, he will not starve, but I cannot afford to take him from Missensham House and I cannot go there to care for him. I suppose the separation is what I fear the most.'

'I'm sorry, Grace,' said my mother quietly, 'but you know that I...'

Mrs Cuthbertson nodded quickly. 'You have nothing, I know, and it would be an insult to you to ask for your help.' She sighed deeply. 'It is funny – I would have had you and your daughter out on the streets all those years ago and now it will happen to me. It is a kind of justice, don't you think?'

My mother did not give her an answer as she did not need one.

'But you will offer me this refreshment in your house, Lily,' Mrs Cuthbertson continued. 'I take comfort in that.'

My mother nodded and Mrs Cuthbertson looked to me for the same reassurance, but I did not give it.

'Well, I mustn't stay,' she said briskly. 'The time has come for me to return home while the law still permits it.'

She stood up and stretched her long elegant limbs. She still had a fine body, but I wondered what good it would do her now – there would not be many men who would marry a widow of her age and her manner was too barbed to win her many lovers or friends who would help her.

She picked up her bag and handed her husband's Will to my mother. 'For your fire,' she said. She took a little torch from her bag and shook it to get the batteries connecting. Then she peeled the masking from the head, flashing the rings of light around the walls. 'The batteries should last long enough to get me home.'

'You should get away with it tonight,' said my mother. 'The blackout wardens will not be out in this weather.'

'I shouldn't think so,' she said, 'but the snow clouds will also keep the bombers away.' She nodded to herself. 'Yes, tonight I think that all is at peace.'

The women nodded to each other, with neither of them attempting a parting gesture or raising a hand to shake, but the look that passed between them was more than any embrace could have meant.

I stood in the doorway of my mother's little house and watched Grace Cuthbertson move slowly down the road, her tall silhouette fading into the shadows, but the light from her torch still a bright circle until she reached the bottom of the hill. Here the light stopped moving as if she was pausing for breath, bracing herself against the biting wind, and then she vanished into the darkness.

I rubbed my hands to warm them, feeling the ridge of rough skin across my palm and I remembered the last time Mrs Cuthbertson had called and felt the cut of the knife on my skin once more. I no longer held the knife, but as I looked at the puckered skin, I knew that the scar would always remain.

LILY

40

December 1943

Ivy stood in the doorway for several minutes as she watched Grace Cuthbertson make her way down the dark street. Then she shut the door against the flurries of snow, walked slowly across the room and sat down heavily on the stool opposite me, where Grace had sat just moments before. I marvelled at how small she looked; she had removed the belt and apron from her nurse's uniform and her slight frame seemed lost inside the loose fabric of her dress. She seemed so young and vulnerable and I was reminded of the little girl I had once known. She rubbed her hands, not in the warmth of the flames, but in a way that seemed to trouble her, her fingers tracing slowly across her palm as she winced with pain.

'It is over now,' I said. 'You can stop your fretting.' I was her mother, but it had never been my way to comfort her and, even now, I could not find the right words and she continued to stare at her hand. 'I know it must have been a shock for you to see Mrs Cuthbertson here,' I said, 'but we do not have to fear her any more. Things can be different now. Our life can be different. There is much more that we can...' But she still did not look up and I realised that she no longer heard my words.

Ivy stood up and reached behind the photo frame on the mantelpiece and I saw a little glass bottle in her hand; a small bottle with a blue label, a bottle that was empty. When she finally spoke her voice was shaky. 'I noticed this behind your wedding photograph, Mother,' she said, holding the bottle up to me. 'Mrs Cuthbertson was talking about Clive, so I could not help looking at the photograph of him, and that is when I saw this.'

'Well, I don't know what that is!' I said, but my memory was not what it had been in my youth and I could not think of anything more to say.

'It is funny,' she said. 'I was never sure when this bottle of Luminal had gone missing from my nursing bag. I always assumed that Mrs Cuthbertson had stolen it. She had asked Bridget for the same pills and me too, so I thought her an addict. I was so sure that it was her who had taken them, Sadie was sure that it was her too, but now I know it was you, mother.'

'Oh, the Luminal that I found in your bag!' I said, for at last I remembered. 'Well, that was all such a long time ago and I was only looking for something to help me rest. You know how my legs get tired and I do tend to worry about things.' I leant forward to take the bottle from her, but, as my hand touched hers, I felt that her skin was hot from the fire, but she seemed to sense neither the heat nor my touch. 'I know what Luminal is,' I said. 'I have taken it before when I first went to Elmridge House. I don't need your concern, I know how to use it safely.'

But she still seemed upset. 'You knew what trouble I could get into, Mother, but that did not bother you. You took it anyway.'

I suppose I owed her an apology, but that kind of thing did not come easily to me. 'Well, I must have been suffering...' I began.

But Ivy was not listening. Her eyes seemed to stare through me and her breaths were coming quickly. The bottle slipped from her hand and smashed onto the hearth, but she did not notice the tinkle of glass nor the splinters on the tiles.

'What is it?' I said.

Only then did I realise that her gaze had returned to the photograph in the blackened frame and she reached up and took it down from the mantelpiece.

'I will clean up that glass,' I said quickly. 'You were always clumsy even when you were a girl. You always—'

But she raised her hand to silence me. She took her bag onto her lap and drew out a fold of brown parcel paper, and then a photograph, one which I had seen before – a group of dancers posed round a ballerina with a man on each arm – my last performance as Liliana Postova. She placed the photograph on her lap, next to the picture in the little blackened frame.

'It is the same photograph,' she said. 'But then I suppose I always knew that it would be.'

'I don't know what you mean!' I put my hands on the arms of my chair and started to raise myself up slowly. 'I will get the dustpan from the kitchen and while I am there I will put the kettle on and—'

'No!' she shouted, and I dropped back into my chair.

'This photograph has been here on your mantelpiece my whole life,' she jabbed her finger at the picture in the frame, 'but it has been many years since I looked at it. You said that this was your wedding day and that the man in this photograph was my father.'

'That's right,' I said, 'and now you know—'

'But this is not a wedding dress,' said Ivy. 'I always believed that's what it was – with all the white lace and taffeta and the bouquet you are holding – but it is the same picture as in this other photograph, the one of the ballet. You are not wearing a wedding dress here – it is a ballet costume, the one you wore for *Giselle*.'

I watched the movement of her finger as she moved the tip slowly from one photograph to the other.

The photograph you told me was of your wedding day is exactly the same as this bigger photograph. It is an identical print, but you have cut away so much of it – the fullness of your skirt, all the other dancers, even Len, your brother, who stood to the right of you – you have cut away so much that anyone who looked at it would just see you in a white dress and Clive Cuthbertson in his suit at your side.' She looked up from the photographs and angled the little blackened frame towards me, her hands trembling. 'It was all you needed to do to fool people into thinking that this was a wedding photograph. Maybe you even started to believe it yourself.'

'It does not matter that the photograph was not actually taken on our wedding day,' I said, for that must have been obvious to her. 'I just wanted a photograph of your father to prove you had one and this was as good as any other.'

'Mrs Cuthbertson only had a small postcard with this image on,' she persisted. 'She told Hugo that you already had a print of the photograph. That was true wasn't it, Mother? Because she was talking about this one – the one which you destroyed when you cut it up like this.'

I don't know what you are trying to say!' I cried. 'Maybe you are right about the photograph, but I don't see how it matters.'

Ivy turned away from me and looked into the fire, the light from the flames flickering over her face. I thought that she must be waiting for me to speak, to say something more about the photographs, but there was nothing more to say and apologies were not my way.

At last she turned back to me. 'Over two months ago, Grace Cuthbertson came to see me at the nurses' house to tell me that her husband had died.'

'I know that,' I said indignantly. 'You told me as much.'

'On that day she told me she was looking for a Will. She thought that Dr Cuthbertson might have made a Will in your favour because of the promise that he made to you when you were pregnant. If there was no Will, she knew that, as his wife, she would inherit everything.' She paused and looked at me. 'Which is funny, isn't it?'

I shrugged my shoulders for I had no idea what she meant.

'Well, surely if there was no Will, as Dr Cuthbertson's first and only legal wife you would be the one to inherit his estate, not her. You could prove Grace's marriage a sham.'

'Well, she must have known that I would not come forward,' I said. 'After all, it would be very difficult for someone like me to claim—'

But she would not let me finish: 'You would just have to show a marriage certificate.'

'Well, maybe I would, but I don't know where that would be—' I began.

'Or maybe a real wedding photograph rather than a fake one, or a ring that was gold and not brass. Yet you don't have any of those things, do you?'

'Well, I—' I could have explained it to her, but she did not let me speak.

'In all the time that I was here with Mrs Cuthbertson tonight, she never mentioned a marriage that had come before hers.'

I put my head in my hands, feeling the weight of her words. I wanted to explain everything to her, but I was tired and confused. I knew that the things she spoke of must be somewhere in the house, but I could not recall seeing them.

'You were not his wife,' she continued. 'You never were. You used this photograph to get the midwife to help you leave Elmridge House. You fooled Sadie with this photograph as you fooled me.'

'I was his wife,' I began. 'The wedding was...' The words seemed to come to me automatically as they always had, but somehow the thoughts were not complete. 'He loved me,' I said at last, for that surely was true.

'Dr Cuthbertson spoke of a brass ring when he was dying. Hugo thought that it was a strange thing to mention – a little detail in the middle of such a disturbing story about your escape – but it did mean something, he was trying to say that you and he were not really married. Why would he want to make sure that his son knew that?'

Ivy put the photograph back on the mantelpiece, but this time she turned it to face the wall. 'It is funny,' she said. 'Uncle Len told me that this ballet was about a peasant girl named *Giselle* who dies of a broken heart after discovering that the man she loves is betrothed to another. In a way that is what happened to you, Mother. Dr Cuthbertson was married, but it was never to you.'

'So I suppose you are angry with me now?' I said.

'I am not angry,' she shook her head slowly. 'I pity you. Which is somehow harder to bear but I think that I understand now.'

'No!' I cried. 'You don't understand, you can't!' I pulled myself up from the armchair and walked shakily over to her. I reached out my hand and laid it on her shoulder, patting the fabric of her dress.

Her shoulder hardened to my touch and she removed my hand, a bemused look in her eyes as if I was a stranger to her. 'No,' she said firmly. 'It is too late for that.'

It was too late. Throughout her life I had been scared of showing her affection. My own experiences had taught me that life can be tough, so I had raised her to be hardened to it, and sentimentality would not have helped. Now, as my hand fell back to my side, I wondered if I had been wrong – maybe she had not felt loved at all, just taken for granted.

'Don't bother with any more lies, Mother,' she said, 'because I have this, too.' She took something else from the parcel paper, it was a postcard, and one that I recognised but could not think from where. On the front was a picture of Elmridge House. She handed it to me and the memories started to return.

'Oh!' I said, turning it over. 'I wrote this. It says I am to be married, to Dr Cuthbertson. It did happen after all, you see.'

'Look at it' – she pointed to the postcard – 'not the words, but the other side, the picture.'

It was Elmridge House just as I recalled it, with its pitched roofs and grand flinty gables, even the motor car was parked outside. 'I remember it,' I said.

'I used to think the house so grand,' said Ivy, 'but only because I was used to having so little. In fact, there are many houses like it in this part of the county, every village will have its grander houses, it is unremarkable, so why would there be a postcard of it? It was not until today that I looked at it properly and I saw what is printed at the bottom.'

I took the card from her and fetched my spectacles, squinting through the lenses at the small line of text. 'Elmridge House,' I read out loud. 'Discreet...' but then I stopped for the words did not make sense.

'Discreet care for sensitive ladies of a nervous disposition,' she said the words I could not. 'This place was not a family home back then. In fact it never was while Dr Cuthbertson owned it, he worked at an asylum called St Catherine's in Oxworth, but his obituary told of a private practice. Elmridge House was the place wasn't it, Mother? It is where you were staying, not in your family home, but in a private clinic, one for neurotics – you were his patient not his wife!'

'No,' I said. 'It wasn't like that.'

'Mrs Cuthbertson said it herself – she was jealous that you could be close to Clive, but she only meant as his patient. When she talked about your illness, I thought that she meant your softened hip, but she was talking about your other illness – the one that was in your mind. She behaved badly, but she saw the error of her ways once you had fled. She was not hunting you down, she came looking for you at the nurses' house because she regretted how she had treated you. She was worried about you.' She held the photograph and postcard out to me once more – the group of dancers and the grand house: 'Please, try and remember!'

I did as she said. I looked at all the faces I had once known – I had seen neither Clive nor Len since the year that the photograph was taken and they remained ever youthful to me, as if frozen in time. Grace had sat before me mere moments ago, changed so much in body and spirit that I no longer recognised the sweet energetic girl who had giggled with me as we drank crème de menthe together in my dressing room all those years ago. Grace had talked of the once grand Elmridge House falling into disrepair, but for me it would forever be a place of opulence and finery and I remembered how I would gaze out of the long windows or stand in the garden, marvelling at the views of the village and countryside.

Then I realised that Ivy was staring at my face with the same expression that Clive often had during our long talks all those years ago, and I wondered if she was right, if I had been mixing my memories and daydreams.

'Uncle Len told me he took you to Elmridge House to rest your body and your nerves,' she said, 'but it was more than that, wasn't it? He took you there because you had become fixated with Alexander, a man who did not want you. You almost convinced Len that you were having an affair with Alexander, you even convinced yourself, but you were not.'

'I went to Elmridge House for a break,' I said bitterly. 'That was all. I always thought that I could go back to Alexander. There was something special between us; if we were not lovers it was only because Len stopped me from going back to him.'

'Alexander left because the police came to the theatre looking for him,' she said. 'It scared him enough to leave for good. Len thinks that it was you who called them.'

'What rot!' I cried. 'Len wanted Alexander, that was all, but he could not have him.'

'Uncle Len spoke fondly of you,' she said. 'Yet for some reason he never asked after you and did not want to contact you, even after all these years, and I wondered why that was. I think that he feared what had become of you, because it must have been a difficult decision for him to take you to Elmridge House.' She paused.

'In fact, he could not even admit what had happened. Attitudes have changed over the last twenty years, but, in a way, your brother is still very old-fashioned. I think that he felt some shame in having a family member who suffered from mental illness, and I think that he felt guilty that he brought you to Elmridge House and had you committed.' 'Leonard has told you a load of rubbish,' I said. 'Alexander loved me, he just...' but somehow I could not finish the sentence. Alexander had always been so kind to me and I could feel the passion between us when we danced; he desired me, I could see it in his eyes, even though he could never bring himself to tell me. '... And Clive loved me too,' but my voice seemed weaker now.

'Clive was your doctor,' Ivy said firmly. 'Your psychiatrist, no more.'

'Clive was different to Alexander,' I insisted. 'He cared about me, he wanted to provide for me.'

'Maybe he did,' she said, 'but as a patient, and one that he had failed, because that is all you ever were. You were not the first Mrs Cuthbertson, you were never his wife.'

'I was his wife!' I cried. 'We had a special bond.'

'You need more than a special bond for a marriage,' she said. 'You need banns read in a church, you need witnesses, you need to sign a register, you need to stand before God.' Then she added: 'You need to have a man who is willing.'

'You do not need to be married to be lovers,' I said. 'You are a nurse, you know the ways of the world all too well from that filthy little business you run from the nurses' house. How do you think you came into being?'

She sighed. 'Now I even doubt that, Mother. For all that I have heard of Clive Cuthbertson, an affair with a patient, no matter how brief, seems like the last thing he would have done.'

'You told me that there were lilies all over the gardens at Elmridge House,' I said. 'They have been there for twenty years. He had them planted for me. You see the bouquet I am holding in the picture – they were his way of showing me how he felt.'

It was such a grand show of affection that it should have been obvious to her, if only she had listened, but she did not: 'One day you realised that he was courting your friend Grace,' she said, 'and everything changed. Instead of being obsessed with Clive you became obsessed with Grace. She became evil to you. She had taken away the man you wanted and the life that you thought you could have with him.'

'How can you say that?' I spat. 'You have met this woman for yourself. She has threatened you. Isn't that all you need to know about her?'

'She is not the woman you told me of,' said Ivy. 'Grace Cuthbertson is objectionable and blunt, that is true, but she is not that woman. Hugo shouted something after me as I was leaving Elmridge House, it was something about me not knowing everything and I think he had wanted to tell me more about his mother. He must have known what happened between you and Grace all those years ago and that is why he was not concerned when he learned that his mother was coming here to see you, in fact he thought it good that you would not be alone.'

'You cannot sympathise with her!' I cried. 'Don't forget that I am your mother.'

'Maybe by blood' she said, 'but somehow that does not seem strong enough any more. I know that you are sick, but I am angry because nothing you have told me is true. There is nothing that I can know about you. Even when I was a child you lied about my father dying in the Great War and about the limp you said was childhood polio. None of that was true, was it?'

'Oh that!' I laughed, relieved that she was only talking of trivial matters. 'When I said those things to you it was so long ago. I just thought it easier, you were too young to really understand. I was thinking only of you and I did not want to upset you.'

'And now?' she said. 'Do you still see me as a child? Because there is plenty more that you have lied about since.'

'No,' I said. 'Everything I have told you is true. Len did not tell you anything that I have not, and if you think that he is implying other things, you have to remember that he is still bitter with me over Alexander.'

'Oh, Mother!'

'Well, what about Sadie?' I said. 'You trust her, don't you? She will tell you the truth, after all, she was there at your birth.'

'Sadie believed only what you told her,' she said. 'She has heard it all from your lips, and I know that you can be very convincing.'

'Stop this!' I cried. 'You are upset with me and I understand that but you are not listening, you are only believing what you want to believe.'

'Well, that would make two of us,' she said.

We sat in silence. We had so much more to say to each other, but there had been too much said already and we were weary. After a while, Ivy shook her head and put the photograph and postcard back in the brown parcel paper and tied the strings carefully around them. Then she put them in her bag and stood up shakily.

'Don't go,' I said. 'You should stay the night. It is late and the snow is thick now. We can talk in the morning.'

But she took her coat from the floor and pulled it on. 'I have to go,' she said. 'We both need time to think, but I am not sure how long that time will be,' and the way she said it scared me; there was something so final in her voice.

'All right then,' I said weakly. 'Whatever you think is best.' I pulled myself up from the chair and tried to tuck her scarf into the neck of her coat. I felt I had to do something. After all, I was her mother and she needed to know that I was there for her, but she pushed my hands away. 'Make sure you take the roads,' I said. 'They may be trying to clear them already. Don't cut across the village green.' But there was something about my voice that I did not recognise, for it had never been my way to fuss over her, and the words sounded strange in my mouth.

She gave me a hard look. 'I am not going back to the nurses' house, Mother,' she said. 'I need to go back to Elmridge House.'

'No!' I cried. 'You cannot go to Mrs Cuthbertson!'

She shook her head. 'I do not intend to,' she said, 'for I think no more highly of her than I do of you. I am going back to Hugo for I think that I can help him. I don't know who is to blame for what happened, but some have suffered more than others.' She paused. 'And I want to be with him.' She took up her bag and walked to the door. 'If you cannot tell me the whole truth, Mother, there is just one thing that I would like to know. Please will you tell me because it is important to me?'

'Of course,' I said.

'I would like to know if Hugo and I are related, because if you were not married to Clive Cuthbertson, I need to know if he was my father or was there another? Can you at least tell me this one little thing?'

'Oh, Ivy, I...' I opened my mouth but realised that I could not say anything. Whether it was because I could not find the words, or did not know how to say them, I wasn't sure, or maybe she was right – I could not tell dream from reality.

'Something, Mother, anything?' She opened the door. 'No,' she muttered to herself. 'I didn't think you could tell me the truth.' She stepped out into the cold night and shut the door behind her.

Her words lingered in my head and I realised that she was right; I could not tell her the truth.

41

I listened to Ivy's footsteps in the street, the faint chime of metal as she took up her bicycle and the swish of the tyres on the snow, and then she was gone.

For so long it had just been the two of us – my daughter and I; our little family. I pulled myself up on to the chair and sat down wearily. Christmas was only days away. It was a time of year that I always dreaded because it was a time when I was reminded of what I did not have – a husband at my side and the gifts that I could have purchased with his income. The day had always been a strange one, the war making it even more so – a cheap cut of mutton, potatoes and carrots, eaten silently from plates on our laps so that we could have the warmth of the fire. The exchange of small gifts, underwear and socks, and a bar of scented soap all wrapped in newspaper and string, followed by a game of charades. I had hated those times, but now that Ivy was gone, I realised that they had been all that I had ever wanted, and now I would be alone.

Now Ivy had a new life ahead of her, but it was one that I would not be part of, for I knew that if she went to Elmridge House again, then she would not return to me. I stood up slowly and took the little blackened frame from the mantelpiece, turning it to face me once more. It was only a small photograph, faded and grey, but something about seeing the larger print that Ivy had brought with her had revived my memories and the picture seemed more alive than ever, and I could smell the mustiness of the greasepaint once more. I felt the warmth of him next to me and the weight of his stare, his fingertips brushing against mine and the yearning in his body. He had loved me once, he had loved me first, and Grace had taken him from me.

I could not explain it to Ivy as she stood on the doorstep willing me to speak. I could not say anything because it was all too painful. The man that I had loved had been taken from me by Grace, and now, because of her, Ivy too, was gone.

I rubbed the frame with my handkerchief, but it was badly tarnished and I realised that I could never get the silver to shine again. I put it back on the mantelpiece, at the front this time; in pride of place.

Out in the street there was laughter as neighbours returned from parties, the crump of boots in the snow and the slam of doors. Around me, the patched ball gowns hung from the picture rail like corpses. I thought of each dress as if it was a time that I had lived – the after-show parties, the celebrations in the Lamb and Flag, the dance nights at the Trocadero and the gatherings in the dressing rooms where we had laughed and drank together with friends. When I looked at the dresses again they were limp and lifeless – my party had been long ago.

I hobbled round the room and swept up the shards of glass from the hearth. I did not shut the curtains nor bother with the blackout blinds as the room had faded into darkness, a jagged frost pattern creeping across the windowpane.

A draught of cold air on my forehead brought a new simplicity to the world, my thoughts now clearly defined, and for the first time, I saw my memories as if through the eyes of another. I began to think that the way Clive had looked at me when we stood together in front of the camera had not been one of attraction but of fascination, for I had seen the same expression on his face when he read his journals. I had called myself Clive's wife, but they were words which I could not recall ever leaving his lips, and when I had mentioned our marriage he would always look at me sternly. I had ordered the brass wedding ring when my fingers became swollen, but I had never been able to find the one which it replaced, despite years of searching. There was also the matter of builders who had never existed, Walter's questions about my attempt to end my pregnancy, and the repetitive piano music that had become more of a torment than a comfort. Then there was the other woman who stayed at Elmridge House – one who knitted a scarf for her dead son. There were locked doors and windows, knowing looks and hushed voices.

I had seen these things all along – I had just chosen not to think of them. They were things which had started on one cold night in February 1920, the night of my final performance, when I stood together with Clive in front of the photographer's camera and stared into the little black lens.

I remembered the flash of the photograph which had sealed the moment in memory forever. Then, as the smoke of the flash powder filled the room, I had taken Clive's hand in mine.

But he pulled it away sharply. 'No,' he said sternly. 'I have told you before!'

I had stared at him but his face was hard and I felt the sting of tears in my eyes. I ran from the stage, along the narrow corridors and back to my dressing room, where Edgar waited at the door, still in his long overcoat. He removed his driver's cap when he saw me and nodded respectfully.

'Come in,' I said.

It was the pain of rejection that could only be soothed by another. Edgar had been unsure at first and, as I poured the crème de menthe, he had talked only of the motor car waiting in the alley at the stage door. He had smiled shyly as I removed his gloves and muttered something about his orders to collect me from my dressing room so that he could drive Len and me to Elmridge House. After I kissed him, he had said little more, just dimmed the mantle and lit an oil lamp. Then he went to the dressing room door and locked it.

Neither Edgar, Clive, Len or myself said a word on the long drive to Missensham, but there cannot have been silence in our heads: over the previous two days there had been the drama of Alexander's sudden departure and the policemen searching his dressing room; there had been the posing for the photograph when Clive had torn his hand from mine; and there had been the intimacy Edgar and I had shared on the rug in the dressing room. Yet we drove in silence, all of us lost in our thoughts and secrets.

At Elmridge House I saw little of Edgar, he was betrothed to Hannah, so we were often apart. I would sometimes see him on the driveway as he prepared the car or planted lilies in the flower bed and he would look up to my window, doffing his cap when I waved or blew a kiss, always a sad look in his eyes.

It was only when my pregnancy started to show that Edgar confessed everything to his brother. Clive forbade any contact between Edgar and me. He made sure that Edgar and Hannah were married that very month and moved them out of the servants' quarters and into the dovecote, a run down cottage that I could no more than glimpse if I pressed my nose against my windowpane. Clive kept my secret for me – he never told Hannah who my baby's father was and, despite what she might have suspected, he never told Grace – he said it was his Hippocratic oath, but I knew that he felt responsible for his brother's actions. When it came down to it, Clive was an honourable man.

Clive said that he could not dismiss Edgar when there was so little work about for former soldiers – after all, Edgar was his flesh and blood, and so too was my baby; a new Cuthbertson that he would always provide for, even after death. It was an honourable thing to do and an act of love and, at that moment, I knew that neither Edgar nor Alexander would ever compare to Clive, and no man ever would. I had a new love and this time it was real.

I walked slowly to the window, the ache in my hip a little worse due to the cold weather, and peered out on to the snowy street. The moon had come out, at last giving a little light and the snow had settled into a thick blanket. The trail left by Ivy's bicycle was still clear and dark and I was glad that she had not had to face further snow showers on her journey. Elmridge House still held secrets for her, and it was only a matter of time before she discovered them. When she returned to the house, she would meet Edgar, the new master of the house, and together they would fit the pieces together. Clive may not have been able to name Ivy in his Will, but he had fulfilled his promise to her the only way that he knew and one day she might indeed inherit Elmridge House from Edgar, her real father. Clive had made his amends and would rest in peace. At Elmridge House, Ivy would soon discover a father in Edgar and a cousin in Hugo. She would have a new family and I was happy for her.

In the light of the moon, Grace Cuthbertson's footprints seemed no more than shallow hollows in the snow. The night was clear and I could see the dark horizon and, in the distance the trees on the top of the hill which hid Elmridge House from view. I even fancied that I could see the dark track that led up to the house and the hollies clumped on the lawn. I could not help but think of Elmridge House again – the house as it had been in 1920, and the life that I could have had with Clive. Then I thought of the daughter that I had loved and was now gone. They were things that had been mine but they had been taken from me, and there was only one person that I blamed.

Ivy had been right. I had taken the Luminal from her nursing bag over a year ago when she visited me, but my hips were not so bad these days – the little aches were bearable and I had no trouble sleeping. I had no need for the Luminal – I had taken it for one purpose only, for I had known for a long time that Grace Cuthbertson would come here, and that she would torment me with tales of a life that she had stolen from me; a life in a big house with a man that I had loved. There had been ten pills in the bottle at the start of the evening, and now there were none.

I remembered her as she had been all those years ago, in her billowing white costume as she smoked in my dressing room, and of how we had laughed together as we stumbled through the corridors of the theatre. I remembered her at Elmridge House, pirouetting in my driving coat and I remembered the rag doll that she had made for my baby. She had been a friend once, but she was no more.

I swept up the fragments of the Luminal bottle and then took up her empty glass, holding it up to the moonlight. There was a film of green liquid on the bottom of the glass, and a powdery white residue. Grace had always said that crème de menthe could hide the taste of anything – it seems she was right.

I walked back to the window and looked out at the far hill. I fancied that I could see the light from Grace's torch moving slowly up the slope and along the track that led to Elmridge House, the little pinprick of light making its way through the snowy field. But Grace would not make it home that night. I had waited over twenty years for my revenge, and as I looked out on to the snowy landscape, I finally felt at peace. Somewhere in the cold field, the light from Grace's torch would stop moving in the swirling snow, and then the bulb would dim and fade to nothing. Her light would go out.

Acknowledgement

I would like to thank Caroline Ridding and the team at Aria for all their hard work and dedication, my agent Alison Bonomi for her guidance, and my family for their love and patience.

Hello from Aria

We hope you enjoyed this book! Let us know, we'd
love to hear from you.

We are Aria, a dynamic digital-first fiction imprint
from award-winning independent publishers
Head of Zeus. At heart, we're avid readers committed
to publishing exactly the kind of books we love to
read—from romance and sagas to crime, thrillers
and historical adventures. Visit us online and discover
a community of like-minded fiction fans!

We're also on the look out for tomorrow's
superstar authors. So, if you're a budding writer
looking for a publisher, we'd love to hear from you.
You can submit your book online at ariafiction.com/
we-want-read-your-book

You can find us at:
Email: aria@headofzeus.com
Website: www.ariafiction.com
Submissions: www.ariafiction.com/
we-want-read-your-book
Facebook: @ariafiction
Twitter: @Aria_Fiction
Instagram: @ariafiction

Printed in Great Britain
by Amazon